SUZETTE A. HILL was born in East Sussex, and spent much of her childhood playing spies and smugglers on Beachy Head and picnicking at the foot of the Long Man of Wilmington. Hill worked as a teacher in both public school and adult education before retiring in 1999. She now lives in Ledbury, Herefordshire. At the age of sixty-four and on a whim, she took up a pen and began writing. Hill has since published seven novels, including the Reverend Oughterard series.

www.suzetteahill.co.uk

By Suzette A. Hill

A Little Murder
The Venetian Venture

a&b

The Venetian Venture

SUZETTE A. HILL

Allison & Busby Limited
12 Fitzroy Mews
London W1T 6DW
www.allisonandbusby.com

First published in Great Britain by Allison & Busby in 2014.
This paperback edition published by Allison & Busby in 2015.

A CIP catalogue record for this book is available from
the British Library.

10 9 8 7 6 5 4 3 2 1

ISBN 978-0-7490-1660-9

Typeset in 11/16 pt Sabon by
Allison & Busby Ltd.

The paper used for this Allison & Busby publication
has been produced from trees that have been legally sourced
from well-managed and credibly certified forests.

Printed and bound by
CPI Group (UK) Ltd, Croydon, CR0 4YY

To my god-daughter Angela van der Stap

PROLOGUE

'Tell me,' said Cedric Dillworthy, 'does your cousin really inhabit a palazzo on the Grand Canal? You have never mentioned it before.' The professor's thin voice held the merest hint of scepticism.

'Well not *quite* on the Grand Canal,' his friend Felix answered, 'though as near as dammit – a little tributary you might say.'

'You mean some backwater?'

'No, I do not mean some backwater. I mean exactly what I say, a particularly charming canal in sight of the Grand one. The place is by a small bridge and has its own landing stage, thus one does not have to hike suitcases all over the place. *Were* we to go there you would find that a great blessing.'

'Doubtless. But I still do not understand why you have never spoken of this cousin or indeed ever mentioned Venice. Rome yes, but never Venice.' The scepticism had sharpened.

Felix gave a pained sigh. 'I have never mentioned Cousin Violet because she is ancient, testy, and I barely know her. Neither do I know Venice; a large lacuna in my education no doubt, but which I trust will be shortly filled.'

'Yet you seem very familiar with the location of the palazzo.'

'Because it was in the bloody photograph she sent! Now, do you want to come or not?'

Cedric took a reflective sip of a very dry martini and contemplated the cat sprawled at his feet. 'Are you sure she won't be there? I can't say I relish being at the beck and call of an ancient irascible even if she does live in decaying splendour; bad enough having to play lackey to the basset hound.'

'No of course she won't be there! That's the whole *point* of our being invited. I keep telling you – to guard the basset while she gads about in Chicago. The person she usually parks it with has had a fall or something and the backstop has bowed out at the last minute. Hence recourse to yours truly: any port in a storm I suppose . . . A bit of luck really. Just think, three weeks in the heart of Venice and all for free!'

'You forget the penalty,' Cedric observed mildly.

'What penalty?'

'The dog of course.'

'Oh that won't be any trouble. A daily stroll and the occasional bone should do the trick. Minimum of exercise, they have short legs that type.'

'Supposing it doesn't understand English?'

'Bound to be bilingual. Just like the gondoliers I expect. Oh, and speaking of whom, I rather gather . . .' Felix began to smirk.

Thus it was that Professor Cedric Dillworthy and his friend Felix Smythe of Smythe's Bountiful Blooms, Knightsbridge, embarked for Venice on 10th October 1954. Some months earlier they had been embroiled in an embarrassing fiasco in St John's Wood concerning a murdered woman and a coal scuttle. Since then, however, with the help of good weather and the sustained afterglow of the young Queen's coronation (not to mention Felix's newly bestowed Royal Appointment warrant) London life had proceeded with an amiable smoothness and that particular period of their lives was mercifully entering the realm of myth and legend.

Yet courtesy of Felix's cousin, the gadding Violet, here they were shortly to be entangled in a fresh legend: Venice, in all its beguiling charm and brazen beauty.

CHAPTER ONE

It was the autumn of 1954. And Rosy Gilchrist, now recovered from the painful turbulence wrought by her late and dubious aunt Marcia, walked briskly along Great Russell Street to the British Museum. She had worked there for three years, and despite the quirks and tantrums of her immediate boss, the notable Dr Stanley, had grown to love being a denizen of the place; and, in a masochistic way, to being academic handmaid to the capricious Stanley. Eight months previously the scandal of her aunt's peculiar and sinister death with all its personal ramifications had seemed a threat to her job – or so she had feared at the time. But now, with everything ostensibly accounted for and the case sewn up (or at least indefinitely shelved) her life had returned to an even keel. Too even perhaps.

Too even? Yes, for excruciating though the events of that time had been, her now smooth and pleasant days had begun to feel just the merest bit bland. In late wartime, as a mere girl in the ATS manning the searchlights on the south coast and preparing the anti-aircraft guns, she had certainly known excitement . . . and fear. (Dreadful griefs too, with loss of parents and of her pilot fiancé.) And in the war's aftermath Cambridge had also been a challenge, albeit of a different sort. But neither of those periods had been quite so fraught as the six months she had spent enmeshed in the imbroglio of her aunt's murder. To be out of it now was a blessed relief . . . And yet despite the lifting of personal fears, and peace (in every sense) restored, the 'New Elizabethan Age' with its heady hopes and burgeoning freedoms seemed to bring a flatness she couldn't quite define.

'Typical,' she told herself impatiently, 'there you were scared witless and desperate for calm and safety, and now that you've got it you begin to look about for something else to muddle your placid days. Perverse, that's what you are!' She grinned ruefully and started to run to the Museum to be at her desk before Stanley came rampaging in demanding tea and attention.

In fact she need not have hurried, as for nearly two hours she was able to work undisturbed by either her boss or the baleful pleasantries of Mrs Burkiss the office char. But no silence lasts and as the clock struck midday she heard the familiar voice of Dr Stanley booming along the corridor, and the next moment he was in the room.

'Do you want a holiday?' he asked abruptly.

She was startled. 'Er, not especially, I had some leave not long ago.'

'Yes but I think you should take some more,' he replied, pacing the room and scattering ash.

Rosy cogitated, unimpressed by the apparent solicitude. In fact she was more than a little unsettled by it. To show interest in his staff's welfare was not Stanley's style. Was this an attempt to ease her out, a subtle hint that her services were no longer required?

'Ah . . . well,' she said uneasily, and waited.

He swung round and fixed her with a stern gaze. 'You see I want you go to Venice. Soon.'

'*Venice!* Whatever for? I don't know it.'

'Well here's your chance then. You could make yourself useful there.'

Make herself useful there? What did he think she had been doing all this time *here* in London fixing his lectures, editing catalogues, researching projects and mollifying his colleagues – making daisy chains? She returned his gaze with a mixture of wonder and irritation. 'I see,' she said slowly, 'so why do you want me to go to Venice?'

'To find something. A book: Bodger's Horace.'

'*Bodger's* Horace,' she exclaimed, 'what on earth is that?'

He sighed. 'Didn't they teach you anything up at Cambridge? Doctor R. D. M. Bodger, an Oxford Fellow in the 1890s. His edition of Horace's *Odes* plus translation is one of the most notable we have. Except that we don't have it, that's just the point. There are only three copies extant, two in America and one in Europe, i.e. Venice. The Venice one is especially important because it has his signature and a dedication in his own hand, and it's imperative we include it in our spring exhibition of rare nineteenth-century texts.' He paused and leered. 'That'll put a feather in our cap I can tell you – and more to the point, some shekels in the coffers!'

Rosy frowned. 'Really? So what's the financial advantage?'

'Quite considerable. The nephew, Sir Fenton Bodger, is most keen to see that edition retrieved and deposited here at the Museum. If that can be done he is willing to make quite a sizeable donation to the department – *my* department.' Dr Stanley beamed.

'But apart from the signature what's so special about the thing? I mean, is the translation very good?'

Stanley grimaced. 'Pretty awful actually: exact enough but turgid – keeps to the letter but hardly to the spirit of the verse. To call it lumpen might be unfair but it's hardly distinguished . . . No, its value lies in the notes and annotations – now those do show some insight and originality. Bodger was a scholar not a poet. In fact he would have done better to leave the translating altogether and confine himself to the textual exegesis. However, it still has an intrinsic worth, and because of the nephew's interest *extrinsic* as well. Which is why I want it here with us.' He rapped the desk and leered again.

Rosy hesitated, still unclear. 'But,' she asked, 'wouldn't it be simpler if you were to get it yourself – I mean why send me? And in any case where is it exactly?'

'Ah, leading questions. Your revered superior is incommoded on two counts: first I have far too much on my plate wrestling with my new publication – you know the one, *Collections and Curios: Tips for Curators*.' (Rosy knew it only too well. It was, she gathered, to be the definitive guide to the curating fraternity, a *vade mecum* without which no serious custodian could possibly survive.) 'And secondly,' he continued, 'at long last my hip is to be dealt with or so they tell me.'

Without thinking she asked what was wrong with his hip, an unfortunate blunder which elicited a blast of indignation.

'My *hip*!' he exclaimed. 'The one that has been giving me all this agony. Don't tell me you haven't seen my appalling limp!' She had not, though now she came to think of it she did vaguely recall a few grumbling complaints.

'Oh dear. Are they going to operate?'

'They are thinking of it. Bound to be ghastly of course but one has to suffer to be whole.' He assumed a martyred air and added, 'Still, you can assuage the pain by bringing me brandy and chocolates and other essential palliatives.'

'Not if I am in Venice I can't.'

'*Ah* . . .' he replied with evident relief, 'so you will go then?'

'Well yes, in principle.'

'And in practice?'

Rosy hesitated, slightly embarrassed, and then said firmly: 'Well for one thing who will pay?'

'*Pay?*' He sounded startled. 'Oh well . . . uhm, us of course, the Museum. Er, yes that's it, we'll sub your travel *and* accommodation.' He managed to sound at once both vague and magnanimous.

'The Danieli?' she enquired brightly.

'Like hell. You'll be lucky! As it happens I have an old school pal whose sister runs a small *pensione* in the Dorsoduro quarter, plain but decent as they say. It looks out over the water to the Giudecca, you would like that.'

'Would I?'

He nodded confidently. 'Sure to.'

'So where is this book then? Will it be easy to get hold of?'

Stanley paused, frowning slightly. 'Ah, well there could be a small problem. Not major of course,' he added hastily, 'but there may be a couple of little hiccups, though nothing you can't cope with.'

'Hmm. Do I really want to have hiccups in Venice? It doesn't sound terribly romantic.'

'Romance is not the object of your venture,' he said sternly. 'You are there to retrieve the Bodger Horace and bring it back to the Museum amidst joy and plaudits. This is a serious task, Rosy, and I am relying on you. Much is at stake: the honour of the department, i.e. brass and kudos. Now listen carefully . . .'

Rosy listened, making notes. And then watched as,

16

briefing complete, he extinguished his cigarette in her pencil tray, stood up and strode briskly to the door.

'Poor fellow, frightful limp,' she murmured.

Cooking supper in her flat that night she reflected on the terms of her mission. She was to embark for Venice (i.e. catch the Calais steamer for the Simplon-Orient) in three days' time, arriving in the St Lucia railway terminal at the crack of dawn. On the train there would be a reserved couchette; but on arrival in Venice she would be expected to make her own way to the *pensione* via a vaporetto, and then after alighting, negotiate two small bridges '*a piedi*' (as Stanley had carefully enunciated). 'Quite simple,' he had said airily, 'just make sure you are properly shod and don't take too much luggage. Personally I always use a rucksack.' (She had immediately resolved to avoid rucksacks at all costs, and decided instead to blow the expense and buy a smart leather suitcase from Marshall & Snelgrove. She might not be staying at the Danieli but was damned if she was going to turn up in Venice looking like some hobo!)

Travel practicalities dealt with, her instructor had turned to the quest itself. 'It's quite straightforward *really*,' he had told her earnestly, 'it's just that the book's location is a trifle problematic, you may have to do a bit of nosing around first.'

'Nosing around?' she had asked warily. 'What sort of nosing around, and where exactly?'

'Ah, yes . . . well that is the slight difficulty I alluded

to. You see it could be in a number of possible places. My informant, Sir Fenton, is rather imprecise on that score. At one stage it was definitely in a small second-hand bookshop on or near the Rialto called 'Pacelli e Figlio'. Fenton's cousin saw it there by chance and told him. But soon after the sighting, old Pacelli died and his son offloaded much of the stock elsewhere.'

'Where?'

'I gather there is a shop in the Castello district, in Calle di Fiori or some such place; if the book is no longer in the Rialto place there's a good chance of its being there. Apparently they keep a large classical section. Have a good rootle in the stacks, offer a derisory sum and Bob's your uncle.'

'Supposing they don't want a derisory sum?' Rosy had asked.

'In that case you can go up to twenty guineas and tell them the venerable British Museum will advertise the bookshop on a large hoarding in its vestibule. That should do the trick; they like a lot of show the Italians.'

'Are you sure the Museum would sanction that?' she had asked.

'Not for one moment but he's not to know that.'

'I see. But supposing after all this rootling I discover that the book isn't there at all or that somebody has bought it. What then?'

'Then my dear Rosy you ask him where the bloody hell it's likely to be. Come on dear girl, use some initiative. If you could put a searchlight on the Hun in the war then you can surely put a beam on Venice for that damn book. It's not much to ask.' He gave her a look of wounded reproach.

She had flashed a cooperative smile but refrained from questioning the analogy. Training a searchlight on enemy aircraft was undoubtedly the more hazardous, but it was child's play compared with sifting through the whole of Venice for a book of ill-translated Latin poems. Still, if Dr Stanley was determined to send her on a wild goose chase to a beautiful and fabled city then that was his choice; hers meanwhile was to select the new suitcase and some appropriate clothing to go in it. She finished her supper while pondering the prospect, and recalled the smart silk jacket glimpsed in Debenham & Freebody's window only that morning. Yes, a trip to Wigmore Street was definitely indicated . . .

CHAPTER TWO

Edward Jones sat in the bar of the Berkeley and reflected. He couldn't afford the Berkeley but that did not stop him from patronising the place. Standards had to be maintained after all. And in any case normally he contrived to be treated by someone else – occasionally his grandfather but more often than not by those gullible enough to have been seduced by his charm and sleek looks. Actually Edward was not in the least charming (his housemaster had dubbed him putrid) but at the age of twenty-four he had watched others sufficiently well to cultivate the illusion of being so. It was an illusion rarely sustained but could be useful in times of sudden deprivation or to get a girl into bed.

Such a time was now. The girl issue was irrelevant; but he had lost heavily at Kempton, his tailor's bill was pushing astronomical, and the last client he had tried to interest in a used Lagonda had reneged on the deal. (Amazing how shifty people could be!) Added to this, his quarterly rent for the miniscule flat in Pimlico – for which there were no obvious funds – was looming at unnerving speed. Things looked bleak. Bleak but not desperate. Though fundamentally charmless Edward was also a genuine optimist and a firm believer in the principle that luck smiles on those who help themselves. And ever since the age of five Edward had been helping himself with dedicated care.

Thus, draped on the bar stool and sipping his gin and tonic, he gave thought to the latest venture: a venture not enormously lucrative admittedly, but one which if successful would certainly give a nice little boost to the waning finances. Besides, if he played his cards right it might open up further areas of profitable interest . . .

Bodger was the name, Sir Fenton Bodger. He had met him a few days earlier at a party given by his grandfather at Quaglino's. They had exchanged cigarettes and small talk and Edward had mentioned having a sister living in Venice.

'Ah Venice,' Bodger had exclaimed, 'haven't been there since before the war but it's my *almost* favourite city!' Edward assumed he was expected to ask what the favourite was but really couldn't be bothered. New York, Paris? Did it matter? The old cove would only prose on in clichés.

There was a pause, and the man, evidently realising

his cue had fallen flat, asked if he visited his sister often. Edward said that he did from time to time and that as it happened he was due to be with her that very week. (Yes Lucia had been quite generous about this trip, for once offering to pay his travel expenses – an offer that naturally he had graciously accepted.) They had continued chatting about Venice and Edward got the impression that the older man was rather taken by him. He wondered why. It wasn't as if he had been making any special effort to be engaging. There had been no point. Apart from a stick and a lisp the chap had been unremarkable, merely one of those bland indeterminates that act as wallpaper in such gatherings. Was it perhaps his new silk tie (knotted à la Windsor), impeccable haircut and slick cufflinks? Such sartorial niceties so easily impressed! (Subsequently, after making discreet enquiries, Edward learnt that Sir Fenton was exceedingly rich – a fact that not only made him less indeterminate but automatically conferred immediate distinction.)

After a few more words they had been joined by other guests and then separated into the surrounding throng. But just as Edward had been wondering if he could procure one last drink before leaving, there was a tap on his arm, and in slightly ingratiating tones the Bodger fellow said, 'Young man I have a proposition. Your grandfather tells me you are very bright and with strong initiative – in fact from what he was saying I'm a little surprised you're not part of the firm. Pictures not your thing perhaps?'

Edward had smiled politely, omitting to explain that

while he liked pictures well enough it was he who was not the thing with his grandfather. (The trial period spent in his relation's art gallery had failed to win favour with the owner, the apprentice's copybook having been not so much blotted as saturated. The fault, of course, had hardly been Edward's: as invariably, it was the other bastards. However, that was some years ago and now a more cordial relationship prevailed – just.)

'I'll oblige if I can,' he had lied. It was unlikely that the proposition would amount to much; something irksome and unproductive no doubt. Poodle-faking the daughter? God, the last time he had done that he had been the laughing stock of Chelsea – hadn't even managed to get his leg over. Not that he had wanted to. No fear! Jane Ponsonby-Slim had been noted for her girth, her piety and her ear-splitting bellow. She was still on the circuit and to be avoided at all costs . . . He returned his attention to the speaker.

'You see,' Bodger had lisped earnestly, 'as I was saying, the book belonged to my great-uncle, rather a fine scholar, and I am most eager to retrieve it from Venice and have it permanently on display here. The British Museum has shown an interest and a man called Stanley is being most cooperative – sending out some young woman to see what she can do. But you know what girls are like, they lack staying power.' (Huh! Not Jane Ponsonby-Slim, thought Edward.) 'And since reinforcements never come amiss, and since you know Venice and are about to go there I thought you too could do a little research. As said, it doesn't hurt

24

to have more than one person on the trail. Naturally your time would be well remunerated, successful or otherwise. And of course should you by chance find the thing and bring it back I should be *most* grateful!'

How grateful? Edward had wondered. 'Well,' he said slowly, 'I daresay I could manage—'

'And naturally *were* that to happen I think a bonus would be in order don't you?' The man put a hand on Edward's lapel and ran a plump and questing finger down the edge and lightly touched the hip pocket. 'I think I recognise the cut of your jib – Titchbold & Tomkins isn't it? Very wise if I may say. A good-looking young man like you ought always to invest in decent suits. Tell you what, get hold of the book and send the bill for the next one to me. Mind you, I should want to see you in it of course!' He had given a sly chuckle and proceeded to jot down details of where the search should begin.

Thus, in a reflective mood, Edward ordered another gin and tonic and contemplated his trip to Venice. Like thousands of others he had to admit to liking the city, and of course it was very handy Lucia having a tolerable flat near the centre. At least the measly husband had been useful in that respect!

Nevertheless whenever he went there he was conscious of the fact that he was merely the kid brother reliant on his sister's benevolence – charity really. It would be pleasant to have his own place or indeed to afford one of the better hotels: a fortnight in the Gritti would be acceptable. Ah well, one day perhaps . . . meanwhile at least something had come his way via this Bodger fellow. Fee and expenses had sounded pretty good (certainly enough to cover the T & T bill), and who knew, if he really could lay hands on the book a superlative suit could be his. (And oh yes he would make sure it was top notch all right. Nothing less than the finest stitching for Edward Jones!) He smiled at the prospect. The chap had been right: good features did indeed deserve the proper accoutrements. And after all, quite apart from being a source for classy tailoring the contact might just turn out to be of some long-term benefit – boring old ponce.

And thus it was that in a mood of muted optimism Edward Jones set out for Venice and his fate.

CHAPTER THREE

The advent of Felix and Cedric to the Palazzo Reiss had been marked by confusion, noise and rain; conditions which made Felix feel weak and his companion angry.

'I understood,' complained Cedric icily, 'that your cousin's residence was blessed by a private landing stage. Why the boatman chose to drop us off at this distance I cannot imagine.' He gave another heave to his suitcase and stubbed his toe on a cobble.

'Didn't you hear what he said?' Felix snapped, oppressed by the rain and piqued by the implied criticism. 'He said the landing stage was broken and won't be repaired for at least twenty-four hours. Apparently they are working on it now.' The claim was endorsed by a nearby hammering. 'He told me quite clearly and in good English. You evidently weren't listening.'

'Ah well,' his companion sniffed, 'doubtless my ear was more taken with his accent – or its variants.'

'Doubtless.'

They stumbled on damply, and rounding a corner were confronted by the source of the hammering: the broken jetty and three workmen in oilskins.

'Hmm,' Cedric observed, 'anyone would think we were in Padstow. This is not Venice as I recall it.'

'You mean soused in sunlight and its denizens clad in Garibaldi cummerbunds?'

The professor said nothing; and putting down his case scrutinised a heavy oak door set into the wall a few yards from the water's edge. He took out his glasses and peered at a brass plate displaying a short list of names: Bellini, Hope-Landers, Hoffman. 'Who is Hope-Landers,' he asked, 'your cousin?'

Felix shrugged. 'No idea. Violet's name is Hoffman.'

'Then this is the place all right. But what about the other names? I thought she lived alone. Perhaps it's a sort of boarding house . . .'

'It is not a boarding house,' said Felix tightly. 'Now kindly move over.' He nudged his friend aside and put a tentative finger on the top button. 'Let us hope the concierge Signora Whatsername is awake.'

'Probably deafened by all that hammering – or the creature.'

'The creature?'

'Can't you hear it?'

A deep throaty roar emanated from the interior and Felix groaned. 'For a dog that's called Caruso its voice is absurdly *basso profundo*.'

'Hence basset,' quipped Cedric, adding, 'but of course essentially he is going to be your charge; that was the bargain. Perhaps you can practise arias together.'

Felix scowled, and then hastily adjusted his features to an ingratiating smile as there came the sound of locks being drawn back.

The door was flung open, and they were faced not by Signora Whatsername but by a tall man of about sixty in a well-cut suit and carpet slippers. He held a pencil and a copy of *The Times* folded to the crossword. They took him to be English.

'Bit wet out there, isn't it?' he observed cheerfully. 'I'm the lodger, Guy Hope-Landers, and unless you've come to read the meters I assume you are Vio's cousins. Signora Bellini our concierge is off on hols so I'm on duty.' He smiled extending a hand.

'Actually,' said Felix a trifle stiffly, 'I am the cousin; this is Professor Dillworthy, an old friend.'

'Sorry, my mistake. I knew Vio said there were two of you coming and I assumed you were both relatives. She talks so fast I don't listen half the time but one generally gets the gist.' He started to help them in with their luggage and then paused, and looking at Cedric, said, 'You're not one of the Seaford Dillworthys are you? I knew a couple of those once – my God what a crew, wild isn't the word!

Especially that Angela, she'd lead anyone a double dance. I wonder if—'

'No,' Cedric said firmly, 'absolutely not. We are an entirely different branch – from Yorkshire you know.' For a second he closed his eyes recalling the dreaded Angela and the fracas in the hayloft. He just hoped this wretched man wasn't going to address the niceties of consanguinity let alone the contours of the Dillworthy nose, of which his own was a prime example.

However, the wretched man seemed otherwise engaged, for having attended to their bags and closed the door, his attention reverted to the discarded *Times* and its crossword. 'I say,' he said, as they hovered awkwardly in the gloom, 'I don't suppose you would hazard a guess at this would you? It's the last one and it's been plaguing me all afternoon. "Nine letters: *She sells these to pilgrims.*" Any suggestions?' He tapped the page and looked hopefully at Felix who stared back blankly, unused to such threshold conundrums.

'Seashells, I imagine,' responded Cedric coolly, 'though the pilgrim hint seems a little obvious for *The Times*. Perhaps they do a simplified version for the foreign market . . .'

Any intended barb was lost on their greeter who entered the letters with a triumphant flourish. He beamed. 'Fits exactly. Just the job! Now, I expect you would like to see the dog. I'll bring him out.'

'Not *just* at the moment,' said Felix hastily, 'perhaps we might see our rooms first. And, uhm, actually I'd quite like to . . .' He glanced enquiringly towards the nether regions.

'Have a slash? Of course, of course. It's en route, follow me.' Picking up one of the bags the man led the way down a dark, uneven passage to a curved stone staircase lit bleakly by a single grilled window. The air was grey, dank and dusty, and Felix's unease was now rather less physical than mental. Some palazzo! an inner voice grumbled.

'You could use that one if you're desperate,' said Guy Hope-Landers, gesturing towards a door at the foot of the staircase, 'but the plumbing is dicey and it is full of the dog's bones; it's his lair. Bloody cold too. You'd do better to use the one in your own quarters.'

Felix assured him he was not desperate; and following their leader the visitors continued up the winding steps to a landing of large proportions and small appeal. The chequerboard tiles were cracked and faded, a tarnished chandelier with uncertain pendants hung in lopsided solitude; and a tired chaise longue sprawled redundant in a corner, its days of hurly-burly long since passed. Other than such features all was bare – and drear. As a prelude to their 'quarters', or indeed their holiday, the landing held little enticement. Felix could see Cedric's lips beginning to purse and wished to God they had gone to Brighton.

'So that's it,' declared their guide, indicating a pair of flaking double doors. 'I would show you round but time and tide wait for no man and I've got to dash – meeting a couple of chums at Harry's. You can expect a visitation

31

from Caruso in about ten minutes, it's his pottering hour. See you later I daresay,' he added vaguely, and the next moment had turned and disappeared down the staircase, leaving them alone confronting the double doors.

'Have you a key?' Cedric asked.

'What?'

'A key,' he repeated, 'they might be locked.'

Felix sighed. 'No I do not have a key, and we shall have to find out won't we.' He approached the doors and turned one of the handles. Nothing happened. He turned the other with no effect.

'Doubtless your cousin has taken the key with her. Probably completely forgot you were coming,' his friend observed helpfully.

'Nonsense,' Felix replied, turning pink. 'Of course she didn't forget. Bound to have left it with that Hope person. Suppose I shall have to hike down to find him before he capers off to Harry's.' He paused. 'Who is Harry anyway, some crossword boffin?'

'Unlikely. Most probably the rather superior bartender – owner actually – in the Calle Vallaresso. I will introduce you there at some point if you behave, *and* assuming we survive this rather unsavoury tenement.' An insistent bladder stopped Felix venting his fury, and containing both, he hastened to descend the stairs.

'Just a minute,' Cedric called, 'one could try brute force, a good kick for instance.' He extended a well-shod foot and lunged briskly at the doors. They creaked open immediately, leaving the assailant wrong-footed and teetering.

At first they could see nothing, all swathed in darkness; but a darkness sweetly redolent of lavender and lily.

'Delicious,' breathed Felix, 'but where's the damned light?'

They fumbled and stumbled and eventually found a set of switches which did the trick. Brightness blazed upon them, and with the brightness revelation.

They were in a very large room, not grand exactly but imposing: its walls covered in Venetian fabric, a high ceiling figured with a delicate *trompe l'œil* and furniture of an austere elegance – suggesting French provenance rather than Italian. But the curtains were clearly Venetian: thick lavish brocade, boldly patterned in intricate swirls of greens and coppery pinks, their heavy folds trailing carelessly on the floor. In one corner stood an open harpsichord, in another a large and assertively modern drinks cabinet parading a regiment of variously hued bottles. Everywhere were large vases of pale lilies and dark lavender whose scent, now that its source was revealed, seemed doubly intense.

'Hmm. All very fragrant,' Cedric observed.

'Yes,' added Felix eagerly, '*and* well equipped.' He gestured towards the bottles.

Cedric nodded. 'Let us trust the contents are fresh.'

'Well the flowers certainly are, so I think you can assume the drink is,' replied Felix defensively. 'Anyway we'll soon find out, but first I simply must . . .' He scanned the room looking for another exit, and then disappeared through a door at the far end.

Returning some minutes later much relieved he found the room empty and the curtains drawn back. French windows stood open revealing a veranda and Cedric's back.

He joined his companion and surveyed the view – the ornate balconies opposite, elegant patrician façades cheek by jowl with time-worn crumbling garrets, the plethora of jumbled rooftops and sporadic bell towers, a narrowly glimpsed stretch of the Grand Canal, its waters choppy and fuscous green; and immediately below them their own small tributary with its defective jetty and hammering workmen. The rain had ceased, sun was slyly gleaming through the clouds and the men had removed their oilskins. Felix gazed down, took out his cigarettes, and as one of the hammerers glanced up on impulse gave a languid wave. Rather to his surprise it was returned. He smiled, inhaled his cigarette and turning to Cedric murmured, 'Rather a nice view don't you think?'

'Most agreeable,' the other assented. 'Now, presumably in the course of your quest you have made a general reconnaissance. I take it there is a habitable bedroom or two?'

'Several,' Felix replied carelessly, 'plus two bathrooms, a dining hall, a kitchen plus breakfast room, storeroom, a small study with a balcony and staircase adjoining the main one . . . Oh yes, and there's a sizeable billiards room should you require it.' Noting Cedric's look of surprise he began to feel so much better. 'I'll give you a tour,' he said graciously.

Tour complete, with Felix smug and Cedric reassured, they attended to the task of unpacking and adjusting to their new abode, which, while not opulent, was indeed spacious and aesthetic.

Cedric nodded approvingly at the choice of Turner prints and original Canalettos, raised a quizzical eyebrow at their hostess's choice of literature (Proust, Raymond Chandler and Winnie the Pooh) and took pleasure in toying with the Kirkman harpsichord before lightly pronouncing it hopelessly out of tune.

'Doubtless the damp from the canal – one has to be so careful with these things, they can't be neglected,' he remarked; before adding hastily, 'but the flowers are lovely of course. Presumably the concierge's parting touch; we must remember to leave her a full envelope. I must say your cousin certainly shares your floral instincts!' He gave Felix a genial smile, relaxed now that matters appeared more hopeful.

'Yes, they are lovely,' Felix agreed. 'Perhaps she had learnt of my recent good fortune and it's her way of offering congratulations. Amazing how word gets around.'

'You mean learnt of the Royal Appointment plaque? But surely you must have told her that yourself.'

'Well no actually. I had been so busy arranging things for this little jaunt that it quite slipped my mind.'

'Good gracious,' Cedric exclaimed, 'you must have been busy!'

'*Exactly*. So busy in fact that I now deserve a very stiff drink.' He went over to the cocktail cabinet and inspected its display. 'Perhaps we should deviate from our usual and try something a little more exotic, something specifically Venetian. After all, when in Rome as it were . . .' He scrutinised the labels. 'Oh *this* looks rather interesting, especially if one adds a slug of gin. I wonder if—'

Cedric coughed. 'Before you get too engrossed I think you should remember your visitor.'

'My visitor? What visitor?'

'The opera singer of course. According to Hope-Landers this is his hour, so he is due for arrival at any minute.'

'Oh Lord, the bloody dog!'

'Precisely, and if I'm not mistaken that could be the creature now.'

There was an unmistakable scratching at the doors, a muted whine, and the next moment a stout and flop-eared basset had nosed its way across the threshold. Caruso had made his entrance.

CHAPTER FOUR

As with Felix and Cedric, Rosy's arrival in Venice a few days later had also been damp. Alighting at the St Lucia railway terminus she was enveloped by what optimists might term an early morning mist but realists a deep fog. Expecting sunlight and panorama Rosy was ill-prepared for the pall of dankness. Voices were muffled, figures blurred and she was engulfed by a grisly clamminess – a condition the Canalettos had ignored and the guidebooks failed to describe. She felt a stab of irrational pique: was this the vaunted Venice with its romance and vivid pageantry? Where were the gondolas, the sparkling fountains and charming bridges? Where for that matter was the Grand Canal and a vaporetto? She fumbled in her pocket for Dr Stanley's scribbled directions and peered into the fog.

'*Signora, posso lei aiutare? Lei è perduta?*'

Rosy was startled by the sudden voice so close to her ear. 'What? Sorry, I—' she began.

'Ah, the signora is *Eenglish*,' the man exclaimed, 'I thought maybe; you have the look.' He beamed.

What look? Rosy wondered, not sure whether to be flattered or annoyed. '*Mi dispiace*,' she faltered, '*non parlo Italiano. Dove—*'

'Do not trouble dear lady, I speak excellent Eenglish. You want vaporetto, yes? I take your case.' Without waiting for a reply he had seized her suitcase and walked off quickly.

Rosy followed, plunged in apprehension. She had paid a lot for that case. Was it now to be appropriated by some glib-tongued foreigner? Her mind whirled. At best he would expect a large tip; at worst she would never see the case again. If the former, did her purse contain enough loose lire? If the latter, what the hell was she going to do? She pursued him doggedly along the platform, across a concourse, through an archway and then down a flight of shallow steps.

At the bottom of these he set down the case and flinging out an arm announced, '*Eccolo, il Canal Grande!* Here you wait, the boat come, you pay. *Benvenuta* in Venezia, dear madam.' He bowed deeply from the waist, and with a stream of '*arrivederci*'s disappeared into the murk leaving Rosy ashamed and relieved.

As the vaporetto chugged its course down the broad channel, weaving from bank to bank picking up early workers, Rosy gazed around at the tall spectral façades rising steeply from the leaden waters. They loomed on either side in unending lines, shrouded and stately in the wafting mist. Yes, this was like the postcards all right; but postcards overlaid with centuries of dust – colour and detail lost in a film of grey. And despite her earlier sense of anticlimax Rosy felt a stirring of interest, awe even, as the canal widened and opened into a theatrical curve, its serpentine contour giving a cold majesty to the looming palazzi. A few of these she thought she recognised from photographs. Were those the crenelated walls of the Ca' d'Oro, or that the famed Foscari? And could the Byzantine building to her right be the Palazzo Loredan . . . ? Hazy air and knowledge made identity uncertain.

Gradually the worst of the fog lifted, leaving a veil of mist which while still damp held hints of pallid sun. Rosy checked her watch and saw it was a quarter to eight and hoped that her hostess would not be bothered by the early arrival; although, she reasoned, running a guest house the woman must be used to such disturbance. And in any case, from what little had been gleaned on the crackling telephone in London there had been no objection.

But concern for her landlady's convenience was quickly eclipsed by the sight of a bridge ahead – a bridge heavily ornate yet stonily solid and crowned with graceful arches. Surely it could only be the Rialto! Rosy experienced a surge of excitement as she surveyed the fabled edifice. So this was Shylock's stamping ground, the spot where Antonio sought word of his foundering ships and Launcelot Gobbo capered; where deals were clinched, schemes hatched, lovers trysted and gossip flourished into alluring scandal. 'What news on the Rialto?'. . . Like generations of visitors approaching the city by this route, Rosy recognised the bridge and with a start of pleasure knew she was nearing the heart of things.

She had disembarked further down at the stop for the Accademia. And following Dr Stanley's casual instructions had heaved her suitcase over a couple of small bridges and through a perplexing network of squares and alleyways, until rather to her own amazement she confronted a door set in a high wall and bearing the required inscription *Casa Witherington*. Underneath were four directives: *Suonate*; *Hier klingeln*; *Sonnez*; and *Kindly Ring the Bell*. Meekly Rosy did as she was bid and waited in some nervousness. Two minutes later, with a creak and a rattle, the door swung open; and a very small lady in a very large hat beamed a welcome.

'Come in my dear, how clever of you to arrive exactly at half past eight! This is when we commence breakfast – a most soothing meal I always think. My regulars rarely appear and those who do rarely speak. *Such* a peaceful time. It quite sets me up for the rest of the day and prepares one for the garrulous supper. And since you have had to travel all the way from ghastly Victoria station I daresay you will be grateful for the quiet.'

Rosy nodded and gave what she felt might be an appropriately silent smile, while inwardly wondering if

40

her hostess always wore a hat at breakfast. (She did; and at most other times too.)

Miss Witherington led her across a small courtyard into the house and up a steep flight of stairs, which, burdened with her suitcase, Rosy found rather more of a challenge than did the seemingly agile chatelaine.

'I have given you the corner room, it's quite large and well away from Mr Downing – poor man he does snore so! I always think it must be agony for the children, probably keeps them awake all night.'

'What children?' Rosy asked uneasily. She hadn't bargained on being billeted with a crew of infants.

'Oh Mr Downing is a resident master at a prep school in Worthing. He comes here in the holidays to recover.'

She led the way into a semi-darkened room redolent of gardenias and Mansion Polish – the latter presumably specially imported from England. Opening the shutters Miss Witherington exclaimed, 'Oh look the sun after all. I *knew* it would break through. I win my bet.' She clapped her hands trilling gaily, '*I'm in the money, come on my honey . . . !*'

Rosy was startled, both by the song and its occasion. Was Miss Witherington a bookmaker on the side?

Seeing her surprise the other explained, 'You see I am awfully good on weather. You don't live in Venice for thirty years without learning something about its climate's whims and vagaries – or those of its residents for that matter.' She gave a laugh and added, 'And with such *meteorological expertise* it does seem a waste not to put it to some lucrative use. Wouldn't you agree my dear?'

Rosy said that she entirely agreed, while making a mental note not to be so rash as to bet on anything with Miss Witherington: quite possibly the lady harboured expertise in other areas equally gainful.

When she had gone Rosy unpacked and stared out of the window at the wide expanse of water. Was this still part of the Grand Canal? Surely she had left its banks some time ago. She consulted the guidebook and realised that it was of course the broad inlet south of the city, the Canale della Giudecca, forming part of the lagoon and named after the long island mentioned by Stanley. Over to the left she could discern the dome and spires of the great Redentore, admired by most and hated by Ruskin. To Rosy's untutored eye it looked pretty damn good . . . ten times better than Battersea Power Station that was for sure! She powdered her nose, combed her hair and prepared to go down to partake of the 'soothing' breakfast.

In fact it was not so much soothing as torpid. Quiet most certainly: two other guests, male and female, and a cat. The former were engrossed in newspapers, the latter fast asleep. The fare was moderate: some very un-Italian cornflakes and porridge, rolls not quite desiccated and a pot of decidedly weak tea. Looking in vain for coffee Rosy wondered if after all she should have held out for the Danieli.

'Don't worry,' the male guest volunteered, 'it gets better

in the evening. In fact the old girl is a very good cook when she chooses but she never chooses at breakfast. It's as well to accept that otherwise nerves are fretted and one starts the day at a disadvantage.' He smiled politely and glancing at the woman said, 'Wouldn't you agree Daphne?'

The woman nodded. 'Yes. Submit to circumstance and then compensate with excellent coffee and ice cream round the corner at Tonelli's. If you try their house speciality Bomba Garibaldi you'll never touch a Lyons wafer again.' Having delivered so practical a tip she returned to silence and her paper.

Rosy glanced at the clock: nine-fifteen. A little early in the day for frozen explosions but something she might well try later on. Meanwhile there were more pressing matters to pursue: Horace and the Pacelli bookshop. Best to start immediately before being seduced by the guiles of ices and architecture. She opened her handbag and consulted Stanley's plan of campaign.

As explained, your first port of call should be the Pacelli bookshop. This is where Sir Fenton's cousin saw the volume originally. He says that from what he remembers the owner is a little dour but should be cooperative in aiding your searches. There is a remote possibility that he may still have the book – in which case snap it up straightaway and return here three days hence allowing yourself time to visit St Mark's, Torcello and the Gesuiti church. Viewing these is essential to your education; but unless you are still without the book on no account linger longer as I shall want you here to organise my new set of lectures.

However, if – as is the more likely – the book is not with Pacelli then you will need to make further enquiry (probably at the other shop in the Castello quarter, assuming it's still there). This may necessitate a longer stay. But the essential thing is to bring back the goods. Thus do not flag or be sidetracked by frippery. A telephoned progress report would be appreciated. You should have no difficulty in tracing the first bookshop: I gather it's somewhere in the Rialto area – bound to be easy enough to find.

'A model of usefulness,' Rosy said to herself dryly, 'and how touching to be concerned with my cultural enlargement.' She finished the cornflakes, scowled at the weak tea, nodded to her fellow guests and walked out through the now sunny courtyard to begin her quest.

Via a series of turnings and mis-turnings she arrived at the Accademia Bridge, climbed its steps – pausing like all visitors and artists to admire the *belvedere* on either side – and descended in the direction of the Ponte di Rialto. At least, that was what the sign indicated. But she soon discovered that 'Per Rialto' was where all street signs pointed in Venice regardless from where you had come or intended to go; indeed sometimes you would be torn in two, frowning over opposing arrows. Initially Rosy was exasperated: 'Ridiculous!' she protested to herself. But again like all visitors, diverted by the intrigue of a fresh new world she slowed her pace to a saunter and left it to fate as to where and when she might reach her goal.

In fact the goal appeared quite suddenly, unmistakable and so much bigger than when seen mistily from the vaporetto. It was also much busier: shops, largely jewellers, flanking its sides, while bevies of people scurried, chattered and pottered upon its ancient steps. There was a murmur of voices, Italian mainly, some German and occasionally an exclamatory American. No English an omission which gave Rosy a perverse satisfaction. She joined the potterers, intrigued by the window displays of pearls, coral, silks and silver. Books? None it seemed unless you counted a rather chi-chi-looking stationer's. She stared around hoping to see the name Pacelli writ large over some ancient doorway. There was nothing of course. Bound to be near, she thought, trying to share Stanley's airy optimism, and decided to postpone matters with a coffee. This did much to assuage her breakfast deprivation and she sipped it gratefully on a terrace beside the Canal.

As she sat watching the scene of boats and busyness, suddenly, and for no apparent reason, there slipped into her mind an image of the current Pope. Rosy was startled – she was not in the habit of dwelling on the Vatican and its incumbents. What on earth had made her think of that fellow? . . . Ah of course! His name: professionally Pius;

privately Pacelli. No wonder those ascetic features had filled her memory. She was amused by the coincidence and wondered idly whether somewhere in the papal cousinship there might indeed lurk a Venetian bookseller. Well pope's cousin or no, she certainly hoped she could find the wretched man. It had already occurred to her that Stanley's phrase 'on or near' held multiple meanings. If the latter, was the shop left of the bridge or to its right? North or south? On the Canal bank or in some shadowed offshoot . . . and in any case, exactly how near was 'near'? She sighed, and leaving some lire on the table set off to investigate.

After ten minutes of aimless wandering she knew that there was nothing for it but to use her meagre Italian and make enquiries. The first person she stopped looked puzzled and then said, '*Mi scusi*, no understand English,' and hurried on. Rosy was mortified, having felt that while her vocabulary might be sparse her accent was good. In this she was clearly mistaken!

A couple were approaching and she tried again, enunciating her words with greater precision, but this too produced a negative response. 'Say,' an American voice rang out, 'not Italian, kiddo. We're from Texas *USA*!' They smiled genially and also hurried on. Had she been in England the obvious course would have been to approach a policeman, but no such person seemed in evidence; and in any case she rather doubted whether a Venetian *poliziotto* would be quite as ready as a London bobby to deal with the perplexities of witless tourists.

'*Signor*,' she said nervously to a small and sharp-suited man on her left, '*Può aiutarmi? Cerco una libreria si chiama Pacelli e Figlio. E qui in vicino forse?*' She smiled hopefully.

The man regarded her solemnly and then said in impeccable English: 'For one from Perfidious Albion you speak extremely well. My compliments, signora.' Rosy didn't know whether to feel flattered or furious. Perfidious bloody Albion indeed! The cheek of it! Her indignation must have shown for with a light chuckle he said quickly, 'A little joke of course. Your country is charming, I know it well . . . And yes, I also know the bookshop you seek.' That was something at any rate and she asked if it was far.

'Not at all. It is the second turning on the right and then straight ahead to the end of the cul-de-sac. If you permit me I will be your companion.'

'Be my companion?' she thought. 'No fear!' And then realised that of course he was merely suggesting he should show her the way. She smiled her thanks and they set off.

As they walked he enquired whether the signora was looking for something special; what was her interest in this particular shop? 'Since his old father's demise not many serious tourists come to Giuseppe – he caters for what one might call esoteric tastes.' He eyed her quizzically and for a moment Rosy felt that something was being implied that she didn't entirely understand . . . or rather she hoped she didn't.

'My boss has sent me to look for some poems by Horace,' she explained stiffly. 'It's a rather special edition.'

'Really? A special edition?' He frowned and seemed to look puzzled. But after a slight pause gave a laugh: 'Ah Horace! Yes of course: "*Quis desiderio sit pudor aut modus tam cari capitis? Praecipe lugubris cantus . . .*" Your boss must share my tastes: I used to read a lot of Horace at Eastbourne, I became quite a specialist.'

Rosy stopped in her tracks. 'At *Eastbourne*! Why on earth should one want to read Horace at Eastbourne?'

'Ah but not the town itself, some miles outside. I was a prisoner of war in the area for three years. One had to do something.'

'Oh – yes. Yes I see . . .' She didn't particularly but by this time they had reached the bookshop doorway, and wishing her a happy and fruitful time in Venice her guide took his leave.

Anyone less like the pope would be hard to imagine. Giuseppe Pacelli possessed neither the height nor the El Greco features of his namesake. Squat, bald and snub-nosed, he resembled rather Charles Laughton playing Quasimodo – though judging by the speed at which he rushed to greet his new customer, without the latter's handicap. He beamed unctuously. '*Signora – bellissima donna – c'e cosa posso fare per lei?*'

Taken aback both by the speed and effusiveness, Rosy stammered, 'Er . . . *per favore, parla Inglese?*'

The smile broadened and the voice took on an ingratiating lilt. 'A leetle, a leetle, my lady.'

Rosy cleared her throat and spoke slowly and firmly,

as befitted an Englishwoman explaining something to a foreigner. 'Good, because I am trying to find a book of poems by the Latin author Horatius Flaccus.' She took a card from her pocket and laid it on the counter. 'These are the details and I gather this bookshop may once have had such a copy.'

He glanced down at the card. The smile waned somewhat and there was a brief silence. Then picking it up for closer scrutiny, he said, 'Of course, of course, we do have such a book. You would like to buy?'

'Very likely,' she answered.

Without a word he disappeared into a back room and was gone for some time, presumably raking the dusty shelves. 'Well,' she said to herself, 'couldn't be simpler. Just shows, occasionally things do work. With a delayed report to Dr Stanley I can spin out another four days here in art and fun. *And* return with the goods!' Grinning in triumph she glanced casually at the titles on a nearby table. These were not quite as she had expected – translations of Hank Janson, Frank Harris, Henry Miller, a lavishly illustrated Marquis de Sade, something called *Tales My Mother Should Not Have Told Me* and a book with no author but entitled *Histoire d'O*. She was about to see who O was but was interrupted by the return of Giuseppe with the Horace. He flourished the volume under her nose and immediately began to wrap it.

'Just a moment, signor,' Rosy said hastily, 'if you don't mind I'd like to take a look.' She started to give it a cursory scan, and then stopped. The editor's name was certainly

Bodger but there was no sign of a signature or an inscription. She trawled the pages. Nothing. No handwriting anywhere, whether in quill, nib, or even pencil.

She sighed. 'I am so sorry, but this is not what I am looking for. It is essential I have the signed edition with its inscription. This has no mark at all.'

He gave a blank stare and shrugged. 'But there is no other, signora.'

'But I gathered that there certainly was . . . Perhaps it got sent to another shop. I was told that—'

'Who told you?' the man interrupted sharply. 'A person here in Venice?' The obsequious tone had assumed a hostile edge.

'Well, no. You see . . .' She trailed off, knowing her Italian was not up to explaining the situation and doubting his English could cope. She rather suspected, too, that whatever lingo was adopted such efforts would be futile.

'You want?' he asked curtly, pointing to the book.

'No, no I do not want,' she replied firmly.

He shrugged again, and reverting to Italian said indifferently, '*Va bene. Grazie, signora. Buongiorno.*'

Sensing a dismissal she moved to the door, but as she turned the handle he called out in English: 'Signora, I assure you no other copy. This one only. Do not look more.' Rosy gave a brief nod and left the premises.

'Lying,' she muttered to herself as she retraced her steps along the cobbled alley. He might not have stocked the one she sought but how could he possibly be so sure that another did not exist? Of course he couldn't. And as to his injunction to look no further, she very much doubted it had been prompted by concern for her feet or time. Not so much a piece of advice as an order. Damn cheek!

She sat on a piece of wall and brooded. Fallen at the first fence. So what now? Presumably Plan B, i.e. visit the Castello establishment. She took out the map and checked its position. Yes, walkable: along the Riva degli Schiavoni in the direction of the Arsenale, on to the Via Garibaldi, turn left at the John Cabot house and with a bit of luck the Calle di Fiori should materialise somewhere on the right with the shop at the far end. Well at least she could combine business with pleasure. The route passed a whole gamut of famed landmarks: the Doge's palace, the Bridge of Sighs, the celebrated Danieli, church of the Pietà . . . and oh, of course, the very house where Henry James had completed *The Portrait of a Lady*! A splendid itinerary, especially as she would have to walk through St Mark's Piazza to reach the waterfront.

She stood up, impatient to get going before the shop shut for lunch and to start her acquaintance with so lovely a city.

CHAPTER FIVE

Rosy's curiosity had been more than satisfied by her morning ramble, the places she passed stirring her impatience for further pleasures.

However, such pleasures did not include her time at the Castello bookshop, which lasted for approximately one minute. The place was closed; the notice in the window advising intending browsers that the owner was taking his annual holiday. The blinds were drawn and a mesh covered the door. Rosy was so frustrated that she stamped her foot – twice, an action which made her feel foolish. She glanced around hoping no one had witnessed so absurd a display, and then recalled that this was Italy not England: eyes were less alert to personal oddity. She started to go back the way she had come and then decided to cut to the right to explore more widely – at least something might be gained from the fruitless mission! She crossed a small campo, selected a street displaying a direction for San Zaccaria and found herself beside a narrow canal and a bridge.

Preoccupied by her recent frustration and envisaging a restorative drink, Rosy did not see the dog at first – but she heard it all right: an explosive throaty woof like a grumpy cannon. She jumped and nearly tripped up the steps of the bridge; and then looking down encountered the mournful eyes of a stout basset hound. It stood four-square gazing up at her, brows furrowed and feet splayed.

She cleared her throat wondering vaguely what 'good dog' was in Italian. '*Buono cane*,' she enunciated carefully, moving to circumvent it. Evidently it did not care for that, for it also moved and continued to impede her path. The expression (impassive) remained the same, as did the resolutely spread paws.

'Oh come on,' she protested in English, 'do get out of the way!'

'It won't,' a voice said from behind her, 'whatever language you use.'

She spun round and was confronted by Felix Smythe, holding a dangling lead and wearing the harassed look of one in pursuit of a dog.

'Good Lord, Felix,' she exclaimed, 'what on earth are you doing here?'

'I could ask the same, Miss Gilchrist,' Felix replied, 'but

as a general answer to your own enquiry I am here on holiday; more precisely I am trying to secure this hound. Would you be so kind as to hold its collar while I clip on the lead?' This was less of a question than a directive, and Rosy did as she was bid while Felix bent to fumble with the creature's neck. As he did so he received an absent-minded lick on the cheek. Felix recoiled. 'Can't think why it does that,' he complained.

'Obvious. He must like you,' said Rosy. 'Some dogs have peculiar preferences. I remember we once had a Labrador who—'

Felix gave a dismissive sniff. 'Fascinating I'm sure, but one doesn't come to Venice to hear of the idiosyncrasies of your erstwhile pets Miss Gilchrist. Now, what exactly are *you* doing here? Don't tell me the BM has dispensed with your services, I was given to understand you were its essential lynchpin, a veritable clerical *sine qua non*!' He gave a sly titter.

'Not by me, you weren't,' retorted Rosy, stung by his sarcasm. She shouldn't have made the quip about canine tastes. Really, Felix Smythe could be so hoity-toity! She flashed him a dazzling smile and said sweetly, 'Actually I am no more a clerk there than you are Eliza Doolittle. But tell me, how's trade since the great accolade? I haven't had a chance to congratulate you.'

That did it as she knew it would. To have a 'By Royal Appointment' warrant displayed above the threshold of Smythe's Bountiful Blooms had been one of Felix's dearest wishes and a source of endless hope and speculation. Its eventual award, just at the close of the grisly murder case they had all been involved in, could not have been better timed. Temporarily away from London, Rosy had been unable to congratulate him in person. But now was her chance and she made full use of it. 'You must be thrilled,' she exclaimed.

Felix's taut features relaxed, and leaning a nonchalant elbow on the stone parapet he proceeded to give an animated account of his triumph. 'Yes,' he said modestly, 'it was most gracious of Her Majesty to remember me, most gracious. But then I've always thought that the dear Queen Mother and I have a special bond where flowers are concerned: she is *very* discerning you know.'

He continued to enthuse for a while, and then prompted by a yawn from the dog stopped in mid-sentence, and said, 'But *what* did you say you were doing in Venice?'

Rosy started to explain and had just finished the bit about Bodger's mediocre translation but distinguished commentary when the air was rent with an excruciating melange of leonine rumbles and peahen screeches. A small poodle and its large owner had mounted the steps, and the basset hound had clearly taken exception to both. The ensuing altercation, both human and canine, was raucous and embarrassing. However, peace and honour eventually restored the interlopers went on their way, the poodle casting scandalised glances over its shoulder.

Felix mopped his brow and glared at his charge. 'Bloody dogs,' he observed, 'the sooner I get back for a siesta the better! Tell you what, Miss Gilchrist, Cedric and I will meet you at Florian's tomorrow evening at nine o'clock, they do the most wonderful cakes . . . You know it do you?'

'Er, yes. It's in the Piazza isn't it? Underneath the arches,' Rosy replied, slightly surprised by the invitation.

'Yes, beneath the *portici*,' Felix confirmed. 'So we'll meet there then. Good. Now I really must go and take a rest before Cedric returns from the Accademia demanding tea. One gets so exhausted . . .' He yanked at the lead, and dog and minder trotted down the steps and were soon lost in the shadows of an archway.

Undecided whether to be pleased or disturbed by the encounter Rosy bought an ice cream, sat in the sun and brooded. It was not that she disliked Felix and Cedric, simply that she felt no particular affinity – a negative which she sensed was reciprocated. Until the business of her aunt they had been little more than passing acquaintances – figures occasionally encountered at a cocktail party or a private view, where exchanges had been polite yet distant. But the business of her aunt's murder with all its attendant horror and embarrassment had perforce pulled them into a mutual orbit. For a period she had been thrust into a collusive intimacy and shared a knowledge it would have been rash to reveal . . . Mercifully that was all over now, and the painful phase firmly (if not deeply) buried. Nevertheless did she really want to rekindle false intimacies, to renew a link which had been none of their choosing?

She licked the cornet's melting dollop, savoured its silky texture and decided that on the whole she did not . . . And yet even as she reached that conclusion she knew full well that come the following evening she would sally forth to Florian's eager for chat and gaiety, however brittle. Already, like thousands of such neophytes, she had fully succumbed to the Venetian spell; and also like many was content to absorb the city's charms alone. But it was content not averse to companionship; and the prospect of sharing cocktails and a moonlit Piazza, even with Felix and Cedric, did have a certain appeal. Besides, who knew, they might suggest something useful re the errant Horace!

'So why on earth is Rosy Gilchrist in Venice?' enquired Cedric. 'I should have thought Frinton would be more her style.' He flashed a superior smile.

'Something to do with tracing a book I gather. That Dr Stanley person sent her here.'

'Really? What sort of book?'

Felix frowned. 'Uhm . . . not sure. Something called Hodge's Boris I think: a collection of poetry. Can't say it sounded frightfully exciting but she seemed keen. I wasn't really listening as Caruso was squaring up to attack a poodle and I had to throttle him while being charming to its owner. Quite a manoeuvre and I really couldn't attend to a third party as well.'

'Hodge's Boris? Whatever's that? I've never heard of it.'

Felix shrugged. 'Well dear boy, I don't suppose you've

heard of everything, but that's what she said. I am merely relaying information.'

'Hmm. Ought we to ask her here for a drink? It would be a civil gesture I suppose. Is she alone?'

'She is alone and I have already done that – well not here but to Florian's. Tomorrow evening at nine.'

'Florian's? That's a bit excessive isn't it, even for Miss Gilchrist. Should she wish for a second zabaglione I trust you will be the one doing the honours.'

'Oh come now, Cedric, we're in Venice not penny-pinching in Mayfair! I think we can permit Miss Gilchrist a second drink on the house – *our* house. And anyway you know how I adore Florian's; any excuse to dally at one of those little gilt tables.'

'Or indeed to dally with the little gilt waiters.' Despite the acerbic tone Cedric lowered his left eyelid. Such ocular gestures were rare with the professor and Felix giggled.

CHAPTER SIX

The two friends had rapidly taken to their new abode (and indeed its glorious context); while even Caruso was proving less of a penalty than Cedric had feared, being on the whole fairly cooperative. Thus a few days into their sojourn they were enjoying a leisurely breakfast on the veranda before gathering themselves to visit the Frari, leaving the dog to dream of bones and arias in the autumn sun.

'We don't have to stay long,' Felix said, 'there's so much stuff there it might be indigestible. I suggest we stagger our visits, just a bit at a time. Today could be a little *aperitivo* as it were.'

'Yes,' agreed Cedric, 'but we must make time for the two great Titians. First things first. And then of course we might just glance at—'

'The barber shop? *What* a good idea.'

Cedric was startled. 'Er, I was going to say the Bellini *Madonna and Child* in the sacristy, but if you have a hankering for a haircut I suppose that must take precedence.' He broke off and sighed. 'Ah, light dawns: it's not a hankering for a haircut as such but a yen to inspect the premises of the two gents we met in that bar last night. What were their names? Paolo and Pucci or some such. A bit Marx Brotherish I thought, especially the one with frizzy hair, a sort of taller version of Harpo.' He gave a mild chuckle.

'But you must admit they were very charming; and they did say we should drop in any time we were passing.'

'But we shan't be passing, the shop is in the opposite direction from the Frari.'

'Oh only a few bridges away,' Felix said dismissively, 'and besides don't you want some more of that Fontini cologne?'

'I might.'

'Good, that's settled then: pictures then scent – or should that be *pittore poi profumo*?' Felix leered and tilted his panama.

But their schedule was to be interrupted. As they approached the Accademia Bridge, seeking espressos prior to the Frari, Guy Hope-Landers came down the steps accompanied by a slim tawny-haired young woman, striking in cream Capri pants, matching ballerina pumps and cerise sweater. She was twirling a long cigarette holder and talking animatedly to her companion.

'Ah,' muttered Felix, 'our fellow resident. Too early in the day for niceties, perhaps we can circumvent . . .'

'Too late, he's seen us. Prepare to charm.' They composed their features.

Hope-Landers gave an expansive wave. 'Hello,' he exclaimed, 'the custodians. All goes well I trust? No problems – escaping gas, escaping dog, boiler buggered?'

They assured him that everything was exactly as they might wish, and smiled politely at the lady.

The man launched into introductions. 'This is Lucia Borgino,' he explained, 'granddaughter of the venerable Gideon Vaughan, he of the splendid Mayfair art gallery. Lucia has inherited his eye – always on the *qui vive* for new talent. And just like grandpa, a word from her can make or break any budding Picasso.' He shot her a glance half mocking, half reverent.

The discerning Lucia gave a casual shrug, and, inserting a cigarette into her holder, observed that with so much dross flooding the market it was as well that somebody was prepared to take a stand. 'Although actually,' she confided, 'it's not so much the would-be Picassos that you have to watch but those dreary suburban flower painters whose pathetic offerings cram the Summer Exhibition year after year . . . God how I loathe vapid lilies, in whatever medium, alive or framed. They are always the same: pale, etiolated and *totally* uninteresting.' She gave an affected sigh and with perfectly formed lips did a fair imitation of a Brigitte Bardot pout. Felix, who harboured a passion for lilies and a distaste for Miss Bardot, hated her immediately.

It was too bad of Cedric. But baulked of his morning caffeine and seeking alternative stimulus, he said casually, 'Oh Felix adores lilies, an expert in fact. I can tell you that since our arrival the Palazzo Reiss has turned into a veritable *giardino dei gigli*; so fragrant, and the dog loves it. He and Felix visit the flower market every morning and come back laden with the things.'

Lucia raised an already perfectly arched eyebrow and, regarding Felix with polite disdain, remarked, 'How quaint.'

There was a brief silence, during which a cat screeched and Felix scowled. And then Hope-Landers said, 'As a matter of fact I was just telling Lucia about your friend and her quest for the Horace book. At least I assume that's the one Mr Smythe was referring to yesterday, the Horation odes as edited by R. D. M. Bodger.' (Felix nodded vaguely.) 'Lucia thinks she might know the man who has it and could make an introduction.'

'Oh really?' Cedric replied with sudden interest. 'That would be helpful. One gathers Miss Gilchrist is becoming just a mite *agitato* about the whole thing. Thinks she is letting her boss down if she returns to the BM empty-handed. Felix thought she was distinctly on edge about it. We will probably be seeing her from time to time so if the matter could be resolved it might be of universal relief. Wouldn't you say so, Felix?'

But Felix, still stung by the attitude of the lily-hating

Lucia, affected not to hear, being too engrossed in the scudding clouds over the dome of the distant Salute.

'Well,' Hope-Landers replied genially, 'I daresay something can be arranged. We can probably fix a meeting with Carlo, assuming that he actually does have the thing. Not that that in itself means anything. By all accounts he can be quite tricky – well, according to Lucia he is.'

'I didn't say he was *tricky*,' Lucia corrected him, 'merely that he is fastidious as to whom he deals with.' Her glance hovered briefly in the direction of Felix, and then addressing Cedric, she said, 'I mean, what exactly is this lady like? Presumably she speaks Italian.'

'Er, not as such,' Cedric murmured, 'but she is eminently respectable.'

Lucia grimaced. 'How sad,' she sighed. 'No Italian and eminently respectable. What on earth is she doing in Venice?'

'As explained,' Cedric replied stiffly, 'seeking the Horace – and like thousands of others with or *without* Italian, admiring its beauty.' The acerbic note was familiar to Felix and he felt pleased with his friend. That should settle her hash, he thought.

It didn't of course. Lucia Borgino emitted an indulgent laugh, and patting her companion's arm said, 'Oh well I expect I can fix something – anything for you, Guy darling. Now let's get going, we've *so* much to do. Come on!' Without another word she started to walk away.

Her escort gave an apologetic smile. 'She's right, we are rather pressed. Her brother is coming to stay. But don't worry. She'll fix it with Carlo all right.' He lowered his voice: 'Rather influential you know.'

'How nice,' said Cedric coolly.

'Worry?' Felix expostulated after they had gone. 'Who said anything about being worried? Frankly I couldn't care a damn about that beastly book. If Rosy Gilchrist imagines I have come to Venice to be patronised by the likes of Lucretia Borgia or whatever her name is, she has got another thing coming. Really, it is too—'

'Be fair. Miss Gilchrist has never met the woman and she didn't exactly arrange this encounter.'

'No,' Felix retorted, 'and I don't exactly take the dog to the flower market every morning. We have been once, that's all!'

Cedric smiled. 'Ah but doubtless you will cultivate the habit . . . Now, let us pursue our plans that were so tiresomely interrupted: a peek at the Frari followed by a delicious late luncheon at Alfredo's; and then, who knows, perhaps a fragrant visit to the two Marx Brothers. What could be nicer?'

CHAPTER SEVEN

Her hostess had been right. Unlike breakfast, supper at the Casa Witherington proved to be, if not garrulous, at least moderately animated. In their amiable gentility Rosy's fellow guests made easy company and she listened with interest to their talk of Venice and its quirks and pleasures. Most were middle-aged and evidently habitués of the establishment, though there were a couple of young Germans who spent most of their time gazing at each other in rapt absorption. Clearly honeymooners.

'Is this just a pleasure trip or are you here on dreary business?' Mr Downing asked. 'Last week we had a chap staying whose firm had something to do with London drains. Apparently he had been sent on a fact-finding mission connected with the Venice sewerage system. He said it was for purposes of comparison. I don't think he saw a thing of the city above ground – a somewhat subterranean sojourn I should think; or, as the punsters might say, a bit of a waste!'

Rosy laughed. 'Yes I am on business in a way, but my pursuits are entirely above ground. I'm trying to trace a book of Latin verse for my boss at the British Museum.'

'Ah, a *literary* mission; certainly more edifying than drains one would imagine.' Mr Downing sniffed and helped himself to the last of the zucchini and shovelled up the penultimate tomato. Rosy felt sorry for his prepschool charges: poor little brats, probably all starving.

'You don't mean the Bodger book do you?' Miss Witherington asked.

Rosy was surprised. 'Yes, do you know it?'

'I know *of* it, most people do – well a few at any rate. But it's all such nonsense.'

'What, the poetry? Oh but I should have thought . . . Though of course I gather the translation is unremarkable.'

'No, no. Not the content; the price on its head. Well over a million I believe. Is that your interest?'

Rosy nearly dropped her fork. A *million* pounds for that book? She was astounded. Whatever was the woman talking about?

'Er, well no,' she stammered. 'It's Dr Stanley, my head of department. He's mounting an exhibition of rare nineteenth-century first editions and wants to include it. He told me to offer twenty pounds for it – well guineas actually. I doubt that he had anything much higher in mind.' She giggled. 'So where is it and why does it cost a million?'

'Its whereabouts are not known and much disputed. As to its value, that is not the price-tag but the amount of reward offered to the lucky finder.'

'How extraordinary. So who on earth is offering such a sum?'

'A man called Berenstein. Rather eccentric – as also, given the association, is his first name. It is a bold parent who christens his son Farinelli, but his did and he seems happy enough with it. The boy is now an elderly recluse living in Padua with warped tastes and childish humour. Hence the nonsense of a million pounds.'

'What's wrong with Farinelli?' Rosy asked.

'Nothing at all, in fact a very illustrious name – though as a schoolboy in the playground the bearer stands the risk of being dubbed Il Castrato. Evidently you are not a follower of opera, Miss Gilchrist.'

Rosy acknowledged that she wasn't; and was about to ask why Farinelli Berenstein was so ready to dispense a million pounds for a poorly translated volume of Latin poems, when Miss Witherington exclaimed, 'Oh my goodness, I must flee: the orange soufflés will have hit the ceiling!' She leapt to her feet and scurried in the direction of the kitchen.

'She's good at those soufflés,' observed Downing musingly, 'but frankly I prefer the tortiglione . . . although of course her great triumph is the Monte Bianco. Now that really does take the biscuit! Unfortunately they don't make it in England, it's a speciality of . . .'

But Rosy was as indifferent to Mr Downing's culinary preferences as she was to Signor Farinelli's deficiencies. What mattered was the Horace and the man's involvement with it. She must find out more. Perhaps after supper with the drama of the soufflés subsided she could pin her hostess down to further revelation.

And then of course she remembered. No she couldn't buttonhole Miss Witherington after supper, she was due at Florian's to meet Felix and Cedric. Still, with luck she could corner her after breakfast. Meanwhile the prospect of a wander to the Piazza San Marco and a nightcap in stylish surroundings was rather appealing. She could wear the filigree silver earrings bought earlier in the day. Felix, at least, might appreciate them.

With time in hand she had taken the opportunity to stroll along the Zattere before striking inwards towards San Marco. The mid-October night was mild, warm even, and the Giudecca straits so smooth that the moored boats scarcely moved, only rarely the rhythmic slap of wood on water breaking the silence. One or two people were still about, dog-walkers and the occasional strolling couple, but in their quiet meanderings these somehow deepened rather than dispelled the tranquillity. Rosy gazed around at the dark waters and the distant gleams from the Giudecca, smelling the hints of late jasmine wafted from an unseen garden. She wished she could stay longer; but to the east the twinkling lights beckoned, and obediently she quickened her pace to reach the Gesuati church and take the left turn which would lead her to the Ponte Accademia and onwards to the Piazza.

She walked past the Campo Sant'Agnese lit only by stars and a gas lamp, and would have continued straight on but was stalled by a cat who seemed intent on making her acquaintance. Doubtless it was full of fleas, but it was rather a cute, fluffy little thing and she couldn't resist stooping to tickle its ears.

As she bent down whispering coaxing words she heard voices a little further ahead, and looking up saw a couple of men standing by a bench. They were engaged in lively conversation – heated really, as she could hear one of them insisting, '*Rivedi il tuo prezzo! Fai pagare di più l'Americano,* molto *di più,*' while the other gave what sounded like an oath and threw his cigarette to the ground.

'*Impossibile,*' he retorted.

'*Si, si,*' the other urged.

They broke off at her approach and muttered a peremptory '*Buonasera.*' Rosy responded politely and was about to walk on briskly, when the shorter of the two suddenly cried, 'Ah, it is the English signora who come to my shop! You wanted book, you want Horatius. You remember me?' She most certainly did, and he was no more appealing in the dark than he had been in daylight. She gave a cool smile of recognition.

'Madam has found her book?' he enquired slyly.

'Er, no not yet,' Rosy replied. She looked pointedly at her watch. 'Excuse me, I am in rather a hurry.'

'Perhaps the lovely lady has a date?' the other man had the cheek to ask; and added, 'Dates more fun than silly poems. Forget it, pretty girl!' He leered.

Rosy said nothing, sidestepped smartly and walked off. The air behind remained mute but she could feel them staring after her. She marched on – or as much as one could march in high heels. She had worn them to spend an elegant evening in Florian's, not to hobnob with frightful men in dark corners! Suddenly the prospect of seeing Cedric and Felix became oddly reassuring.

'Presumably she *will* come,' Cedric said, 'one never quite knows with Rosy Gilchrist: one of those contrary types whose intentions are difficult to assess.'

'You mean like me?' his companion asked coyly.

'Dear boy, your intentions are invariably transparent and just occasionally charming.'

Felix smirked, lit a cigarette and settled into his chair. Perhaps Rosy Gilchrist's presence might be a trifle otiose after all . . .

'Ah,' Cedric announced, 'here she is.' He waved towards one of the glass doors where Rosy stood diffidently, surveying the maze of velvet alcoves. It was a few months since Cedric had seen her and he felt that on the whole she passed muster. Rather smart in fact. He stood up, ushered her to their table and signalled the waiter.

Felix executed a neat bow and said, 'We rather like sidecars after dinner but have anything you choose – lemonade if you must.'

Rosy laughed, relaxed by the warm lights and convivial ambience. 'I think I can manage without the lemonade thank you. A sidecar would be delicious.'

Like all visitors to Venice inevitably they talked of the city: their impressions, experiences and favourite places. Or at least Cedric and Felix did. Rosy, newly arrived and diverted by her task, had less to contribute but she listened eagerly to their views and anecdotes. 'Oh dear,' she sighed, 'I haven't even been inside St Mark's yet, so goodness knows when I'll be able to fit in anything else. Dr Stanley wants me back by the end of the week complete with the wretched book!'

'Oh ditch the book and admit defeat,' counselled Felix, 'Torcello at dusk and San Giorgio at sunset are surely worth more than some Victorian hash of the Horace person! Spend your time wisely Miss Gilchrist.'

'Actually – you won't believe this and I hardly do myself – but that Victorian hash as you call it may be worth a great deal of money. Stupendous in fact.'

'Stupendous?' queried Cedric sceptically. 'And what might that mean – five hundred?'

Rosy shook her head. 'A million.'

Cedric was not easily shocked (or at least generally contrived to conceal such reaction) but at Rosy's words he almost did the nose trick into his cocktail. Felix too gave a gasp of incredulity, and then turning to Cedric rather thoughtlessly blurted, 'She's got it wrong!'

'No she has *not* got it wrong,' Rosy retorted, stung by his dismissal. 'I am merely passing on what my landlady told me this evening. Apparently there's some crank tycoon in Padua who . . .' And she proceeded to give them the few details she knew.

Felix tittered. 'Well that does put a different complexion on things. I think for a million one might consider missing both Torcello and San Giorgio!'

'So typical,' Cedric sighed. 'I always knew you were a philistine at heart.'

'Ah, but think of the exquisite paintings that could be purchased for one's own private delectation – to gaze upon daily if one chose and without the hordes getting in the way.'

There ensued an animated discussion as to which paintings might be selected and indeed whether such possession would justify the transaction. The issue remained unresolved and the topic concluded by another round of sidecars.

'Just think,' Felix said to Rosy, 'when you find the thing you and your boss will be able to retire early and live in clover – though I am sure you won't forget old friends in such good fortune.' He winked.

Rosy suspected that the wink contained a pinch of seriousness. *Old friends?* That was a new term all right!

'Yes but she won't find it,' said Cedric coolly. 'If what the landlady says is true others will have already looked;

and if nothing has so far emerged then I can't see why it suddenly should now. It's a dead duck.' He looked at Rosy: 'Felix is right. Forget the thing and enjoy Venice – or as the ineffable Horace would say, *carpe diem*!'

'Well I'd like to *carpe diem* with some zabagliones and coffee,' his friend declared.

'Good idea,' agreed Cedric. 'And then we'll escort the millionairess back to her lodging and a good night's rest. Pursuit of Art and Mammon is always fatiguing, don't you find Miss Gilchrist?' He gave a benign smile.

Rosy was grateful for the suggestion. Normally she wouldn't have thought twice about walking back on her own, but despite the distraction of Florian's and her companions' good humour, she still retained the image of Giuseppe Pacelli and his sidekick being mocking in the darkened square.

'Well that's a fine tale,' Felix laughed as he and Cedric made their way back to the palazzo. 'Do you think there's anything in it?'

'Not a jot. The landlady is probably batty and spinning her a line. Or it's one of those old canards that periodically flourish when nothing much else is going on, something to lighten the damp evenings when the tourists have left. The Venetians are noted for their inventiveness . . .'

CHAPTER EIGHT

Tired from her evening at Florian's and taking her cue from other residents, Rosy decided to skip breakfast and to remain a little longer in bed. She stretched and reviewed her progress. There had of course been none; none plus a slightly upsetting incident. However, one thing was useful: with nothing to report she was at least spared the tiresome job of telephoning Stanley. An undoubted bonus.

But one could hardly be content with so negative a gain; and she pondered her next move. To do as Felix and Cedric had recommended, i.e. abandon the whole project and take the opportunity to explore and enjoy Venice instead? It was certainly tempting. But was it ethical? After all as an employee of the Museum she was being paid to carry out an assignment. If that assignment proved unviable surely it was her bounden duty to admit defeat, curtail the expenses and return to London empty-handed but virtuous. The alternative was to return empty-handed having exploited her trip for all it was worth! The latter seemed cavalier, the former feeble . . . Indeed it was the thought of being feeble that galvanised Rosy. Surely it was pathetic to give up so quickly – and if she was going to indulge herself in Venice then such pleasures must be *earnt*, she told herself sternly.

Thus resolved she got out of bed and dressed hastily, intent on pursuing Miss Witherington to learn more of the Berenstein fellow and his connection with the Horace book. If nothing else it would at least show willing and be a positive enquiry, however unproductive.

'What a wonderful supper last night,' she enthused, carefully avoiding all mention of the meagre breakfast, 'that risotto was superb!'

'Oh well one doesn't live in Venice for years on end without learning something handy,' Miss Witherington replied modestly. She adjusted her hat and her eyes twinkled. It was obvious she had been gratified by Rosy's words.

'Uhm . . . you were talking about Mr Berenstein yesterday and his desire to get his hands on the Bodger edition of the Horace odes. Is he really offering so much money?'

'Oh yes,' Miss Witherington laughed, 'and I have a stake in it myself.'

'*You* have?' Rosy exclaimed. 'I'm sorry, I don't quite follow—'

'The offer of the reward has a time limit. It was set for four years and has only another few days to run. The project itself is absurd – an obsessive fantasy typical of Farinelli. The odds on fulfilling the offer's conditions are very long indeed, though the chances are still there of course. And thus being a realist I have placed a modest bet with a dear friend of mine that the four-year period will pass without anyone coming up with the goods. So far it's all been very promising and I'm clearly on to a winner. Just think, very shortly I shall have won my bet and gained enough funds for two new hats and a week in Paris at the Longchamp racecourse! Now how's that for excitement?' She clapped her hands in gleeful anticipation, and then wagging a finger added, 'Now my dear I trust you are not going to queer my pitch by finding the wretched thing after all this time. That would be really too bad!' There were further squeaks of mirth.

Rosy laughed too and said that she rather assumed that the Longchamp racecourse could indeed expect the pleasure of Miss Witherington's company before too long. 'But,' she queried, 'are you seriously saying that *were* I by some remote chance able to find this book that I could claim the million pounds?'

'Well not unless you have the other thing of course.'

'Other thing? Whatever do you mean?'

'Oh how silly of me – didn't I tell you? The Murano vase. The two go together, like love and marriage as the song says. Without the glass thing the book's price is considerably reduced, a mere few hundred lire or so. Same with the vase.'

Rosy was perplexed. 'I am sorry – I don't really understand.'

'Not many would,' Miss Witherington remarked dryly, 'you would need the addled mind of Farinelli Berenstein. He wants the book on account of its dedication – something to do with his dead mother I gather. Apparently in the old family home years ago this book was kept on a table in the study and served as a sort of plinth for the glass goblet – a rather gaudy little gewgaw by all accounts but apparently of some sentimental value and also treasured by the mother; though whether for the same reason as the book I don't know and don't care particularly. Anyway, the point is that as mothers do she died. The house was sold and much of its contents disposed of or lost. Son Farinelli came to Italy, led a dissolute life with various mistresses of both sexes, made a lot of money selling dubious antiques at outlandish prices to the Nazis, and now in his dotage and prompted by amusement and sentiment has issued this ridiculous challenge.'

'So what does he propose doing with the items assuming they are found?'

Miss Witherington shrugged. 'I have no idea: put them on his bedside table next to his false teeth and monkey-gland tablets perhaps . . . Goodness, I do trust he takes the latter, it is essential he remain extant until the period is up, because at his death the whole deal is scuppered and the prize money goes to the state. That would render my bet null and void and I should forfeit the fun of new hats and the delights of champagne at Longchamp. Thus he *must* continue alive for that period (not much longer!) and during this time the two items must *not* be found. So to that negative end, Miss Gilchrist, I trust you will not be too assiduous in your searches!' She laughed, and discarding her hat and rolling up her sleeves announced she had to prepare some 'super-duper' puddings and lagoon-fished trout for the evening meal.

Minutes later from the kitchen could be heard the clatter of dishes and the distant warbling of '*We're in the money* . . .' Feeling slightly dazed it struck Rosy that an early elevenses of Bomba Garibaldi might help to put her thoughts in order. She set off for Tonelli's.

The Daphne woman had been quite right: the ice cream was totally luscious. And after a chaser of a double espresso Rosy began to toy with the possibility of ordering another. 'No,' she told herself sternly, 'behave yourself and don't be such a pig; there are pressing matters to consider.' So forgoing the ice she ordered another coffee and lit a cigarette; and gazing out over the serene water reflected upon Miss Witherington's rather bizarre words.

Clearly if the book had not materialised over the last four years, the chances of herself alighting on it in the next few days were slim to say the least . . . as indeed Cedric had pointed out. The task was proving even more pointless than she had originally thought. So much for

81

Dr Stanley's bright ideas! The prospect of his reaction when she returned to her desk bookless and defeated was grim indeed. She pictured the scene: a chiaroscuro of reproachful melancholy and hectoring angst. The eruptions would eventually die down of course, but for days – weeks even – she would be haunted by hangdog looks and baleful sighs. Charming.

As she brooded it also occurred to her that the probable reason why the book had not already been brandished at Farinelli Berenstein was that the Murano vase remained undiscovered. As Miss Witherington had explained, one without the other was useless. To secure the prize both items had to be produced together . . . Well she didn't want the prize: just the damn book on its own, safe in her suitcase. The perishing vase or goblet, or whatever it was, was an irrelevance. She sighed. And then as an antidote to irritation opened her guidebook and became immersed in the finer points of St Mark's Basilica.

Five minutes later concentration was interrupted by the arrival of a rather smart couple in their early thirties – or at least the woman was, her escort looked younger. They settled at a table behind Rosy and she heard the waitress take an order for biscotti and coffee. 'Oh and you can bring me a cognac as well,' said the young man. Rosy was slightly surprised to hear the English words and voice. For some reason – perhaps the sleeked hair and over-pressed trousers – she had assumed him to be Italian.

She resumed her reading, the couple's presence registered only by a muted burble. But something must have been said to quicken the mood for she heard a gasp of impatience from the woman and the voices sharpened.

'I've told you, he's definitely got it,' the woman said.

'Are you sure?'

'*Yes*, I've seen it – on the mantelpiece. It's been there for ages.'

There was a protracted pause; and Rosy was about to gather her things and ask for the bill when she heard the man say, 'Well in that case you had better do something about it.'

This was greeted by a caustic laugh. 'Oh yes – what exactly?'

'Get hold of it of course, idiot!'

'And just how do you propose I do that?'

'How should I know? Sleep with the bugger or something.'

'Hah! It'll have to be "or something" – I don't think he's up to the other.' There came another mocking laugh.

Rosy experienced a flare of prurient curiosity and she cocked her ear for more. But at that moment a beaming Tonelli bustled over, full of grateful blandishments and urging her to visit again to sample further confections. 'My Chocolate Mussolini is vairee good, signora. *Diabolo!* You will like. *Everybody* like Tonelli's Mussolini!'

'Oh I am sure I will,' Rosy replied enthusiastically. It occurred to her to ask if he also did a Vanilla Fascista with nuts on, but thought better of it.

Thus by the time cash and compliments had been exchanged, Rosy's guidebook dropped and ceremoniously retrieved and felicitations sent to the 'so sharmink' Signorina Witherington, the couple's table had been vacated and they had vanished. Rosy felt a tickle of disappointment. It had been an intriguing little exchange, and she wondered what the fate of the item on the mantelpiece would be and whether its owner proved up to anything after all!

With her head filled with such frivolity she turned her steps in the direction of the Piazza San Marco to be sobered and uplifted by its great basilica. If she had nothing else to report to Stanley at least she could assure him she had seen something wondrous. Besides, who knew, she might even pass an open bookshop along the way.

CHAPTER NINE

The relationship between Lucia Borgino and her brother Edward Jones was fractious. It was always the same: their first few days together were generally good, verging on the congenial in fact. And then the tensions and bickering would begin, the exasperated sighs and mutual jibes. They were good at jibes; always had been, ever since childhood when each had learnt the pain and curious pleasure of rivalry and had honed their weapons accordingly.

At ten years old Lucia had been Queen of the May – amusing, wayward and precociously self-possessed. She had been adored and indulged by parents and grandparents alike, and had been bossily possessive of her brother five years younger. It had been so satisfactory teaching, correcting, and guiding the toddler through the snares and riddles of infancy while at the same time flaunting her own undoubted superiority. The grown-ups were impressed by her solicitude and patted her curls exclaiming what a wise little sister she was. They praised her talents, her wit and her prettiness; frequently. And Lucia had basked in their attention and flattery.

A few months after her tenth birthday things changed. Little Edward had started to show signs of independence and a growing self-assurance that would question Lucia's dictates. Indeed, not only question but ridicule them. Like herself he developed, even at that early age, a nice line in childish invective which he would practise assiduously not only on other children but also on his sister.

To her fury he also developed the knack of turning cartwheels considerably better than her own. Sometimes too he would raid her money box, helping himself liberally to the sixpences and threepenny-bits and even to the boiled sweets occasionally secreted there; and with a face of cherubic innocence would blame such depredations upon the dog. Two of her mother's friends kept exclaiming how attractive the little boy was growing (ridiculous, *she* was the pretty one!) and he would flutter his stupid lashes and give a sickening smirk . . . There were no two ways about it: dear little Edward was turning into a tiresome little bastard. It was not actually a term she knew at that stage, but the sentiments behind it settled deep in her psyche; and the phrase, once learnt, was applied frequently and with varying degrees of force and embellishment.

Edward too had found his sibling irksome. It was the patronage he couldn't bear: the put-downs, the snubs, the tone of dismissive mockery when he got his sums right, swam a length at the swimming baths or when, years later, he was found canoodling with the girl next door (shrieks of caustic laughter). She was stingy too. She got twice his amount of pocket money but never offered him a penny; instead would berate him for being extravagant while she spent her own shillings on sherbet and lollipops which she would make a point of guzzling in front of him. Mean and arrogant that's what she had been!

And yet, and yet. Despite such hostilities there remained between brother and sister a bond of fragile intimacy, a relationship based less on affection than on a tacit recognition of a shared affinity – an affinity defined by a firm sense of their own worth and a disregard for most things not pertaining to their personal ends. For Edward the end was money; for Lucia status and social prestige. The two ends are not incompatible and often go hand in hand . . . as indeed, metaphorically, did the siblings when circumstances suited. On the whole the current circumstances did suit and Edward's stay at Lucia's flat, initially at least, was congenial to both.

'So this Sir Fenton,' Lucia had asked him, 'is he a knight or a baronet?'

Edward replied that he really hadn't thought about

it and that provided the chap had the dosh, which he obviously had, he couldn't care less.

'Oh I agree,' she had laughed, 'when push comes to shove dosh takes precedence. Still, a decent title doesn't come amiss. You had better introduce me when I'm next in London. Who knows, I might like him. Is there a wife?'

'I rather suspect not. And actually, Lucia, I don't think he would care a fig if you did like him, it's *me* he likes. Likes the cut of my jib, as the old bore said. I tell you, if I play my cards right I could become quite useful to him and have him eating out of my hand. There may be other areas of lucrative possibility. So don't come pushing your nose in, sister dear!'

She laughed again. 'Wouldn't dream of it, not if he's like that; my interest has vanished instantly. You'd better be careful about what else he has in mind! Anyway tell me a bit more about this book and what he wants you to do.'

Edward outlined his brief. 'So you see on the face of things it's fairly straightforward. He's given me the name of a bookseller to contact who he thinks might know something and can point me in the right direction. Can't think of his name at the moment but it begins with a P and—'

'Pacelli? Not that old rogue!' she snorted. 'He's a greasy piece of work. Still I suppose he may be useful. But he'll want money – won't do you any free favours!'

'A man after my own heart,' Edward said.

'Well I trust it all works out for you. But frankly with the size of your debts I can't see this man's fee being of stupendous help. And even if you do find the thing and get a hundred-guinea suit thrown in, apart from pleasing your vanity that's not going to take you far; keep the bank manager sweet for a couple of months maybe. But you really need other strings to your bow I should have thought.'

'Thanks so much for the sterling encouragement,' Edward replied. 'The point is, as I have explained, if successful this little venture could earn me not just coppers but kudos. It's an investment. You know the proverbs – from little acorns et cetera, and nothing ventured nothing gained. Sir Whatsit's taken a shine to me and I'm going to—'

'Exploit the old bugger?'

Her brother raised a quizzical eyebrow. 'I am not *sure* that you are the one to talk of exploitation. Did pretty well out of your ex, didn't you? Certainly enough to afford this flat and swan around Venice in Dior suits. Rather took him to the cleaners I seem to recall.'

'I did *not* take him to the cleaners, he owed me the damned stuff and in any case it was what he deserved! And I have only one Dior suit,' she snapped. 'As usual you exaggerate.'

They glowered at each other.

And then Lucia relaxed. 'I think we might call a truce,' she said graciously. 'I expect you're tired after your flight and personally I've had rather a tedious time being charming to grandfather's clients. They come to Venice not having clue what they're supposed to be looking at and he expects me to show them the Guggenheim and explain the paintings. He seems to think that in their gratitude they'll remember to buy more stuff from him when they're next in London. It's such a bore.'

'But he pays you,' retorted Edward, still nettled by her earlier attitude.

She pouted. 'A pittance . . . Look, I suggest you go and unpack and get yourself straight and then we might go out and have a coffee and decide where to lunch. Nothing heavy mind you, we're dining with the Canellis this evening.'

She settled on the sofa and switched on the wireless. It was the weekly programme 'Tales of Venice', a mildly amusing hotchpotch of local anecdotes, personal reminiscence, snippets of history and bits of current gossip. But she paid little attention; her mind was elsewhere, i.e. on Guy Hope-Landers. She really quite liked the man, and in view of what he had let drop the other day felt she could get to like him even more. Quite a bit more in fact. Yes definitely worth a try. She stretched out a graceful hand and regarded the ring with some disdain; a paltry little thing really. Angelo had always been mean; but despite their split she wore it anyway – a signora without a ring on her third finger was unheard of! Still, she didn't want to be stuck with that one all her life . . . No, not at all. What was the thing Edward had quoted? 'Nothing ventured nothing gained'? Well at

90

least he was right there she supposed; and like him she could do with a bit of gain!

She powdered her nose and was about to switch off the wireless when her ear was caught by the last part of the programme's final item and the jocular tones of the announcer:

And so, listeners, to claim the million pounds from Signor Farinelli Berenstein his solicitors declare that finders of the genuine Bodger Horace must also produce that distinctive antique vase we were describing earlier: the mauve-and-yellow Murano piece with the scrolled lettering and flawed handle. But remember, ladies and gentlemen, one without the other is like a vintage wine without a corkscrew: useless!' The compère gave a mocking laugh. *'Tune in this time next week, my eager friends. And meanwhile enjoy your wanderings in cloud-cuckoo land – or as the English might say, don't stab your fingers with that needle in a haystack!*

His concluding chuckle was drowned in a blast of dance music.

Lucia switched off the set. How absurd she thought. But an extraordinary coincidence all the same. She must tell Edward – when he had finished preening himself in the bathroom mirror. 'Do hurry up,' she called, 'I'm dying for some coffee!'

* * *

They strolled arm in arm towards the Zattere and Tonelli's café in a rare mood of sibling amity. (Doubtless the warming effects of the sun and the water's azure indolence.)

'You know your commission for this damn book?' Lucia said.

'Hmm.'

'Well oddly enough, while you were unpacking I heard the most ridiculous item on the wireless. It involved the Bodger thing, and do you know . . .' And she proceeded to tell him the outlandish tale.

'Huh, fat chance of that I should think. It's one thing searching for the book – now that is a practical proposition – but to expect to find the vase as well is a fool's errand. Like looking for the proverbial needle.'

She laughed. 'Exactly what was said on the radio. One of those popular fantasies put about by Murano glass-blowers to promote sales I shouldn't wonder!'

'Except from what you said this one isn't contemporary; it's meant to be an antique isn't it? And from the sound of it not a very valuable one either. If the handle is skewed it was probably a reject. Colour sounds a bit dodgy too . . . what did you say, mauve and yellow? Ugh! Anyone with taste would have thrown it out years ago!'

'Ah but not everyone has our taste.'

'You can say that again! Do you know, on the plane coming over there was a woman wearing the most . . .'

But Lucia was not listening. She had suddenly stopped and was gazing fixedly across the water to the Giudecca.

'What are you looking at?'

'Nothing,' she replied faintly. 'I'm thinking.'

'Yes well don't think too long, I want a drink.'

Detaching her arm she turned towards him. 'Do you know I think I may have seen the thing. Good Lord,' she said slowly, 'I think I know where it could be . . .'

CHAPTER TEN

Edward lay sprawled on the sofa, eyes closed. Though he had only had a single glass of wine at lunch he felt tired. Presumably the effects of the early flight followed by the large cognac at Tonelli's. They were going out that evening and perhaps he should take a nap . . . Take a nap? Christ that's what old men did. He wasn't going down that road yet! But he kept his eyes closed all the same. And stretching long legs he kicked off a shoe and put a softer cushion under his head. It was pleasant in the sun. At this time of year London had started to get so damn draughty. He reflected on what Lucia had said in the café. It had been an intriguing idea but hardly likely, although she had seemed very certain. Still, it didn't do to take too much notice of what Lucia said: her mind had always been vivid.

She had gone off somewhere; no doubt to hobnob with some American or German client of their grandfather. Probably showing off as usual, being oh so droll and witty. She liked doing that – attracting sly admiration from the men and intimidating their wives. She found the process gratifying regardless of any monetary gain (though was invariably quick to grasp such bonus). Personally he preferred to save his energy for something tangible: what was the point of being charming if there was nothing concrete to be gained? It was exactly the same when they were children. Lucia would pirouette in her taffeta frock in front of the grown-ups lapping up their praise and laughter; the attention was reward itself. Whereas his own antics had been largely aimed at the acquisition of a shiny half-crown or new Dinky car – something *heavy* in the pocket. He mused: a general difference between the sexes? Or a specific difference between himself and Lucia? It hardly mattered; the essential concern was the heavy pocket. Blow the psychology.

He brooded, picking over what she had told him. Yes it had sounded pretty dubious. And in any case acquiring the Murano piece would only be relevant if he could get his hands on the Horace. The book was the *sine qua non*. And if Lucia was wrong about the location of the vase (as she probably was) then at least the book held some value of its own. His acquisition of it would impress Sir Fenton and thus be likely to secure further commissions – and of course it would get him that rather exquisite suit (and maybe others.) Yes, first things first: find the book and then see.

Edward opened his eyes, and gazing at the ceiling in fact began to see quite a lot. Spread out above him lay a vista of possibility: all the stuff of leisured wealth, e.g. yachts, girls, exotic beaches, a permanently reserved table at the Ritz, weekly flights to the Riviera, dining with film stars and Prince Rainier, a team of Maseratis, the whole of Savile Row fighting for his custom and fawning over his lapels, a cellar of cognac, a larder of caviar . . . and the prospect of never having to chat up old prunes like Fenton Bodger again! And as for Lucia, well she could be told to stuff her economy-class charity – a million quid would probably get him a share in a private plane!

It was a happy reverie. But Edward was fly enough to recognise the dangers of such daydreams. Despite what Lucia had said about the location of the vase, the chances of laying hands on both objects were negligible. Nevertheless he had stirred his own imagination, and the idea of the tawdry vase grew more insistent. But it was an insistency tempered by his grandfather's words: 'Never succumb to fantasy; you'll be a fool and miss all the best chances.' Ironic that one who made his living from the artistic fantasies of others should preach such pragmatism. Still, he was probably right, sniffy old sod. (His grandfather's success was a perennial source of annoyance to Edward. As far as he could make out the man possessed few discernible talents – except to direct and correct the activities of others, a skill he exercised with tireless persistence: his forte one could say.) Edward scowled, and pushing the vase to the back of his mind returned to the task in hand.

What was it Lucia had been saying about those two English chaps she and Guy had met recently? Apparently they were staying in the same place as Guy himself, old Violet Hoffman's palazzo . . . And yes, that was it: they had a friend visiting Venice, some female attached to the British Museum and also looking for the Horace. Huh! Ten-to-one she was the person Bodger had mentioned back in London. He smiled at the memory. The old boy had made it clear he wasn't expecting much from her – a rather lightweight emissary for such a serious mission! Still, pretty galling if she found the thing. After all he hadn't embarked on this caper to be pipped at the post by a woman, or by anyone for that matter . . . The Horace was going to be his prize dammit!

In fact Edward did sleep (exhausted by his reveries?), and well rested he went out that evening on sprightly form. The Canellis were always good value. Their supper parties were convivial affairs and this time was no exception. The wife cooked well and the husband had been lavish with the wine. And very good it had been, a vintage Barolo to which Edward had done more than justice. By the time they left, well past midnight, he felt and looked distinctly unsteady. Lucia was unsympathetic. 'I suggest you take a long walk before coming back to the flat. I don't want you throwing up over my new rug, you can do that in one of the canals.'

'I have no intention of throwing up anywhere,' he had told her angrily.

'You said that last time,' she retorted, 'one can't take the risk. Don't worry about me, Maria and Pietro are going in our direction, I'll walk back with them . . . Oh and by the way, try not to bang the door when you come in.'

Worry? he fumed after Lucia had gone. Why the hell should she think he would worry? God that girl could be so selfish! He sighed and lit a cigarette, but after a few puffs threw it down. Actually he did feel a little sick. Perhaps she was right – a walk might do him good. He hesitated, not sure which way to choose . . . Ah yes, he could go via the Rialto and take the opportunity to check Pacelli's opening times. Apparently the bookseller kept erratic hours and was in the habit of posting his schedule on the door. It would be annoying to turn up the next day and find the man not there. He set off slowly – it didn't do to rush things.

Gradually the night air and exercise started to take effect and the pangs of nausea subsided. By the time he reached the right spot (having stumbled down two wrong turnings) he was feeling better though still rather muzzy. She was right, he really had had a skinful!

He made his way up the darkened passage. The shop was in the cul-de-sac at the far end, and as he drew nearer he was surprised to see a dim light from inside. Was the bookseller a night owl? It was nearly two o'clock, quite late for Venice. Perhaps the thing had been left on by mistake. He took a few more steps. And then the light went out, and moments later the shop door banged and the figure of a man came running out, clearly in a hurry. In fact so much in a hurry that he collided with Edward who, still in a fragile state, had to cling to the wall for support. The man said nothing but rushed on oblivious of the staggering form he had left behind.

'Bloody hell!' Edward exclaimed rubbing his arm. He stared angrily after the figure, the noise of pounding feet echoing in his ears. The collision must have stirred things up for he started to feel unwell again. A wave of nausea swept over him and he was violently sick.

His head ached, he felt cold and it had started to rain. To hell with the book and Pacelli. All he craved was the benison of bed and a packet of aspirin! He turned and slouched back down the now silent alley.

CHAPTER ELEVEN

It was six o'clock and Felix had just returned from his shopping spree in the Merceric: three Fortuny silk shirts, a cravat, a pair of braces with embroidered gondolas (vulgar but irresistible!), some monogrammed lawn handkerchiefs for Cedric, a Commedia dell'Arte carnival mask and an enormous treasure trove of handmade chocolates. Eager to dazzle his friend with his purchases he went straight into the salon, where the wares were exhibited, discussed, gloated over and four of the chocolates consumed.

'Well you've certainly been busy,' Cedric remarked, 'but what you propose doing with that mask I cannot for the life of me imagine – hang it in the spare loo to frighten the clients?'

Felix pouted and then winked. 'Actually I thought I

could wear it on Walpurgis Night – it might give Sloane Street a stir.'

Cedric smiled and then said, 'As a matter of fact while you've been buying up half of Venice I've had quite an eventful time myself; made a discovery in fact. Odd really.'

'Oh yes,' said Felix pouring the drinks, 'why odd?'

'It's something I found wedged behind *Alice in Wonderland* on one of your cousin's shelves. She keeps her books in such disarray and it seemed to have slipped down.' He took the proffered martini. 'Somewhat curious.'

'What, like Alice?'

'No. Like Rosy Gilchrist – or rather her researches. You see it appears to be the Horace thing she's after.'

'*Here?* How odd!'

'Precisely, just as I've said. Take a look, *if* you can tear yourself away from those shirts.' He passed a small leather-bound volume to Felix, its dark cover worn and shabby.

The latter flipped through the pages and then scrutinising the outside, observed, 'Well it may be a first edition but it's hardly pristine. I doubt if the dealers will be impressed.'

'Immaterial. It's not for the dealers but for that Stanley man at the British Museum. Rosy implied he was mad keen to get it. And so is she – angling for promotion I daresay. She was terribly cut up when the Rialto bookseller tried to fob her off with the wrong one; whereas this seems definitely the right one – a first edition *and* with the required signature and inscription.'

Felix bent over the title page examining Dr Bodger's sepia flourish and the faded words underneath. 'Like all academics,' he said pointedly, 'handwriting totally indecipherable; it could be anything.'

Ignoring the jibe, the professor replied, 'It could be something were you to wear your glasses. Perhaps you would like me to be your amanuensis?'

'Be anything you like old stick, I'm for another drink.'

'No doubt, but listen to this first. It says: "To Bella B. Ah what joyful days!"'

'How very original,' observed Felix dryly. 'And who was Bella B – the wife?'

'From what little I've read the good doctor was unmarried, led a bachelor existence in Christchurch.'

'Presumably somebody else's wife then.'

'Presumably . . . unless of course it was that chorus girl Bella Biloxi. She was all the rage in the 1890s. Men would go up to London in trainloads to see her, young and old alike, mad keen to get a glimpse of a swelling bosom or gartered knee: you could say she was the Marilyn Monroe of her day.'

'So you think Bodger was one of the smitten and thus dedicated a set of ancient Latin poems to her? It seems a trifle unlikely.'

'Ah but you never know with academics. Not only is their handwriting indecipherable but their minds too are hard to fathom.'

Felix raised his eyes to the heavens. 'You can say that again! Now what will it be, with or without an olive?'

* * *

They dined in that evening. And after a light supper of antipasti, cold roast mullet and late strawberries in kirsch and cream (all fastidiously prepared by Felix) they settled to coffee and the topic of Cedric's find.

'It seems very likely that it is the one Rosy Gilchrist has been making all the fuss about,' the professor remarked, 'but what a singular coincidence it should turn up here in your cousin's palazzo. You didn't mention she had classical tastes.'

Felix shrugged. 'Don't know what her tastes are except dogs and music; haven't clapped eyes on the old trout since I was an adolescent. But presumably if she likes Latin poetry there would be similar stuff somewhere. Have you looked?'

'Nothing on the shelves that I can see. Mainly books on Venice, its history and architecture and so on. The rest is a hotchpotch – Bulldog Drummond cuddling up to Proust, but nothing that might be termed classical.'

'In that case we might as well hand the thing over to Rosy . . . perhaps her gratitude will rise to a bottle of bubbly.'

'It might,' Cedric agreed. 'But don't you think you should square it with your cousin in Chicago first? After all we don't want her to think we had pilfered the thing, might not get asked back again. Besides I am quite intrigued to know its provenance – how did it get here and why?'

Felix lit a cigarette and consulted his pocketbook. 'Really,' he muttered, 'the things one does for Rosy

Gilchrist . . . Ah here's the number. But, from what I recall my mother saying of Violet, she is as likely to be on the town with a group of Negro blues players as resting quietly in her hotel suite; but worth a try I suppose.' He stood up and left the room. Ten minutes later he returned grinning broadly.

'So you got her?' Cedric asked.

'You bet. Having her nails done in readiness for a date with Louis Armstrong. So I wasn't so wide off the mark was I?' He proceeded to give a detailed account of his elderly cousin's projected evening, which apparently was to commence with cocktails at the La Salle, followed by dinner at the Drake and culminating in some exclusive jazz dive where her companion would serenade her with one of his own compositions.

'Not bad,' conceded Cedric, 'not bad at all . . . And amidst all this jollity did you by any chance get on to the subject of the book?'

'Briefly. She remembers it vaguely and thinks someone called Carlo may have left it here by mistake but can't be sure. Anyway she didn't sound very interested, more concerned with Caruso; wanted to speak with him.'

Cedric was startled. '*Speak* with him?'

'Yes, it's a ritual they have whenever she is away apparently. The dog is hauled to the telephone and she coos down the line and he grunts. Touching really.'

'Good God! . . . So did you facilitate this, er, conversation?'

'No. The dog's out with Hope-Landers. I bumped

into him downstairs and said I was too fatigued after my shopping expedition to walk the hound and would he mind doing it instead. Quite an obliging fellow really, wouldn't you say?'

But Cedric's thoughts were elsewhere. 'Carlo,' he murmured, 'wasn't that the name of the chap who Lucia Borgino thought might have the Horace?'

'Well if it's the same one then he's obviously lost it; though I daresay there is more than one Carlo in Venice. Still, now that we've got the book and Violet doesn't seem concerned it really doesn't matter. We can give it to Rosy and cancel the meeting with this Carlo, whoever he is. Can't say I have any yearnings to see the Borgia woman again.' Felix's features puckered into an expression of pained distaste.

'Hmm we may have to. I meant to tell you, Hope-Landers has invited us to a small gathering at Harry's Bar tomorrow lunchtime. She's likely to be there but it might be mildly amusing all the same.'

'If he's paying – yes.'

'Oh he's paying all right. It's to celebrate some windfall from shares. Not a large sum but enough to keep him in fags and booze for a while and presumably to keep paying rent to your esteemed cousin.'

They turned to other matters, i.e. where they might go for a postprandial *digestif*. 'How about that bar where we met Paolo and Pucci?' Felix suggested.

'Couldn't be nicer,' beamed Cedric.

CHAPTER TWELVE

It was nearly time for dinner and Rosy had joined the other guests in the little lounge next to the dining room. Two of the women were discussing their purchases of lace tablecloths from Burano.

'It's all very well their being so exquisite,' one said, 'but you do have to clean the damn things. I mean, can one boil them in Tide for example or would you suggest Dreft?'

'I really wouldn't know,' replied the other indifferently. 'Fortunately it's not something I have to bother about. Our char does all that sort of thing.'

There was a silence and Rosy suspected that any burgeoning friendship had been smartly nipped in the bud. She smiled at Mr Downing who promptly began to speculate about the imminent menu. '*I* think that our talented hostess has something special for us tonight,' he announced conspiratorially. 'She has been in that kitchen for much of the afternoon, and if I am not mistaken there is something very fishy brewing, *very* fishy. If it's the Venetian version of bouillabaisse I shall be in seventh heaven!' To Rosy's distaste he made slurping noises and smacked his lips.

'In that case,' said the Daphne woman putting down her Italian newspaper, 'you will be going in the same direction as Signor Pacelli – although with him it's more likely to be the eighth circle of hell. *Not* one of nature's gentlemen I should say.' She sniffed.

'Don't quite follow,' Downing murmured, his mind evidently still absorbed in culinary nirvana.

'According to this he expired in the early hours of this morning,' she said, tapping the paper.

'Pacelli!' Rosy exclaimed. 'Do you mean that bookseller near the Rialto? Goodness gracious!'

Dr Burgess gave a brisk laugh. 'Presumably a heart attack from all that racy reading. I must say some of his books did look a bit close to the knuckle!'

The Daphne woman shrugged. 'Oh no, not a heart attack. He was bashed on the head by the proverbial blunt instrument – that tasteless metal paperweight he kept on the counter; you know the one, the rampant satyr. Death virtually instant one gathers but brains all over the place.' She turned to Downing. 'Do you really think we might be having fish stew? Now that would be a treat . . .'

As they trooped into the dining room Rosy picked up

the discarded newspaper, deftly tore out the page and stuffed it into her handbag. Something to peruse after the bouillabaisse.

Back in her room she tried to make sense of the newspaper article and, as on a number of occasions since her arrival, wished she had opted to do Italian at school. But at least she had no difficulty in spotting the item itself – 'Giuseppe Pacelli, libraio famoso, trovato assassinato,' was the stark headline. Reading slowly and with frequent recourse to a dictionary she was able to establish the essential facts.

These seemed to be that the bookseller had been discovered by a neighbour at eight o'clock that morning. The body, fully clothed, had been glimpsed through the glass door, sprawled on the floor in front of the counter. Seeing a bottle and a couple of glasses upturned beside him, the neighbour assumed the victim to be in a drunken stupor. However, after hammering on the door for some time and seeing no movement, she tried the handle and found the door unlocked. On entering she was horrified to see that the man was dead with his head battered in. The police were called and in the course of their examination of the premises removed a large paperweight which had clearly been the weapon. Some sort of scuffle was assumed to have occurred as a chair was knocked over and a number of books and papers lay strewn on the floor . . . The report ended by saying that the police were anxious to interview anyone who had seen or spoken to the victim on the previous night or in the days leading up to the murder.

Naturally Rosy was shocked by the account, but it was the request for witnesses that she found perturbing. She read it again carefully. *The previous night or days prior to the discovery.* Yes, in theory that would certainly include herself. But in practice? Well she was merely a visitor, an ephemeral tourist whose grasp of Italian was shaky to say the least. Surely she didn't count; what could she possibly offer of interest? After all it wasn't as if she knew the man – she had only spoken with him for ten minutes, less than that probably, and the topic had been exclusively professional.

She frowned, recalling the second encounter in the Campo Agnese when she had seen him with the other man – quarrelling; or so it had seemed. Oh hell, was that material? No of course not. They hadn't really been quarrelling . . . raised voices merely, a minor spat quickly dispelled when she had appeared. True she hadn't liked their attitude towards her – damn rude it had been! Still, a trivial incident surely and one hardly relevant to the present matter; it would be officious to mention it. No, the last thing she wanted was to spend her precious time in Venice traipsing to police stations and making statements of little worth in fractured Italian or pidgin English. Doubtless there was a host of far more useful witnesses available – local people more knowledgeable than she and keen to do their civic duty. Thus persuaded Rosy retired to bed satisfied that she had no role to play in the inquiry into Giuseppe Pacelli's unfortunate fate.

It was only much later in the night that she awoke and

began to think about the death itself. She hadn't liked the man, that was for sure; but a violent bludgeoning was a dreadful way for anyone to go, however impolite they had been. She visualised the scene: a caller (Known to him? The two glasses might suggest so), an argument and accusations, perhaps threats of blackmail (probably running a brisk trade in illicit erotica!); a sudden flare-up and tussle, the seizing of the paperweight and the violent attack followed by a swift exit. Clearly the killing hadn't been premeditated – a spur of the moment thing, the product of blind rage. Was the attacker glad that his victim was conveniently silenced or appalled that a moment's passion could result in such a nightmare?

She rolled over, adjusted the pillows, and shutting her eyes dismissed both scene and speculations. None of it was to do with her and she was hardly the investigating officer. Why burden the mind with pointless questions? Her task in Venice was to hunt for the wretched Bodger, not play detective in a case of squalid murder.

Yet it was the issue of the book that returned her mind to the dead man. *Why* had he been so churlish and dismissive? Indeed not just dismissive but positively hostile. Rosy winced, recalling the mocking face and voice at their last encounter. All most unpleasant! She stared into the dark reliving the details and becoming increasingly certain she had been right in her earlier suspicion – that both Pacelli and his companion had been deliberately warning her off. Quite possibly they were after the book themselves, knew where it was and were protective of their interests.

111

Perhaps Pacelli had been commissioned to acquire it by some other avid book collector . . . after all, Dr Stanley and Sir Fenton might not be the only ones keen to lay hands on this particular bit of Victorian scholarship. There were supposed to be a couple of unsigned Bodger editions in America. Perhaps an obsessed academic over there also wanted the embellishment of signature and dedication and was willing to pay rather more for it than the British Museum's measly twenty pounds – or was it guineas? Besides, according to Miss Witherington and her Farinelli Berenstein story, if both book and glass goblet could be produced simultaneously mammoth money was at stake. But in either case why let some officious foreigner muscle in on the act? Send her off with a flea in her ear, that's what!

A foghorn sounded far out in the lagoon, and not much the wiser the officious foreigner sighed, kicked back the blankets and fell into muddled sleep.

Caruso had been such a tiresome pain. First he had demanded to be let out at four in the morning if you please, then at breakfast he had been most disagreeable with a neighbouring cat. And following that, in an access of maudlin sentimentality he had slobbered all over Felix's newly pressed shirts. It really was too bad! The custodian glared at the hound who retorted with a slowly wagged tail and mighty belch.

Thus when Cedric looked up from his newspaper and announced that someone had been murdered close to the

Rialto Felix felt so much better. 'Really?' he exclaimed. 'Was it a cardinal?'

Cedric lowered the paper and regarded him over the rims of his glasses. 'Now what on earth has put that idea into your head?'

'Well according to literature and history that sort of thing goes on all the time in Venice doesn't it? Or it certainly used to. Prelates and other eminent rascals were always being knifed or seduced. Par for the course.' Good temper resumed, Felix winked at the dog.

'I don't think this chap was seduced,' Cedric observed mildly, 'and from what I understand neither was he knifed: the weapon was his own paperweight, a statue of a priapic satyr. Curious tastes some people have. Still, as it happens quite a coincidence: the victim was that bookseller Rosy Gilchrist was so annoyed about – Pacelli his name was.'

'There you are then,' Felix declared triumphantly, 'I told you it was to do with the church.'

Cedric smiled. 'But quite intriguing you must admit. Perhaps the Italians get more het up about matters literary than we do in England. I don't imagine such hostilities are enacted in the boardroom of Foyles . . . although who knows, maybe they are. The public is always the last to hear of such things.'

'Hmm,' replied Felix thoughtfully, 'I daresay when Rosy gets to hear of it she'll be bursting with curiosity and *Schadenfreude* and eager to share her excitement with us. She does have our phone number. I wouldn't object except that after Caruso's boorish behaviour and my broken sleep I am feeling a trifle jaded. Might it be politic if we were to forfeit the drama and leave Venice for a day and visit Vicenza? I've always had a hankering to see that splendid Villa Rotunda and I gather there is quite a good train.'

'I think you exaggerate Rosy Gilchrist's yen for drama. But since it says here that the police want to interview anyone having had contact with the victim recently she may be considering her position and want our advice on the matter. So perhaps—'

'Exactly! I haven't recovered from our last engagement with Rosy Gilchrist in a police matter. So don't let us take the risk. A quiet day and a low profile is the answer. I'll look up the train times.' Felix bustled to the door and then stopped and tittered. 'You never know, since she was so furious with the bookseller perhaps this is her revenge. All the more reason to keep out of harm's way!'

'Hold on,' Cedric exclaimed, 'I've just remembered: it's today that Hope-Landers is holding the little gathering at Harry's Bar. I told you – he invited us a couple of days ago. We can't duck out now; Vicenza will have to wait.'

Felix pulled a face. 'Honestly, the sacrifices one makes!'

CHAPTER THIRTEEN

'Now, I'm in the chair,' declared Hope-Landers expansively. 'What will it be – Bellinis? This *is* the place you know.'

He turned to Cedric who said he did know and would prefer a negroni.

'Wise choice,' said the host. 'Outside New York this is the best place for them.' He lowered his voice leaning forward conspiratorially. 'And I can assure you they have the edge on the Gritti's – less Campari more gin.'

Felix opted for the same and glanced round appreciatively at the understated surroundings: the bare floorboards, high windows and plain wooden tables. In fact the only item of any note was the bar itself – an Aladdin's cave of gleaming spirits and vivid concoctions.

Amid the room's austerity it led the eye like a magnet. The bartender, shaker in hand and svelte in a cream jacket, smiled discreetly as Caruso detached himself from Felix and waddled to the far end and settled himself beneath a bench in the corner. Evidently his customary place.

'You see,' chuckled Hope-Landers, 'the dog selects the spot. So that's where we had better sit, the others won't be long.' He ushered them to a table where their drinks were delivered and a saucer and biscuits brought for Caruso.

'So who else is coming?' Cedric asked. 'I think you mentioned Mrs Borgino . . . Is there a—uhm—a Signor Borgino?'

'Not any longer, she sent him packing years ago. But she keeps the name – Lucia Borgino sounds rather better in Venice than Lucia Jones.' He laughed, and turning to Felix said, 'Don't you think?'

As one who had substituted a *y* for an *i* in his own name, Felix was inclined to agree but he had no intention of siding with the likes of Lucia Jones, whoever her grandfather might be. Old snubs died hard with Felix.

'As a matter of fact though,' Hope-Landers continued, 'she won't be coming unescorted. Her brother is staying with her. He visits periodically from London. I *quite* like the chap but he's not to everyone's taste.'

'Really? What does he do?' Felix asked.

'Well . . . it seems to vary. A versatile cove you might say, though I get the impression without much staying power. He went into his grandfather's art gallery when he left school but that didn't last long. Annoyed the customers, too cocksure. Apparently Montgomery went in one day looking for a Cecil Aldin dog picture; and young Edward, thinking he was being clever, had the gall to ask the Field Marshal if he had seen any war service.' Hope-Landers chuckled. 'That didn't go down very well, I can tell you. Not well at all! Still he's always perfectly civil to me. But frankly just *entre nous*, I rather think there are some hefty debts in the background, but it's a topic I studiously avoid. After all hard enough keeping one's own purse in the black without having to be concerned for others'!'

'Most wise,' Felix agreed. 'And anyone else?'

'Yes a rather nice American. He paints. Obsessed with the Grand Canal and indeed with Venice generally. You'll like him. A couple of others may look in. And of course Dilly and Duffy are coming but they are always late, bred in the bone you might say.'

'Dilly and Duffy? Who are they – friends of Caruso?' Cedric enquired.

Hope-Landers laughed. 'Oh no, perfectly human I can assure you. They are twins of the inseparable kind, though I must say at sixty-plus just a trifle old to dress in the same frocks but I gather it's something you can't avoid, psychological I suppose. Anyway they are very civil and jolly – that is, until they've had a few and then they're fiendish.'

'I see. And are they likely to become so today?'

'Shouldn't think so; the cabaret is most spectacular on Sunday evenings. At other times they are largely docile. Although they're not too keen on Lucia's brother – take rather a dim view, so you may detect an element of *froideur*.'

'Really? What don't they like in particular?'

Hope-Landers paused. 'Well . . .' he began.

'Not in particular just general,' an American voice said close to his elbow. Cedric looked up and was confronted by a big man with a beard, forage cap and smiling blue eyes. He bore an uncanny resemblance to Ernest Hemingway in his better days, and the context certainly seemed apt. (Yet another twin perhaps?) He was introduced as Bill Hewson, a painter from Boston. 'Yes I came here some time back to do a watercolour of the lagoon. Sargent had done it so why shouldn't I? As it is, I stayed six years and I'm still here.' He grinned.

'And is the watercolour finished?'

'Nope. Never begun. Too much other stuff to catch the eye. Can't get enough of it; you should come to my studio some time, the place is full of the garbage.'

'Oh no garbage there I assure you,' Hope-Landers said, 'all damn good stuff.'

Cedric smiled politely and said they would be delighted to pay a visit.

'Weren't you saying something about Mrs Borgino's brother,' Felix asked inquisitively, 'what's the difficulty?'

But he had to wait to find out, for at that moment the door at the far end was pushed open and in came Lucia accompanied by a tall young man with sleeked hair and sunglasses – an addition which, given the greyness of the day, seemed a trifle redundant. Clad in dazzling

118

white Lucia too seemed indifferent to the weather. For a few moments the siblings stood poised on the threshold surveying the room. They were a handsome pair and made a striking tableau. And then with a light laugh and a wave to the barman, Lucia advanced towards their host whom she kissed lavishly.

'Ah, I think you've already met Cedric and Felix,' he began, 'though we were all in such a rush the other day, didn't have time to . . .'

'Have I?' Lucia threw them a smile of little interest; and then added vaguely, 'Oh yes, I think I remember, on the bridge wasn't it?' She turned to Hewson and exclaimed, 'Lovely to see you Bill. I took Edward to your spring exhibition last time he was here. He adored it, didn't you Eddie!'

'Of course,' her brother said, 'as I always do. Bill's pictures are charming – and *so* reassuring. The familiar never palls; it induces such feelings of confidence.' He whipped off his sunglasses and gave the older man a challenging grin.

'Confidence in what,' enquired Cedric who had overheard the comment, 'your judgement?'

'Sorry? Oh . . . well in life I imagine.' The young man shrugged, and turning away called, 'I say Guy, Lucia said something about some fizz. Any hope? I thought we had come to toast your windfall. Don't be slow in coming forward!'

'Any minute now old chap, Marco's just bringing it over,' replied his host. 'But we might just hang on for Dilly and Duffy, they'll be here soon.'

As indeed they were; for just as the young waiter had put the bottles on the table two grey ghosts came gliding through the door: ghosts in identical mackintoshes and smiling benignly. They greeted Hope-Landers and Hewson warmly, were less warm towards the brother and sister, and appraised Cedric and Felix with mild eyes.

'You're new here aren't you?' said one of the ghosts.

'Where are you staying,' fired the other, 'the Sandwirth? Or slumming it at the Metropole?'

Cedric coughed and said that actually they were in a private residence.

'Which one?' demanded the first.

'The, uhm, Palazzo Reiss,' Cedric replied politely.

'Oh, *Vio's* place!' they chimed in unison; and approving looks were exchanged.

'Isn't there a cousin of some sorts?' Dilly or Duffy enquired.

'Yes,' said Felix, 'I am it.'

'*Really?*' was the collective response. One of them clapped her hands and exclaimed, 'Felix the Florist – we've heard all about you!'

Her sister nodded vigorously. 'We have indeed.'

Cedric was amused, Felix taken aback. What on earth had Cousin Violet known to impart to these two? He barely knew her. But he was flattered all the same and experienced a flush of pleasure.

'Oh yes, you were a *very* naughty little boy,' said one, 'always stealing jam and destroying your mother's flowers.'

'But,' cut in the other, 'redeemed yourself recently we hear. Secured the Queen Mother's approval – one of those By Royal Appointment warrants no less; most commendable.'

'Yes it's amazing how well some turn out isn't it,' observed Dilly or Duffy, 'but by no means *all*.' She cast a pointed look at Edward. The latter was on to his second glass of champagne and affected not to notice. She waved her own glass at Hope-Landers. 'Good news about the lolly, Guy; always nice to have a little spare. Here's to plenty more where that came from. You never know your luck! Happy days everybody!'

Glasses were raised, clinked, and an air of merriment ensued; in the course of which Edward, seated next to Felix, whispered, 'Such tiresome old bats, but one has to indulge them I suppose.'

Felix pursed his lips. 'One has to indulge a lot of people in this life, it's something one learns.'

He had the impression that the response was not appreciated – which was exactly as he had intended. Yet slightly to his surprise Edward continued: 'Oh by the way, I gather from my sister that you have a friend who's after that set of Horace translations. I can tell you she's backing the wrong horse. Waste of time; she won't find it. I know for a fact the thing's no longer in Venice.' He spoke with an air of careless confidence. But then pausing fractionally he laughed and added, 'Or at least I'm pretty sure it isn't. Maybe I am hopelessly out of date and she's managed to find it after all. Living in London one is never entirely abreast of Venetian affairs. Sniffing it out is she?' He gave an enquiring smile.

'Well funny you should say that because if it's the one you mean I rather suspect it is still—' Felix began, but stopped abruptly having received a sharp kick on the ankle from Cedric opposite. Pain not compliance silenced him, and to alleviate the former he took a large gulp of champagne and hobbled off to the Gents.

'So what the hell was that about?' Felix protested as the three weaved their way back to the palazzo.

'Not sure really,' mused Cedric, 'a hunch I suppose . . . Do you think that dog will need any more food or will the bar biscuits be enough for it?'

'Dog be damned!' cried Felix. 'What about my ankle? Any more hunches like that and I shall be in a wheelchair before long!'

'Sorry. Foot slipped.'

'I should think it did. So what were you playing at?'

Cedric frowned. 'Well . . . actually I also wonder what that Edward person was playing at. The sister too for that matter.'

Felix snorted. 'Beyond me I'm afraid. Must have been that second grappa: wits aren't quite what they should be.'

'Well I heard what Master Jones was saying to you – that his sister had told him about Rosy searching for the Horace. Yet five minutes earlier when I had been trying to make polite conversation with the girl she affected supreme indifference to the whole topic and said it was highly unlikely that this Carlo chap would know anything, and that in any case he was currently in New York.'

'But he's not. The American mentioned that he had been at his studio only yesterday.'

'There you are then. It is slightly odd too that when we met her and Hope-Landers on the way to the Accademia she said something to the effect that the one person who might know something would be Carlo and that she would organise a meeting. But in the bar just now she was conspicuously dismissive of the whole subject, and yet—'

'And yet had obviously discussed it with her brother.'

'Precisely. It's as if she is now deliberately trying to sink the matter. And as for the brother: well one moment, *entirely* unsolicited, he emphatically tells you the book is not in Venice and at the next seems eager to know whether Rosy has found it. It all seems a bit contradictory to me and therefore odd.'

'So that's why you bashed my foot?'

Cedric sniffed. 'Personally he struck me as graceless not to say slippery, and I do not think we need divulge any information to types such as that pair. Probably pursuing the Horace to get that prize money – *assuming* Miss Gilchrist's tale has any substance!' He gave a sardonic laugh.

'Well if that's the case let's give the wretched thing to Rosy Gilchrist, if it *is* the book, and then she can scuttle back to the British Museum while we get on with more pressing researches – the Lido perhaps or opera at the Fenice. They have rather a delightful programme I gather.'

Felix paused, and then added, 'But I agree with you, a most unengaging pair; especially the girl, though he was quite handsome I suppose . . .'

'But not as handsome as Paolo,' Cedric said slyly. 'Ah that reminds me! We can't possibly take the book to Rosy Gilchrist tomorrow. Don't you remember? The two Ps are treating us to a *motoscafo* tour of the lagoon and Torcello and then on to Burano for lunch at that splendid restaurant. First things first I fancy!'

'Rather,' exclaimed Felix. 'Shall we take Caruso?'

While the two visitors were thus engaged in contemplating future jollity the 'unengaging pair' were drifting home to Lucia's flat.

'Considering your disability this morning,' Lucia laughed, 'you managed to put up quite a good show, even made one of those ludicrous twins smile – though don't ask me which one! You were hardly at your brightest earlier on and I thought I should have to go to Harry's on my own.'

'Would I be so ungallant?'

'Easily. Anyway, where did you go last night – or did you just sit by the canal doing nothing?'

'I did exactly as you told me: went for a walk towards the Arsenale to clear my head and then on to the Giardini Pubblici,' Edward lied.

The news that morning of Pacelli's murder had been relayed to him by Lucia who had heard it from the woman in the bakery. Naturally he had been very shocked but had said nothing other than to remark ruefully that that was one line of enquiry now lost. Instinct had stalled additional comment for he immediately saw trouble looming: trouble perhaps merely tiresome, or trouble disastrous. Either way silence was best. One had to be careful with confidences. Luckily Lucia had been too busy fixing her hair in an elaborate coiffure for the lunch to discuss things further.

The problem was that were he to report what he had recently seen he would doubtless be regarded as a key witness and have to endure the whole dreary rigmarole of police questioning; not the best way of spending his holiday. And were the murderer apprehended he would be required to give evidence with further wasted time and inconvenience. But *far* worse than either was the fact that sod's law being what it was, it was he who might become a suspect. Did he want any of that? No bloody fear! Thus when in doubt say nothing, he had counselled himself.

Those had been his thoughts *then* – when he had been emerging from his hangover and drinking endless cups of coffee on Lucia's sofa in preparation for the next spate of indulgence. Now, however, with the indulgence over he had rather more intriguing matters to consider . . . much more intriguing, and also requiring silence.

CHAPTER FOURTEEN

The following morning found Edward in Florian's. True, the place was fearfully expensive but worth it all the same. After all if one had weighty things on one's mind one might as well reflect in style. Yesterday's downpour had been drear though presumably, now it was autumn, only to be expected. But today things were back to normal and it seemed a pity not to take advantage of the few remaining days of sun. Thus he had chosen to sit outdoors watching the pigeons in the Piazza and sipping a cappuccino to the accompaniment of a medley from *South Pacific* as strummed by the resident quartet.

He brooded. Could he be sure? No of course he couldn't, it might have been anybody! But, he argued, was that really so? At the time – tired, tight and bilious – he had registered nothing of the fellow: it could have been any chap from Adam to Ghengis Khan; or Father Christmas for that matter. Merely an indistinct shape blundering into the darkness. But *now*, sober and clear-headed, details had started to emerge. Edward dwelt on these, and wondered. And the more he wondered the more certain he became. He beckoned the waiter to bring a cognac. Might as well as not; Bodger's expenses had been generous enough.

He sipped the drink slowly, debating his next move, and glanced over to Quadri's opposite: a venerable establishment but in his view without Florian's suave panache. Its tables were filling up he noted – tourists eager to catch the last of the sun. As he gazed he recognised a couple from Harry's Bar of the previous day, the two he hadn't liked very much; the ones with the girlfriend after the Bodger book and whom Lucia had warned him against. Felix and Cedric their names had been. The Felix fellow had been like a superior rat: sharp, tart and inquisitive; and the older one guarded and watchful. Neither had seemed particularly impressed by his own presence, let alone by his subtle overtures re the whereabouts of the book. He scowled across the Piazza and watched as they stood up and shook hands with a couple of other types who had just arrived. God, weren't they the two hairdressers from the place near the Frari? What were they all doing here? Out on a spree presumably. He watched as they moved off in the direction of the Riva degli Schiavoni and its landing stage.

It occurred to him that if this woman from the British

Museum had a couple of minders in tow the prospect of his getting at the Horace might be more difficult than he had thought. His first line of enquiry was now inconveniently dead and the rival had supporters. Tricky. Still, in view of this recent thing the Bodger project might be rather small beer. He recalled his school days. What was it Hamlet or some such dreary chap had said? 'I know a trick worth two of that.' Yes that was it. Well Hamlet or another Shakespearean blighter wasn't the only one: he too might have a better trick stuck up his sleeve. Lucia had told him he should get another string to his bow and perhaps with luck this was just the one! He grinned and applied his mind to logistics, i.e. how best to exploit the new situation.

His mind returned to the fleeing figure in the alleyway, and once more he visualised the form and features. There was no doubt about it: it was him all right. But one couldn't (or shouldn't) draw automatic conclusions. Just because he had been leaving Pacelli's shop in haste and in the dead of night did not necessarily make him the murderer. Perhaps they had had a row and he was waltzing off in high dudgeon. Perhaps he was being beckoned by an urgent appointment (unusual at that time of night admittedly), or maybe he had simply been desperate to answer a call of nature. (Edward's memory of his own physical discomfort at that period had perhaps prompted the last possibility.) The 'evidence' of course was only circumstantial; and while the man's movements might seem suspicious, looked at objectively his own might also seem so. 'Seen loitering in the vicinity of the victim's shop near the time of his death' didn't sound too good. Only marginally better in fact than 'seen running away from . . .' Yet Edward knew of his own innocence and so, conceivably, might the other know of his.

He stared up at the blue sky, tracking the movements of the pigeons. How valid were such conjectures? Was he playing God's advocate? Yes of course he was, he thought impatiently. Why give him the benefit of the doubt? His being there was too much of a coincidence. He bet the chap was as guilty as hell! (Though *why* that should be he had no idea, and for the present purpose motive was immaterial.) And besides, even if the man wasn't responsible would he want to be linked so closely with the crime? His presence there at that hour had looked pretty fishy especially given the haste of his departure: it wasn't as if he had been strolling away with hands in pockets. (Edward rubbed his arm still stiff from the knock it had received.) Yes, the chap was in a tricky position all right, more than a touch vulnerable one could say.

So how should he proceed – by hint and innuendo? A slyly worded note? Or would a direct confrontation be best, bold and stark? Still, he warned himself, it didn't do to be hasty in such matters: 'slowly, slowly catchee monkey' was the name of the game. He would watch carefully and adapt his strategy to circumstance . . . His mind wandered back over the years. He had once handled a similar challenge, less serious of course, but not without profit. Admittedly the outcome had been tedious (God hadn't the school cut up rough!) but the technique itself had worked a treat. And what had worked then could surely work now – always provided, of course, one took the utmost care. Slowly, slowly . . .

So absorbed was Edward by this new source of gain that the matter of the Murano vase with its attendant dreams took a back seat in his imagination. Once more he recalled his grandfather's diktat. 'Never succumb to fantasy; you'll be a fool and miss all the best chances.' Well here was a good chance all right and Edward Jones was no fool! He paid the bill, downed the last dregs of his cognac, winked at the girl at the next table and sauntered off humming, like Miss Witherington, *We're in the money* . . .

CHAPTER FIFTEEN

Back from their gallivanting the two friends were half way along the passage to the staircase when Cedric said, 'I think it would be kind if you went and relieved Hope-Landers of Caruso, he's had the creature most of the day. We did say we would be back at six and it's now seven.'

'Oh lor,' muttered Felix, 'so we did. I'd forgotten all about it. He'll be bellowing for his food by now though with luck Guy may have given him something – a passing sop to Cerberus you might say.'

'Actually he's been most obliging with that dog of yours and one wouldn't like to think he felt put upon. It's time we asked him up for a drink, especially after the lunch he organised at Harry's Bar.'

Felix inwardly agreed but there was a small matter that

needed to be established first. 'The dog,' he said slowly, 'does not belong to me as you very well know. I am merely its temporary supervisor, a role which in no way confers possession.'

'No but it confers commitment. And besides, I have observed that the creature has grown quite fond of you – a curious fact admittedly – but one which requires certain obligations.'

There was scant light in the passage but Felix knew that his friend's face wore a look of smug amusement. 'Huh,' he retorted, 'so that lets you out then; it can't stand your guts.'

'It most certainly can!' snapped Cedric indignantly. 'Why only the other day it . . .' He broke off as the door to Hope-Landers' apartment opened and they were assailed by a blast of pipe smoke.

'I say,' he said cheerfully, 'what a fearful racket. I thought Signora Bellini had come back early with her fancy man.'

'Ah,' cried Cedric, '*there* you are! We were just talking about you and that splendid lunch you gave. Might you be free tomorrow night for a little champagne with us? Come at about six and we can catch the last light on the veranda, it's still warm enough.'

'Nice idea but I've got Bill Hewson coming. We've a couple of things to discuss including one of his paintings. I'm trying to beat him down on price but I don't hold out much hope. He's a tough cookie when he wants to be.' He chuckled.

'Well once you've finished your business bring him up too, all the more the merrier. In fact you may find Miss Gilchrist with us. We've got a surprise for her – at least I think it will be. We've found something she's been looking for.'

'Really? You don't mean that book she was after do you? I thought it no longer existed, or so Lucia said. She seemed very sure.'

'It may not be the one but who knows . . . Anyway, can we expect you both tomorrow?'

'By all means. Sounds good.'

Hope-Landers withdrew to his sanctum and Felix and Cedric continued up the winding staircase debating the dog's dinner.

Meanwhile, deliberately putting all thoughts of Horace aside, Rosy had spent an indulgent time exploring and getting lost. She had no set itinerary – which might have been sensible – but was content at this stage just to absorb the general ambience of the city, delighting both in its quaintness and its grandeur. One day she would come back and do the job properly (were such an achievement possible in a lifetime) but at the present she was on general reconnaissance, roaming the bridges and alleyways and storing up future treasures.

Yet agreeable as such ramblings were they were shadowed by thoughts of the bookseller's death and the nagging sense that perhaps after all she should be contacting the police. But she drew the same rationalised conclusions as before: she had nothing to offer. Then inevitably, as the morning wore on, thoughts of Pacelli brought her back to her 'mission'. Gloom descended: still nothing to report to Stanley. But she would have to telephone him all the same if only out of courtesy. More gloom.

Returning to the *pensione* she was greeted by Miss Witherington bearing an envelope. 'Such a nice man brought this for you,' she chirped. 'He said I should give it to you as soon as possible.'

'Oh? What was he like?'

'He was thin, hair *en brosse* and accompanied by a dog with exceptionally long ears.' Felix.

After reading the note Rosy felt more cheerful, hopeful even. It was an invitation to their palazzo the following evening, which in itself would be interesting, but even more interesting was the hint contained in the concluding lines: *We think we may have found exactly what you have been after. Fingers crossed. Come and see.* She sighed in amused exasperation. Could it really be the Horace? Why on earth did they have to be so gnomic? Yet surely that's what it meant. If so how incredible! She wondered if this was the time to telephone her report to Dr Stanley but dismissed the idea: she was too tired from her wanderings (one needed stamina to engage with Stanley), and besides far better to wait and relay the good news when she had the damn thing – a bird in the hand etc. etc.

She gazed out over the smooth waters, seductively blue in the autumn sunshine and wished she could stay in

Venice for weeks . . . But at least if the Horace search was over she would have a couple of days spare to explore in greater depth. She checked her guidebook to learn more of the Church of the Miracoli that Cedric had been raving about; and of course there was the incredible Doge's Palace – though that would take at least half a day; and what about the Robert Browning casa, and Tintoretto's little house in the Cannaregio? And surely she ought to do at least a couple of rooms in the Accademia . . . So much to see and so little time: she must make a select and disciplined list.

She took out her notebook and with pencil poised debated which should be first on the agenda. But she was nagged by the thought of Dr Stanley and his insistence that she telephone a report. Perhaps if she delayed any longer he might himself call and doubtless at a time of maximum inconvenience. She closed the notebook and sighed. Best get it over with. She went downstairs and squeezed into the cramped telephone booth in the hallway.

It proved a laborious business and once a connection was eventually made the recipient was said to be engaged (shorthand for having a gin and tonic with a crony). Shoving more lire in the slot Rosy waited impatiently. At last she heard the rasp of his voice, and taking a breath commenced her report.

This of course didn't amount to very much, which given the shortage of lire was just as well. Omitting all reference to Pacelli and his fate, Rosy concentrated on the contents of Felix's note. 'Of course one can't be certain but it does sound promising,' she assured him.

'Excellent. But you are keeping your eyes skinned for the Bodleian bugger aren't you? We don't want him messing things up.'

'The Bodleian bugger?' she gasped. 'I am sorry I don't understand.'

'But I told you: our rival. Sir Fenton let slip that Oxford is also interested and he had tipped them the wink. If you ask me he's a bit of an old tart – flashes his favours in all directions. If the chap from the Bodleian gets the Bodger we're sunk: the Museum loses Sir Fenton's patronage and *we* forfeit the funds. So just watch it, Rosy!'

'Actually,' she said irritably, 'you didn't tell me.'

There was a pause and a cough. 'Oh, didn't I? Ah, no perhaps not. Come to think of it the sod only mentioned it after you had left. Anyway, the honour of the department is at stake so trust no one let alone smarmy academics. Which reminds me – I've had the most frightful bust-up with Smithers. He's had the cheek to query one of the footnotes in my recent publication, says the quotation I cite is of dubious authenticity. Disgraceful!'

'Disgraceful,' Rosy agreed. 'But, er, this Bodleian man, I don't quite see—'

'Yes, at all costs keep the swine at bay . . . Now Rosy if you don't mind I've got pressing stuff to attend to and—' At that point the lire ran out and the line went obligingly dead.

Keeping a sharp lookout for librarians and smarmy academics, the next evening Rosy embarked on the

Palazzo Reiss. Here she was greeted by Felix wearing what she could only conclude was his cocktail garb: a richly green velvet jacket with silk lapels and swirling motifs. At his neck was a pink cravat. Colourful though the combination was, his thin features and short spiky hair did little to enhance the Byronic mode. On the whole, Rosy thought, he looked like a quizzical parrot.

'Welcome to our humble abode,' he laughed. 'Rather drear down here I'm afraid but I can assure you it gets all right in the end; quite nice really – though *getting* to the end takes some stamina. We lack the luxury of a lift.'

Rosy followed him along the ill-lit passage and up the winding stone steps. He was right, the ascent was both gloomy and taxing, and arriving slightly breathless on the empty, dusty landing she felt a squeeze of disappointment. If this was the *piano nobile* the noble element was hard to discern! But as with Felix and Cedric earlier, her impressions revived the moment she stepped inside the main salon. To quote Felix's own words, the accommodation was indeed 'quite nice'. Her eyes swept the flower-bedecked room with its exquisitely ornate ceiling, Venetian wall brackets and elegant proportions. Yes definitely better. The longer of the two sofas contained Cedric and the basset hound – one at either end – and each rose at her entry to pay the customary attentions, the dog sniffing her ankles and Cedric (soberly suited) to compliment her on her dress and offer a drink.

'We have our fellow resident and an American friend of his coming in later,' he explained, 'but first we wanted to show you this in the hope that it just might be what you are looking for.' He went over to the desk, rooted around and then returned thrusting the book into her hands.

The volume was subjected to a 'close forensic analysis' – pages leafed through, signature examined, dedication discussed and laughed over and edition date checked. 'Well,' she said, 'it looks to me as if it's the one all right; seems to tally with what Dr Stanley described. But how extraordinary that you should find it here. I wonder how your cousin came by it.'

Felix shrugged. 'No idea; and when I phoned her she seemed pretty vague about the whole thing. I think her mind was on other things – the jazz probably. Anyway not much interest shown so you may as well have it with our compliments. I very much doubt if she will be clamouring for its return the moment we have left. And if so I shall tell her it is safe in the British Museum being gloated over by one of London's most distinguished scholars.'

'Hmm, I suppose that's one way of describing him,' said Rosy dryly. But she felt in high spirits, pleased she could return triumphant and, for a short time at least, bask in Stanley's respect and approbation. It wouldn't last of course but she would jolly well make the most of it while she could. She grinned and accepted another dose of champagne with which she toasted her two benefactors.

She quite liked Guy Hope-Landers – personable, as her mother would have put it. And the painter Bill Hewson was easy company and full of amusing tales about the

Boston art scene. They showed polite interest in her recent acquisition and toasted her good luck. But both were cynical of the Farinelli Berenstein rumour. 'Can't say that I ever got wind of it,' remarked Hope-Landers, 'although now I come to think of it I did hear Lucia's brother mentioning something like that the other day – something Lucia had heard on the radio, though she hasn't mentioned it to me. But I don't take much notice of what he says anyway, there never seems much substance. He talks for effect most of the time, silly ass.' He gave a dismissive laugh.

'Huh,' muttered Hewson, 'if you ask me he's an insolent young puppy,' and turning to Rosy added, 'and that's putting it nicely Miss Gilchrist. Not one of my favourite people.' For an instant the bonhomie vanished but was quickly replaced by his next remark. '*On* the other hand, the sister's all right – wouldn't you say so Guy? Lucky chap, she's crazy about you!' And he gave a guffaw of laughter.

The lucky chap smiled politely, looked slightly uncomfortable and muttered something about exaggeration. Cedric steered the conversation to less personal matters, such as the state of the American presidency and Eisenhower's war record, Mr Churchill's likely successor and the Guggenheim art collection.

'But what about this murder?' Felix asked after a while, tired of such generalities and relishing a little gossip.

'Which of the many?' enquired Guy Hope-Landers.

'The one here in Venice of course, that bookseller.

Rather surprising I should have thought. One has always heard the city to be rather law-abiding; something to do with its location I suppose, restricts flight.'

'Ah you mean Giuseppe Pacelli,' Hope-Landers said. 'Yes a bit peculiar really. Nothing has emerged so far. They say he had an awful battering but no cash taken. A private vendetta I should think; one gathers he had certain sidelines of a questionable kind. Probably double-crossed someone; one wouldn't be surprised.' He laughed and turned to Hewson. 'Did you ever buy anything there?'

The other shook his head. 'You bet I didn't,' he declared. 'I wouldn't throw a dime in his direction – a nasty little toad by all accounts! Probably deserved his end.'

'But not quite like that,' Rosy murmured.

'What? Oh . . . no I guess not. No certainly not like that.'

They turned to other things and the time passed convivially. Indeed when the two guests took their leave, Hewson declared in a slightly slurred tone that they must all meet the following night at Florian's or some other watering hole to re-celebrate Guy's recent good fortune and Miss Gilchrist's lucky find.

'Huh,' sniffed Felix after they had gone, 'tomorrow night? I very much doubt that. Out for the count I should think for at least two days. I've never seen anyone put it away so smartly!'

Rosy giggled and Cedric wagged a finger. 'Are we being

just a *mite* prissy, dear boy? You must admit he was quite entertaining.'

'Mildly, I would say,' was the response. 'And why he should think so well of that Lucia girl I cannot imagine.' He turned to Rosy and in kindlier tones said, 'Now Miss Gil—Rosy, what about a little cheese soufflé to round things off? The kitchen facilities here are really very good, and though I say it myself the chef is—'

'Remarkable,' Cedric said.

'Precisely,' purred Felix.

CHAPTER SIXTEEN

The next day, returning from their evening ramble (or *passeggiata* as Felix preferred to call it), they found a small white envelope on the table by the front door evidently left there by Hope-Landers. Cedric glanced at it casually and then turning to Felix said, 'Oh, this would seem to be for you.'

Felix was startled. 'For me? Really? Perhaps it's from Cousin Violet, though I can't think why she would want to—'

'Oh there's no postmark, it's local; delivered by hand. Look.' Cedric handed Felix the envelope.

Signor Felix Smythe,
C/o Signora Hoffman,
Palazzo Reiss.

Puzzled, Felix scrutinised the meticulous script. 'How odd. Surely not a bill already! We've only been here a short while.'

'Could be I suppose; although in England tradesmen's envelopes are invariably brown – and in my experience crumpled. This is pristine. Though I daresay Italian style permeates all classes.'

Releasing the dog Felix pocketed the letter and they embarked on the stairs.

'So who's it from?' Cedric asked as they reclined on their separate sofas in the salon.

'What?'

'The letter, who's it from?'

'Oh yes of course, the letter. I'd quite forgotten that. All this sightseeing it quite tires one out!' Felix fished in his pocket and reaching for the paperknife on the bureau slit open the envelope.

My dear Sir, the words ran,

Forgive my impertinence but I believe you are a relation of my esteemed friend Signora Violet Hoffman and are currently residing in her abode while she is away. I should be more than grateful to make your acquaintance and to discuss with you a small matter regarding a book she has of mine. Alas, circumstances dictate that I should reacquaint myself with this book; and thus, much to my embarrassment I require its return. If you could

accommodate me in this matter I should be most
obliged.

As a visitor to La Serenissima you will doubtless be
busy admiring its myriad gems. However, if you were
by chance 'a casa' at six o'clock tomorrow evening I
should be happy to call on you. Unless I hear to the
contrary I shall assume my suggestion is convenient.

Carlo Roberto
Cannaregio 49612006

'Not sure what this is all about,' Felix said, 'but it's from a chap called Carlo who wants to come here tomorrow night. Seems to think Violet has a book of his. What do you think?'

He passed the note to Cedric who read it through carefully. 'I wonder where he acquired his English, Miss Prendergast's Academy for the Cultured & Aspiring? I like the myriad gems bit – very dulcet!'

'Blow the style. What do you think he wants? And shall we be "*a casa*" tomorrow evening?'

'No reason not to be. Doubtless we can squeeze him in amidst the *myriad* demands of our social whirl!' Cedric scanned the letter again. 'Carlo Roberto,' he mused. 'You don't think it's the same Carlo that Lucia Borgino was talking about, the one she was going to introduce Rosy to and then changed her mind?'

Felix shrugged. 'Possible I suppose: he appears to read books. Ring the number, it won't hurt to confirm.'

Cedric tried the number but there was no answer. 'We'll

just have to wait and see,' he remarked. 'Meanwhile I must get ready.'

'Get ready for what?' Felix asked.

'I told you: the soirée musicale at the Goldoni. I think there are still tickets if you'd care to come.'

Felix shook his head. 'Too fatigued from the rigours of the day, dear boy: one needs a soothing evening. I'll have a light snack and then curl up with Caruso and my embroidery.'

'Don't tell me you brought that with you!'

'But naturally – I take it everywhere. After all, music isn't the only thing that soothes the savage breast.'

'But you don't have a savage breast.'

'I might just develop one if you don't hurry up and leave me in peace!' Felix closed his eyes.

Snack, dog and embroidery did their work and Felix was suitably soothed. In fact after a couple of hours he was soothed enough to contemplate a short stroll and a *digestivo*. He glanced at his watch. Cedric wouldn't be back for at least an hour; time enough to have a little wander and explore that rather charming little campo behind the palazzo . . . And he *might* of course drop in on that corner bar the gondoliers seemed to patronise. After all one was always being encouraged to fraternise with the locals . . . He smiled and sleeked his hair in the mirror.

When Felix returned he found that Cedric had preceded him and was lying on the sofa with what could only be described as a beatific expression on his face. It was a face that was normally fairly immobile, but that night it was suffused with a look both barmy and inebriated.

'Good concert was it?' Felix enquired.

'*Fantastico*,' Cedric sighed.

'Delighted to hear that. So what was so good about it?'

'What wasn't?' came the slurred reply.

Felix went over to the cocktail cabinet and mixed himself a drink, carefully omitting to offer one to Cedric.

'But what in particular?' he persisted. 'You clearly enjoyed it.'

'Oh yes, dear boy, but not something you would understand.'

'Try me,' Felix said evenly.

There was a lengthy pause as Cedric evidently mused. 'It was,' he pronounced, 'a sort of exquisite harmony of Bach, Borodin, and Noël Coward; a melange so potent I thought I would lose my mind!'

'I think you have,' retorted Felix dryly.

'Hmm, per . . . haps,' Cedric replied, and passed out.

On the dot of six the following evening the bell sounded and a voice on the intercom announced itself as Carlo Roberto.

'*Un momento. Scendo subito!*' Felix announced with a flourish. And feeling rather pleased with himself trotted down the staircase to welcome his guest.

He pulled open the heavy door and was confronted by a small man in a raincoat bearing a sheaf of pink gladioli.

He gave a brisk formal bow and stepped inside.

Felix was startled. He hadn't expected bouquets and was both flattered and flustered.

The visitor beamed and with the faintest of accents said in perfect English, 'Forgive this little liberty Signor Smythe, but your cousin once told me of your floral pursuits and the prestigious emporium in London. Please accept these with my compliments on your recent royal honour.'

Felix felt even more flattered. (How news travelled: that was the second person who had alluded to his warrant!) He especially liked the term 'prestigious emporium', a most fitting description of his modest establishment. He smirked inwardly and made a mental note to repeat the term to Cedric.

Upstairs he took the man's raincoat and made introductions. Drinks were poured and lighters clicked.

Carlo Roberto nodded appreciatively as he swept his eyes around the salon. 'Such a lovely room I always think. Violet has delightful taste. It is an invariable pleasure to be here – so restful. Alas my own apartment though large is too full of books to seem truly spacious. I dwell in what I believe the English call organised chaos! And as for charming pictures' – he gestured to the Canalettos – 'I fear such embellishments perforce give way to printers' ink.'

Cedric was amused. The man's oral delivery was as formally poised as his verbal. (And certainly preferable to the mutual discomfort of fractured grammar and tortured idiom. Fluency, even of an old-fashioned kind, made communication so much easier!) From the reference to his books the fellow could very possibly be the same Carlo that Lucia had spoken of.

Felix too had made that assumption. 'So you're a book dealer, are you?' he enquired a trifle baldly. 'Someone mentioned your name only the other day. She said—'

The man winced and cleared his throat. 'No I am not a dealer. I do not do deals. The commercial element plays little part in my interest – although I will occasionally procure an item for a friend. I am a *collector*: one of those oddities who cherish books for their own sake and cannot keep his hands off the beautiful, the quaint and the rare. My volumes are my children and I have far too many of them!' He gave a soft chuckle. 'And like children, from time to time they become wayward and unruly and must be restored to order: summoned or (dare I say it) *called to book* and re-catalogued. A laborious process and one I am currently engaged upon.' He spread his hands in a suddenly very Italianate gesture: 'And thus my mission here. I come in the hope of finding a lost child.'

'Which one?' Cedric asked.

Carlo explained that a couple of months earlier he had dropped in at the palazzo to partake of a coffee and a nightcap with his dear friend Violet Hoffmann. ('She mixes the most ethereal Bat's Wing,' he confided.) And on that particular evening he had been returning from a bibliophile convention in Verona. He had with him several new acquisitions which he was eager for his friend to

151

admire. They had spread the books out on the coffee table and he had commented upon each, detailing its content and provenance. Unfortunately such had been the potency of the Bat's Wing and the lateness of the hour that he had lost his usual alertness; and thus when he had scooped up the books prior to leaving he had carelessly left one behind. The following morning Violet had telephoned pointing out the error and he had assured her he would call back to collect it. In fact, 'things being what they so often are,' he had omitted to do this and subsequently forgot all about the book. 'Until now.'

'Why now?' Felix asked.

'My annual inventory. As said, October is the month for the Grand Reckoning!'

'Ah yes of course,' Cedric nodded, 'but you still haven't given us its title.'

'Didn't I? How silly of me. It's a collection of nineteenth-century English translations of the poet Horace. Rather a rare edition compiled by one R. D. M. Bodger.'

'Ah yes,' said Cedric, 'that did cross my mind.'

There had followed an awkward silence while the two hosts pondered the best way to inform Carlo Roberto of his wasted journey.

Felix was the first to speak. Hastily offering his guest another cigarette he said, 'Actually, I am afraid the bird has flown.'

Carlo looked puzzled. 'What bird?'

'Well to be exact your book.'

There followed apologies, explanations and earnest assurances that they would retrieve the book from Miss Gilchrist the very next day.

The man took the news well – that is to say he showed no outward sign of annoyance, but made it clear that rather than rely on Felix and Cedric as intermediaries he would approach the lady himself and explain the situation. 'She will be sorry to give it up,' he smiled, 'and thus the least I can do is to go in person and offer my apologies. Perhaps you will be so kind as to tell me where she is staying.'

They gave him Rosy's address; and after a few pleasantries and a polite enquiry after Caruso, Carlo Roberto took his leave and went on his way.

After he had gone they looked at each other in some dismay.

'She won't like that,' Cedric sighed.

'No. What you might call a turn *down* for the books!'

'Actually I wouldn't call it that,' Cedric replied witheringly. 'My days in the fourth form are long since passed.'

Felix was about to agree wholeheartedly with the latter statement but thought better of it. Cedric was right, it wasn't one of his better jests. Besides this was not the time for verbal skirmish, they had to decide what to do about Rosy. 'Do you think we should telephone and tell her the bad news ourselves? Or would it be simpler to say nothing and let her find out from this Carlo? He obviously intends to go there.'

Cedric mused. 'My instinct tells me to do nothing – often the best course in such matters. Leave others to relay the bad news, less stressful.' Felix nodded. 'On the other hand,' he continued, 'I suppose it would be a courtesy; and also less of a shock when friend Carlo makes his approach – forewarned is forearmed et cetera. Not that she needs arming of course, he seemed a very mild little fellow; quite pleasant in fact. Will you telephone?'

'Oh no,' said Felix quickly, 'I've got the dog's dinner to deal with. We're experimenting with some new biscuits. Frightfully expensive; Paolo recommended them. *Wooffo: Biscotti migliore per i cani migliore.* Apparently they are based on a recipe by a Signor Fortnum.' He giggled and went off to the kitchen to prepare the feast.

CHAPTER SEVENTEEN

Rosy was none too pleased to get Cedric's phone call. In fact she wasn't pleased at all. The prospect of admitting defeat to Stanley so soon after reporting the good news was a blow, and already she could hear the torrent of anguished protest echoing down the line.

She brooded on what Cedric had told her. Apparently the man was an obsessive bibliophile and was clearly anxious to reclaim his lost Horace. Well, she grumbled to herself, if it was so damn important to him why had he been so careless in the first place? Fancy leaving it at the Palazzo Reiss and then forgetting to pick it up! Surely if the thing was so precious he would have returned like a shot the next day. Her mind darted back to childhood and she heard her mother's exasperated voice: 'Frankly, Rosemary, if you persist in leaving your toys about like that you don't deserve to have any.' Precisely: such negligence didn't deserve reward. Anyway what about finders keepers? *She* had found it. (Well not literally perhaps, but as good as.) And it wasn't as if this Carlo had put his name in the thing; other than Bodger's own signature there was no stamp of possession. She heaved a sigh staring irritably at the book. One moment she had the damn thing and the next she was expected to give it up. It was a bit much! The cheerful postcards she had been writing suddenly became irrelevant – mocking even – and pushing them aside she gazed resentfully out at the lagoon. Somehow it seemed to have lost its sparkle since she had last looked.

She reached for her lighter, lit a cigarette and brooded. Cedric hadn't said when she might expect the man but presumably his approach would be imminent. Perhaps she could make a diplomatic withdrawal, i.e. scram and spend the whole of the next day on the Lido. Such an absence would at least be a delaying tactic. After all, the Carlo person had made no appointment and there seemed no obvious reason why she should give him the chance of making one. Elusive, that's what she would be. And with luck if she could play the absence game long enough perhaps he would forget about the book altogether just as he had before . . . Yes that was the answer – decline to be 'at home'. Wasn't there a rather fashionable hotel on the Lido which did excellent lunches and where one could swim? Fearfully extravagant of course, but she could put the jaunt on expenses: a necessary means of protecting the literary spoils while confounding overtures from marauding foreigners. She grinned. Yes, put like that Dr Stanley might feel a surge of rare generosity!

Thus the following morning those were Rosy's plans: to quit the Witherington residence early and spend the whole day elsewhere.

Plans of course are made to be thwarted. And so just as Rosy was descending the stairs poised for a quick getaway, she encountered Mr Downing coming up. He held a small white card in his hand. 'Ah Miss Gilchrist,' he exclaimed, 'how fortunate to catch you! There's an Italian downstairs – very polite I may say – who seems anxious to see you. I can't find our hostess so he gave me his card and asked if I would be so kind as to present it to you with his compliments. I told him you were bound to be still in and I should deliver it immediately.' Downing gave her the card, and stood back breathing heavily from his staircase exertions. He had the air of a biddable retriever waiting for a pat. Rosy sighed. Wouldn't you know – foiled by the marauding foreigner! Withholding the pat she thanked her messenger and continued down the stairs and into the lobby lounge to confront the visitor.

At her entry the small man in the raincoat swung round to greet her. She recognised him instantly as he did her. 'Ah the so charming English lady,' he exclaimed, 'you may recall our recent meeting near the Pacelli bookshop. From your friends' description I rather thought it might be you. Life is full of exciting coincidences.'

Coincidences yes, Rosy thought, but as to exciting

she wasn't too sure. 'Yes of course I remember,' she said politely. 'How nice to see you again.' (It wasn't at all nice: the man had come to take her book away!) She gestured to a chair. 'Please sit down, I gather we have something to discuss.'

He gave a rueful smile. 'Unfortunately yes and I wish the matter were less delicate, but as you now probably realise there has been a slight misunderstanding. Your friends gave you a book which by rights belongs to me, and with the greatest respect I ask that you return it.' The eyes smiled and the tone was precise.

'Yes,' Rosy said non-committally. 'You are referring to the Bodger Horace.'

'Exactly. And I have to admit that when you told me the other day you were looking for a copy of Horace's Odes it never occurred to me that it might be this particular version. I had assumed it was one of the many contemporary editions. I don't know how things are in England, but here in Italy there has been an enormous resurgence of interest in the poetry and every publisher seems to be bringing out a collection.'

'I see. Sort of two a penny you mean.'

He laughed. 'And tuppence ha'penny for five. Wouldn't that be the English phrase?'

Rosy acknowledged that it probably was the English phrase, while inwardly cursing that at any moment she would have to go upstairs to fetch the book and place it meekly in his hands. Perhaps if she were tougher and of a more entrepreneurial bent she would hold out: suggest something more transactional or request a token fee as a gesture of goodwill or whatever it was business people did. But she was no businesswoman and would simply make a fool of herself. Besides, presumably if the thing were his, he had every right to take it back.

Thus reluctantly she heard herself saying, 'Well I expect you would like me to get it. I won't be a minute.'

'Yes please,' he said simply.

Book in hand she started to descend the stairs again and was once more waylaid by Mr Downing. (Really, had that man nothing better to do than loiter aimlessly on staircases?)

'Everything all right?' he enquired in a sepulchral whisper.

'What?'

'Your visitor, I trust he's . . . ahem, I mean *all's well* I take it?'

'Oh yes,' she replied airily, 'as right as rain.' (Like hell!) She wondered if Downing expected the front parlour to be a scene of rape and carnage, reflecting bitterly that pillage might be nearer the truth.

She re-entered the room and with a gracious smile presented Carlo Roberto with his long-lost volume.

The man was clearly relieved to be reunited with the book, and nodding in satisfaction ran his hands over the binding and began to leaf through its pages. Suddenly he stopped and she heard a faint intake of breath. He bent his head to make closer inspection; and then reaching into his pocket produced a magnifying glass. Vaguely curious, Rosy watched as he squinted through the lens at the writing on the flyleaf.

Straightening up he pushed the book aside and regarding her intently said, 'This is not my book. This is a fake.'

She had gazed at him bemused. 'But it is the one that was found at the Palazzo Reiss, the one you left there. Whatever do you mean?'

'Exactly what I say, signora.' Rosy noticed a slight change in his demeanour. The smooth genial tone had turned hard. 'I can assure you that this is not the one that I left there. It is not mine and I believe this one to be a forgery.'

'But I—I don't understand,' she stammered.

'No more do I,' he said dryly.

There was a silence as he continued to watch her closely. She felt that she was being assessed, judged. What did he imagine – that she had tried to pull a fast one, had tried to palm him off with some crude imitation while she could scuttle back to England bearing his own as her trophy? What nonsense! But as she saw the sharp expression and noted the impatient twitch of his little finger, she realised that was probably exactly what he did think. She sighed in exasperation. 'How do you know the book isn't yours? I gather you only had it in your possession for a short time – hardly long enough to spill jam on it!' She gave a caustic laugh.

'No not to spill jam, but long enough to write my initials on the third page from the end – underneath

160

the ode beginning *"Phoebus volentem proelia me loqui"* . . . Perhaps you know it?'

Rosy felt like saying that no she didn't bloody know it and why should she, but was determined to keep cool. Thus she said lightly that alas it was not a line familiar to her and added, 'So you put your initials in all your books do you? A sort of secret stamp of acquisition?'

'Yes,' he replied gravely, 'the moment I get them.'

Rosy cleared her throat, and feeling not unlike an inquisitorial schoolmistress said, 'I don't suppose there is any possibility that on this occasion you may have forgotten to do so. Memory plays such odd tricks. I mean you may have *meant* to but were distracted by—'

'I was not distracted, signora. My initials are in the original and this is not it.' He gave a dismissive shrug. 'Besides there is something else wrong: the inscription. In the original the word "joyous" is used; in this one it is "joyful". I may also add that anyone at all familiar with the technique of forging will recognise that this ink, although cleverly dulled, is no more than five years old. The foxing too is questionable.' He paused, and then said: 'Besides there is no BF.'

'BF! What does that mean – Bloody Fool?'

He gave a wintry smile. 'Not in this instance. It was a piece of Bodger's vanity. He did it with three of his publications, this being one of them. The initials mean *Bodger fecit*, an affectation. It was his way of claiming ownership, a stamp of authenticity; rather like an artist declaring it was his own work and not that of an assistant.

161

He wrote it in tiny letters bottom left of the inside cover. As you can see this has none such.'

Rosy shot a cursory glance. 'Well,' she said briskly, 'I am afraid I can't help you there. This is certainly the book I was given by Cedric and Felix and the one they said they had found in Violet Hoffman's bookcase. I cannot see why they should try to foist a forged copy on to me. I never asked for the damn thing, it came out of the blue! And while you may remember putting your initials in your own copy has it occurred to you – memory being so fallible – that perhaps you didn't leave it at the Palazzo at all but lost it somewhere else, left it in some bar perhaps and that the one found by Cedric has nothing to do with you or your collection.'

'It hasn't,' he said and stared at her grimly; while Rosy feared that her truculence had only made matters worse. She had so meant to be cool and detached.

To her surprise his features suddenly relaxed and he gave a bark of laughter. 'My dear lady you seem determined to put me in some early stage of dementia. First I forget whether I have put my initials in the book or not, and then I mistake my evening at the Palazzo Reiss for some city bar. At this rate I shall shortly be sectioned on San Servolo!' He continued to chuckle but Rosy felt uncomfortable and felt herself going pink.

'All right, so what do you think?' she asked.

The mirth stopped but the initial cordial tone returned. 'I should say there are a number of possibilities: a) that you are a woman of supreme guile, ruthless enterprise, and who being in love with her boss at the British Museum will do anything to gain his favour; b) that your colleagues Cedric and Felix are inveterate liars and for some reason want to pass this book off as the genuine article . . . Who knows, perhaps they are fond of you and want to give you pleasure; such altruism is not unknown. Conversely perhaps they simply wish to cause you embarrassment; c) that my dear friend Violet is in league with a forger, and recognising mine to be the original hastily instructed him to fake a replacement while selling the one I left to the highest bidder. Perhaps she needed a little extra cash to fund her Chicago trip and—'

'Oh this is ridiculous,' Rosy burst out, 'these are absurd suggestions!'

He smiled ruefully. 'How disappointing. I thought they were rather persuasive, especially the first.'

'That was the silliest of all!'

'Yes I daresay, I daresay . . . *mea culpa* Miss Gilchrist. I fear I have a suspicious mind. Clearly you are a stranger to such duplicity.'

Rosy wasn't entirely sure whether he was confirming her honesty or implying she was a fool. But assuming the former she said, 'There must be another possibility, something more likely than your list of nonsensical whimsy.'

Carlo looked serious again. 'Oh indeed. There can be only one explanation: someone known to Violet, or in her house, seeing the book there – or being told of it – deliberately made the switch knowing she wouldn't notice.' He raised an enquiring eyebrow. 'Plausible?'

'Perfectly . . . But you are assuming this happened in the past, shortly after you left the book there. How about the present? Supposing the switch was done much more recently, such as between the time of Cedric discovering the thing and his giving it to me.'

'Hmm. I recall Professor Dillworthy saying they gave you the book a couple of days after it was found. Rather a narrow space in which to perform such an operation, wouldn't you say?'

'Yes but it *could* be done.'

He nodded but looked sceptical. 'In principle yes; in practice I wonder . . . Still, I think we are both agreed, dear Sherlock – or Miss Christie if you prefer – that at some point in the last year *someone*, not yourself or Violet or your friends, appropriated the book and substituted another.' He lowered his voice conspiratorially: 'In time-honoured tradition we should perhaps refer to such person as X.'

'And what is X's motive?'

'Nefarious gain naturally. Doubtless it has something to do with that pathetic piece of hokum purveyed by the poltroon Berenstein. That's it, I'll be bound!'

Rosy suddenly found herself giggling. 'Tell me, Signor Roberto, where did you learn your English – not I imagine in that Sussex prisoner of war camp?'

He looked indignant. 'I most assuredly did! What's wrong with it? The sergeant major was a most assiduous reader. He would read anything from Gibbon to James

164

Joyce to Wodehouse and Chandler, and then relay it to us. "You 'orrible little wops," he would roar, "I'll teach you bleeders to speak the King's perishing English if it kills me!"' Carlo grinned. 'I don't know about him but it nearly killed us, that I do know!'

Rosy laughed and then grew serious. 'So if you haven't got the book and I apparently haven't, who has?'

'Frankly I have no idea and to tell the truth I am not entirely sure that I care. Admittedly it would be nice to get it back again, but it wasn't one of my essentials. I have other more precious items. Nevertheless *were* it to come my way I would grab it. As presumably would you, Miss Gilchrist; because as things stand it looks as if you will have to commence your searches all over again. Back to square-bloody-one, as the sergeant major used to say.'

'Yes,' agreed Rosy wearily. 'Yes I suppose I shall . . .'And then a thought struck her: 'But I don't understand why it was just recently that you became so keen to get the book back. Cedric said it was something to do with your annual inventory, but was that all?'

He hesitated. 'No not entirely. It was something the girl said, Lucia Borgino. She seemed eager to find out what I knew about the Bodger, i.e. did I know who might have it. Well of course I knew – or *thought* I knew – that I had it. But that was not something I cared to divulge. On the whole it is best to divulge very little to Lucia; to do otherwise is not always in one's interests.'

His tone had taken on an acid note and Rosy let the matter drop. But something else had also occurred to her.

'This forgery you refer to – who would do that?'

He was silent for a moment and then said, 'Venice has always had her forgers, we are renowned for it. Some are most versatile and will turn their hand to anything from books to porcelain; others are more specialised and very exacting in their clientele. A lot of it goes on, though there are two names in particular that come to mind, or there *were*: one died . . . But I can assure you Miss Gilchrist it doesn't do to sprinkle names around – it never did and it doesn't now. Venetians are above all things *discreet*.' He lowered his left eyelid, and despite the easy tone she knew he wouldn't be drawn.

She gestured towards the book. 'So what about this – do you want to take it?'

He shook his head. 'It has no relevance to me now. Keep it. You can refresh your knowledge of Horace. Check that last ode, you will find it charming.'

Murmuring some formal pleasantries he was about to leave, when he stopped and said casually, 'Signora you have my card. Before you leave Venice please alert me and we will take tea and toast together, I should like that . . . Oh, and by the way, *are* you in love with your boss?'

'Certainly not,' she snapped.

Left alone Rosy glared at the discarded book. 'Tea and toast?' she muttered. 'What I need is gin and ice cream. The cheek of the fellow!' She set off for Tonelli's.

CHAPTER EIGHTEEN

As Felix had correctly predicted, Bill Hewson had been optimistic in proposing supper so soon after his evening at the Palazzo Reiss. Nevertheless, true to his word, he did indeed book a table for a few days hence at one of the newer establishments near the Ponte delle Ostreghe, a charming trattoria fast becoming a favourite with Venetians and tourists alike.

They had sat under a canopy by a canal, the small terrace dotted with candles and lanterns. Rosy had been placed next to Edward Jones who explained that his sister could not be with them owing to a previous engagement at the opera, 'Being seductive with some poor sap in a private box no doubt,' he had said dryly; and then with a muffled hoot added, 'She can't stand music you know!' As a means of breaking social ice Rosy thought the remark a trifle crass. However, she smiled politely and enquired how long he was staying. 'Until my sister boots me out,' had been the curt reply.

Initially it was a fairly agreeable evening with Hewson bouncily expansive, Hope-Landers his amiable self, Felix a little muted (nursing disapproval of the painter's boisterousness?), Cedric relaxed, and Edward, in between bouts of disdain and affection, relatively civil. Yet beneath the general amity Rosy detected a festering tension between the young man and the American. Now and again she had seen the exchange of covert looks and caught the tone of mutual scorn. (A long-held irrational distaste? Or were there deeper hostilities? It hardly mattered.) As for herself, after the disappointment of the book her spirits were not at their best but she enjoyed things well enough and found Guy Hope-Landers' presence on her right an engaging antidote to Edward's somewhat puerile and increasingly bibulous conversation on her left. At one point, draping a confiding arm around her shoulders and nodding towards Bill Hewson, he had whispered slyly: 'Don't trust that one, my dear, he'd cut your throat given half a chance . . . and he's a lousy painter too!' This had been followed by a splutter of mirth but Rosy had not been amused. She disliked being addressed as 'my dear' by one several years younger than herself and in any case had found the comments in poor taste.

But despite such moments the meal itself had been good with copious antipasti, delicious saffron risotto, and sizzling mussels with clam sauce. Hewson had ensured that the Bardolino was more than plentiful, and Rosy couldn't help noticing that both his own and Edward's glasses were continuously replenished; so frequently in fact that by the coffee stage both men were clearly somewhat the worse for wear: the younger shrill and garrulous, the older truculent. It was, Rosy felt, time to leave.

Indeed that was exactly what Guy Hope-Landers was preparing to do. Thrusting a sheaf of lire under Hewson's plate he stood up, and bidding them all good night explained he had promised to call on Lucia when she returned from the Fenice.

'Oh and you can tell my big sister to go hang!' yelled Edward suddenly.

Hope-Landers waved his napkin in salute. 'Will do, old chap,' and he strolled off into the night.

'Christ,' muttered Edward, 'do I want him for a brother-in-law?'

There was an awkward silence. 'Er, is that likely?' Rosy ventured.

The young man snorted. 'God knows, you never know with Lucia, tight-fisted bitch!'

It was Cedric who broke the further silence. Clearing his throat he said pleasantly, 'Oh come now, I daresay she's a teddy bear really.'

'*Doubtless*,' was the caustic reply, 'and miserly with it!' He leapt up, and with face transformed from fury to merriment thumped the table with both fists; and addressing Hewson shouted, 'Remember, Rembrandt,

I've got your number! Come on old man, catch me if you can!' The next moment, chair overturned and wine glasses smashed to the floor, he had shot out of the terrace and was seen racing along the *fondamenta* leapfrogging over the capstans.

They stared after him stunned and embarrassed. And then hastily heaping more lire on the table departed with as much dignity as possible, the cheers and boos from other diners ringing in their ears.

'Do you think he's mad?' Felix whispered to Rosy.

'As a coot,' she muttered.

'Well one thing is definite,' Cedric remarked, 'we can't go to that restaurant again!'

The American said nothing. Too drunk? Too shocked? Or merely peeved at being addressed as 'old man'?

The mist swirling around the quay had thickened and it was damp underfoot. Rosy's *pensione* was some way off and it was agreed that the quickest route for her might be by vaporetto, and Hewson said he knew a shortcut to the landing stage. This involved turning off the quay into a couple of narrow passages, traversing a small campo and then snaking along a side canal from where they could join the Canal Grande and the vaporetto stop. Emerging from one of the alleyways they were confronted by a small bridge. The mist made it difficult to see, but straddling its balustrade there appeared to be a figure flailing its arms. They caught the strains of a song. The words were in English – '*My old man's a dustman*' could just be heard echoing across the water.

'Oh God, it's him,' groaned Hewson.

Whether the figure had seen them was not clear but it certainly seemed to wave, and at the next moment Edward Jones emitted a loud whoop and nosedived into the canal.

'Where does he think he is,' protested Cedric, 'Magdalen Bridge? Really this is too much!'

'Presumably he can swim,' Felix said.

'He can't,' Rosy exclaimed, 'he told me when we were at supper. And look, he's in trouble!' They hastened to the canal's edge and watched horrified as the diver splashed around in eddying circles, his arms frantically churning the water. He sank beneath the surface, the waves subsided and for a few seconds there was an eerie quiet. Then with a violent eruption the surface broke and a head emerged and the threshing started again, and for a sickening moment Rosy thought she heard a faint wail. Yet, whether by effort or luck, the floundering form seemed to be gradually moving nearer the bank.

'Will he reach us?' she cried.

'Not sure . . . Oh Lord he's gone under again,' muttered Felix. 'But it can't be all that deep, he may just make it. Surely there's a lifebelt somewhere, but in this damned fog one can't—'

At that moment there was a loud splash and another body hit the water: Hewson's. He struck out strongly towards the drowning man. The dark and the fog made it difficult to get a clear view. They heard a shout followed by much splashing and thrashing. It seemed to last an age. And then at last through the murk they could see the rescuer back-paddling slowly towards the bank, one arm firmly gripping Edward's shoulders.

'Thank God,' Rosy breathed. 'Is he all right?'

Cedric and Felix knelt down to haul the swimmer and his burden up on to the towpath.

'Sorry,' Hewson gasped, 'he kept going under, I just couldn't hold on – kept slipping away. Afraid he's a goner, poor little sod.'

The immediate aftermath was of course dreadful. Police and press descended, the latter working so quickly as to be able to feature a brief report the following day lamenting the tragic death of the young Englishman and proclaiming Hewson to be 'il pittore coraggioso', adding that Venice was proud to have him in its midst. As witnesses Cedric, Felix and Rosy were asked for immediate statements on the spot and required to remain in the city until further notice pending further enquiries into the cause of death – which in any case everyone knew to be drowning by misadventure. Lucia was notified and Hope-Landers, roused from his quarters, looked bleak.

CHAPTER NINETEEN

Naturally like everyone Rosy was appalled. It had all been so sudden, so horribly raw and shocking. Watching those desperate struggles had been agony, and the raising and dashing of hopes unbearable. She closed her eyes recalling the fateful words *Afraid he's a goner, poor little sod* and seeing Hewson's futile attempt at revival as the victim lay sprawled on the quayside. Staring aghast at the beached body all had surely known such efforts were useless.

For a moment anger replaced Rosy's pain. Foolish boy! Why the hell had he dived in like that knowing he couldn't swim? She gave a mirthless smile. The answer was obvious: that's what you *did* when you were young, drunk and a show-off. It was the sort of theatrical bravado typical of a showman like Edward. Too damned pleased with himself . . . like Icarus, probably thought he was inviolate. Or divine.

She wondered about the sister. It must be awful for her – although from what Felix had said the woman wasn't the softest of characters. His tone had been waspish, but then it often was. Besides, not being soft didn't make you heartless. Yes, she must be going through hell. Rosy hoped that no one would be so tactless as to mention her brother's angry jibe at the supper table. Not likely really unless the comments had been overheard by nearby diners; his voice had been loud enough! And what about Bill Hewson – how was he taking it? It had been such a heroic failure. Poor chap, it must be intolerable.

Wrapped in such thoughts Rosy sat alone in the patio of the Casa Witherington, studying the rusting creeper and listening to the whistling notes of plaintive robins. In England autumn would be well under way; here in Venice its path was only just begun. She sipped her coffee (a solicitous offering from Miss Witherington) and wondered whether it was really worth continuing her quest for the Horace. Somehow after the tragedy it all seemed rather irrelevant . . .

Her thoughts and the calm of the patio were disturbed by the sudden jangling of the bell. Rosy jumped and stared at the door in the wall. Should she answer it or leave it to Miss Witherington? Better the latter, she was only a guest. She waited, expecting to hear capering footsteps. None was forthcoming. The bell jangled again. No response. Diffidently Rosy got up and went to open the door. She just hoped that whoever it was wasn't Italian; her vocabulary wasn't up to it, least of all that morning.

She was confronted by the figure of Bill Hewson, minus his usual cap and looking haggard.

'Hi,' he said, 'good to see you. I hoped you might be here.' He smiled wanly.

She welcomed him in, offered a seat at the wicker table and asked if she could get him some coffee. 'I am sure our hostess could rise to that. I've just had some myself, although tea seems to be the preferred beverage here even at this time of day.'

He shook his head. 'No, no Rosy. I just er—well I just wanted a bit of company. Somebody to rub along with for a bit . . . it's all been kind of a shock. That poor kid . . . I did my best you know.'

'You most certainly did,' she said warmly. 'A ghastly experience. And then all that awful business with the police afterwards and so on, you must be worn out!'

'Yeah . . . yeah pretty well.' He drummed his fingers on the table and sighed. 'I guess it's silly really, but yes it's knocked me back a bit.' He gave a hollow laugh. 'Age I expect. They say you get less resilient. In the war, even though I was in my forties, I could deal with this sort of thing – losing colleagues, seeing them go under. It was tough, but it was part of the job; you got sort of hardened.' He paused. 'No not hardened but *distracted*: there was so much else pressing in on you, there wasn't time for shock least of all for grief.'

Rosy cast her mind back to her time in Dover as a

searchlight operator and knew something of what he meant. 'I think I understand,' she said quietly.

He seemed not to have heard for he continued: 'But this is different. It's peacetime – we're in Venice, the most magical city in the world, and this crazy thing has to happen! I just couldn't pull my weight, I'm too old.' He looked stricken.

'You are not old and there was nothing more you could have done,' she said. 'It's simply one of those senseless things; they happen all the time. He was young, wild and utterly absurd; the rescue was tried and didn't work. Such failures are hell, but it wasn't your fault. Kindly bear that in mind!' She stared at him fiercely.

He regarded her with solemn eyes and then a slow smile spread across his face. 'Say, you can be quite forceful Miss Rosy Gilchrist. My hunch was right: I knew I'd feel better after being in your company for a while. You're quite a gal!'

'I am not quite a gal,' Rosy retorted tartly, 'I am merely voicing common sense. Now what I suggest is that you accompany me to the Mercerie. I want to choose some pearls, and then we can have a light lunch at that café in the Campo San Zulian. Its *spaghetti al funghi* looks most enticing.'

'Yes ma'am!' He stood up and saluted.

As they left and strolled along the Zattere Rosy congratulated herself. Confronting the bright day after the grimness of the previous night was a good thing.

Definitely good for her, and she liked to think for her companion too. Who was it had said, 'In the sunshine, even death is sunny'? D. H. Lawrence she suspected. Given the circumstances rather an exaggeration perhaps, but the sun certainly helped.

Combing the little shops of the Mercerie also helped. Unlike many men Hewson was a patient escort in the shopping ritual and seemed to take a genuine pleasure in the process of selection and rejection. With a pang she thought of her fiancé killed in the war: Johnnie, valiantly trying to conceal his boredom under a weary grin while she had oohed and aahed over shoes and gloves. Oh God, if only she could ditch Hewson's interest for Johnnie's boredom again! There came the stab of the old familiar pain. Funny the way it would strike at the most unexpected moments – often the most banal or humdrum. A decade had passed since the airman's death and yet the hurt still lurked, slyly poised biding its time. Weeks, months would go by – and then, whoosh, out of the blue the arrow would strike and she would reel with the spasm . . . Just as now, strolling among people and choosing cultured pearls in sunlight. (No, she thought wryly, Lawrence had been wrong there: Johnnie's death was surely the exception, however strongly the sun shone.)

For a few seconds her vocal cords contracted. And then turning to Hewson she exclaimed gaily, 'Oh I'm tired of all this jewellery, the pearls can wait. I'm starving! Do let's go and eat. The café's over there and if we're quick we can bag a table in the window.'

'If you say so,' he laughed, 'but remember lunch is on me.' He took her arm and they crossed the square.

At first all went well: the menu was keenly perused, drinks ordered and approving comments made about the attractiveness of the café and its cheerful service. He insisted that she visit his studio 'to view my daubings and the pathetic chaos we artists toil in', and they fixed a time later in the week when he was holding an afternoon of 'open house'.

The sun continued to shine and despite Rosy's wave of pain over Johnnie's memory she started to relax and enjoy herself. Hewson too seemed at ease and talked interestingly about the pleasures and trials of painting, the new techniques he was experimenting with and the challenges of life as an ex-patriot. Venice, he declared, was the most exciting mistress in the world but like all such ladies capricious and wilful. 'You can't take anything for granted here, neither the weather nor the citizens: nothing and nobody are quite what they seem. I tell you Rosy, the carnival mask says it all; it couldn't be a better emblem for the city. Beauty and delusion, that's Venice for you! She sure is just like a tantalising mistress: loveliness, contrivance and treachery!' He threw back his head and laughed uproariously splashing more wine into their glasses, and, she was irritated to note, over her piece of bread.

On the whole she found his views on art rather more absorbing than those on Venice. The latter were platitudes and the bit about treacherous mistresses heavy-handed. However, given the recent debacle it was good to see (though perhaps not hear) him laugh. So she deliberately tried to keep things light, avoiding any reference to the drowned man or the details of the police formalities. Thus she told him of her work in London, the autocratic oddities of Dr Stanley and her hopes of visiting America one day. 'I have a relative in New York – well, not a relative exactly, more of an in-law – he was married to my aunt once. He's keen that I go over sometime. I really ought to. It would be fun to travel "across the pond" – isn't that what you say?'

'Yeah that's what we say. New York's okay but you'd do better in Boston. Now that *is* a city with style – real style, Rosy!'

'More style than Venice?' she asked teasingly.

He didn't answer at first and she noted how his expression had changed, becoming suddenly thoughtful, sombre even. 'Hmm. More real I would say. Less fickle. Less . . .' He paused, searching for the right term. 'Less damn *fake*.' The word was snapped out, all levity gone. His hand had gripped the table with sudden force, his fingers scrunching the cloth. The mouth hardened and a vein twitched at his temple.

The anger was obvious and Rosy was startled. The change had been so swift, the intensity almost violent. Silence seemed the best response and she turned hastily to the menu and pretended to examine the list of desserts. When she looked up again he was gazing listlessly out of the window. For some strange reason she thought of a young subaltern she had known in the war, Roddy Roper. God, she could hear his voice now, so earnestly confidential. 'When in doubt, sweetie, *always* ply them with drink. Works every time!'

Rosy leant forward. 'I say,' she said brightly, 'there's quite a bit left, almost a glass each. Seems a pity to waste it. Here.' She picked up the carafe and began to fill his glass.

Bill Hewson turned to her and grinned. 'Say, you're quite a little toper aren't you Miss Gilchrist!'

Rosy shrugged. 'I do my best,' she murmured.

As they left the café and walked back across the square, Hewson to his studio and she to resume her pearl-fishing, she noticed a man lolling against an archway smoking a cigarette. Hardly an unusual sight and yet the figure seemed vaguely familiar. She was puzzled. Why should she think she knew him? The man looked up, stared at her for a few moments and then turned away. No, she didn't know him but she had seen him before all right – in another square; one lit by the moon not the sun. Pacelli's companion.

Had he recognised her? Quite possibly. His look, though not lingering, had been direct and searching; and was it her imagination or had those rather narrow eyes flashed the merest sign of acknowledgement? . . . She felt ruffled and was anxious to move away and rejoin the cheerful bustle of the Mercerie. Using the pearls as her excuse she said a hasty goodbye to Hewson, and promising to see him again moved off in the direction of the crowds.

Why she looked back she had no idea, but when she did it was to see the man detach himself from the archway and walk briskly up to the painter and tap him on the shoulder. The latter swung round, but evidently recognising the other relaxed. They stood for some time engrossed in close conversation, and then still talking moved gradually out of sight.

Rosy gazed after them. 'How odd!' she muttered to herself. And for some reason both the pearls and the afternoon began to lose their lustre. She felt tired; and to her surprise found herself relishing the prospect of a cup of Miss Witherington's fiendishly weak tea.

CHAPTER TWENTY

Back at the *pensione* and sitting in the lounge nursing the predictably weak tea, Rosy was debating whether to telephone Dr Stanley again. Unless one counted Edward's drowning, Carlo's curious revelation and Pacelli's murder she had nothing of note to report – certainly nothing of note for Dr Stanley. Such events would be significant to him only in so far as they represented tiresome obstacles to her quest. She wondered idly whether she should invent something, something small but telling which would raise his hopes yet confirm nothing: a harmless lie cheering to him and undisturbing to her.

She was just pondering such a possibility when she was interrupted by two of her fellow guests, Dr Burgess and Daphne Blanchett. They looked windswept and a trifle damp.

'We've been round the lagoon in a speedboat,' the latter explained, 'fearfully fast and not to be recommended. I feel quite worn out!'

'It wasn't actually a speedboat,' said Burgess, 'merely a dinghy with a souped-up engine.'

'Well whatever it was I shan't be indulging in that little trip again. Funny once, silly twice!' She glanced at the tray of tea by Rosy's chair and gave a disdainful sniff. 'I don't know how you can drink that stuff'(neither did Rosy)'insipid enough at breakfast, far worse in the afternoon. I am surprised our hostess has the gall to produce it. Curious really when she's such a good cook.'

'It's probably a deliberate ploy to make us admire the food even more,' suggested Burgess.

'Rather a desperate measure I should think,' she said dryly. 'Oh and talking of desperate measures, I read in the paper that that brother of Lucia Borgino fell off a bridge and drowned. I gather he was larking about and slipped. Attention seeking as usual I suppose. Oh well, one display too far this time I fear . . . Tell me, did Guy say anything about it in the boat? The engine was making such a racket I couldn't hear a thing.'

Rosy was too surprised to catch Burgess's response. It hadn't occurred to her that the two should know Edward and his sister, or indeed Guy Hope-Landers (presumably it was he, and she vaguely recalled his saying he had a boat).

'Actually,' she interrupted, 'the poor boy didn't slip, he dived.'

'Hmm. That would follow,' Burgess said.

'How do you know?' exclaimed Daphne Blanchett. 'You weren't there were you?' She regarded Rosy with accusing interest.

'As it happens I was,' Rosy said quietly. 'It was all rather dreadful.'

'Well yes I am sure it was . . . *ghastly*.' She didn't sound particularly aghast but Rosy gave her the benefit of the doubt.

'So you witnessed the whole thing did you?' Dr Burgess asked.

Rosy nodded.

'How unsettling,' he said, and sounded genuinely sympathetic.

'Very strange,' Daphne Blanchett remarked. 'Are you sure Guy didn't say anything about it in the boat? As a matter of fact given the circumstances I'm surprised he didn't cancel our trip. If the thing happened so recently you might have expected him to be busy comforting the grieving sister. Surely Lucia would have seen to that all right!' She gave a caustic laugh.

'Ah,' replied Burgess, 'but perhaps we were the godsend, a means of timely escape.' They exchanged knowing looks.

Dr Burgess turned to Rosy. 'I am sorry,' he said, 'you must think us rather harsh. But we quite like old Guy. He's a pleasant fellow; one of nature's placid bachelors you might say. For some reason Signora Borgino seems to have set her cap at him. There has been a steady pursuit.

I think he finds it rather a trial, though is too polite to say so.'

Rosy smiled awkwardly. She was slightly uncomfortable hearing details of Hope-Landers' private problems but felt a guilty interest all the same. Gossip was so seductive!

'Hmm,' murmured Daphne Blanchett darkly, 'and in view of what was announced last week the pursuit is likely to get all the steadier.'

'What? Oh you mean the *title*.' Burgess chuckled. 'Yes that should quicken the pace I shouldn't wonder.'

Rosy was bemused but not wanting to ask a direct question cleared her throat instead. Perhaps that would be a cue for one of them.

It was. Burgess glanced across at her. 'Don't suppose you would know about that would you? In fact very few people do. Guy's always kept the connection pretty dark. I suspect he's a bit embarrassed by it actually. He is related to some peer who lives a reclusive existence in a croft in the Highlands: a funny old boy, name of Benjamin Ritchie-Hope-Landers. He never married and Guy is a second, or possibly a third, cousin. It seems the chap is on his last legs and demise is imminent, and Guy being the nearest relative inherits the title. It's a vast estate – three fields and a pair of sheep!'

'Yes,' chimed Daphne Blanchett, 'so all style and virtually no substance. Cachet without cash. Not much use to poor old Guy.'

'But possibly to Lucia?' Rosy ventured.

'Most definitely. To be Lady Ritchie-Hope-Landers

would suit Madam very well, especially if money were attached – not that there's much chance of that. Still, one can't have everything.'

'Young Edward thought you could,' Dr Burgess murmured.

'Yes and he came a cropper,' was the tart response.

'Er . . . what does Guy actually do?' Rosy asked.

'*Do*? Well he lives in Venice.'

'Yes but that's not—'

'Not a job? Well it is as far as he's concerned. He is in receipt of a small pension and has the occasional modest windfall from shares – had one the other day I believe. His patience make him popular with old ladies and children, and his charm pleases hostesses seeking a spare man – and since there are several of those in Venice he is much in demand. As to what he does in his spare time: he regularly completes *The Times* crossword, tends his potted begonias and buzzes about in that awful boat. He did once tell me that if he could afford it he would like to sail around the world and visit the Galápagos Islands to view those disgusting newts. But I rather doubt whether funds run to that so presumably it remains a pipe dream.'

She stood up and gathering her bag and jacket announced, 'Well I'm off for my G&T and some shut-eye. I will leave the pallid tea leaves to you Miss Gilchrist.'

Dr Burgess also got up but at the door paused. 'Oh by the way, remember our esteemed chef is away tonight so supper will be a cold buffet. I advise you to get down early otherwise our friend Downing will be at the head of the queue and scoff the lot!' Rosy thanked him for his advice which she suspected was entirely valid.

Dr Burgess had been right: despite Rosy's efforts to get to the dining room on time Mr Downing had indeed secured the head of the queue and already made substantial inroads into the salad. However, she had managed to secure a decent share for herself and had enjoyed Miss Witherington's speciality of stuffed eggs and vitello tonnato. Afterwards she joined Mrs Blanchett and another guest for coffee and liqueurs in the courtyard. Although it was dark the little patio was lit by the lights from the house and it was pleasant to sit chatting under the stars and watching the flitting moths. But when a breeze got up her companions elected to move indoors.

Still feeling wide awake and having finished her book, Rosy decided instead to take a stroll along the Zattere before turning in. It was quite late and the quayside virtually deserted, though as on her previous walk the air was lightly tinged with the scent of jasmine. Pleasurable though this was it reminded her of the evening encounter with the murdered Pacelli and the other man. She frowned. Had the latter really been the same one that she had seen talking with Hewson that afternoon? If so it seemed a rather strange connection; the man had seemed so louche! Yet the more she compared her memories of both incidents the more she was certain the two were one and the same.

She wondered whether he had played any part in the

police inquiry or had volunteered any information. After all if he had been a friend or an associate of Pacelli then he may have had something useful to reveal – unless of course he had done the deed himself!

It was a thought that re-stirred uneasy guilt. Perhaps she really ought to have reported that second encounter with the dead man; it may have had more significance than she supposed . . . Rubbish! Hadn't one of the newspaper reports said the assassin was of 'massive frame'? (By which presumably it meant well built.) This chap was a rather weedy specimen. Besides, if he were the murdering type was he really the sort to have much in common with Bill Hewson? The latter might not be the acme of refinement but he was perfectly decent.

She started to retrace her steps back to the *pensione*, and then nearly jumped out of her skin at the sudden screech from a lovelorn cat. A moment later there was an answering howl and the sound of a can clattering across flagstones – feline impatience? Or were cats just clumsy like human beings? Either way she had had enough of such noises and quickened her pace towards the door in the wall.

She was just taking out her key when she thought she heard a footfall behind and caught the sudden whiff of cigarette smoke. She turned sharply but saw nothing . . . or nothing except a shadow merging into the gloom. Hell, she thought, surely that's not *Le chat qui fume!* She shoved the key into the lock and whipped inside slamming the door – and promptly collided with a pair of garden chairs.

They hit the ground with a crash. She picked them up feeling a fool, crept across the courtyard hoping she hadn't woken the other guests, and let herself in to the house. Apart from stentorian snores coming from the direction of Mr Downing's door, all was silent. She sneaked up the stairs and gained the sanctuary of her own room. Here she switched on the light and sat on the bed feeling quite out of breath. Clearly she was unsuited to such nocturnal ramblings: imagination was far too jittery!

The room felt stuffy; and going to the window she pushed open the shutters and gazed out scanning the stars. The night air was cool and fresh and held no hint of cigarette. She took a few deep breaths and remained standing there enjoying the nearness of the shadowy water with its winking lights. And then as she reached to close the shutters her gaze fell on the track skirting the house and where a few minutes previously she had been walking . . . Yes it was unmistakable: a figure was standing there staring up at her window.

She caught her breath and darted back. Instinct urged that she shut the window and turn off the light. But in the midst of fear reason took control. Appear oblivious, she told herself, seem unaware of the watcher. Move about a bit, return to the window, brush your hair, and only then switch out the light . . . and see what you can spy from a darkened interior.

Thus pressed against the outer wall Rosy squinted through the shutter slats trying to detect some form or movement. At first there seemed to be nothing: absolute dark and stillness. But as she peered things became more defined and she could see something: the figure of a man slowly moving away. He paused for an instant and she saw the faint flicker of a match and the glint of a cigarette tip. And then there was nothing.

'Some bastard Peeping Tom!' She fumed as she lay in bed angry and not a little frightened. In London, of course, one would occasionally encounter the odd creeper but for some reason she had not expected that sort of thing in Venice. Pickpockets yes (they were everywhere the world over), but not this sordid nonsense. She tossed on to her side. How naïve! What had she expected – nothing but opera and romance and carnival cavaliers? Stupid that's what!

Although Rosy had slept surprisingly well she awoke still angry. It really was too bad! The area had seemed so safe and normal. She must be more alert in future. As she dressed she recalled her conversation with Daphne Blanchett the previous night. The woman had been quite helpful about the Horace, sympathising with her disappointment over the wrong version and suggesting another bookshop which might conceivably be useful.

Thus Rosy decided to give that a try, and then, whatever the outcome, to telephone Stanley again. If she were lucky well and good; if not, she would firmly suggest the search be terminated. Too many blanks had been drawn. And what with the murder, Edward's dramatic death and the unsavoury experience of the night before she felt she was hardly in the right state to continue the mission or indeed to do justice to the city. She would come another time – with a congenial companion and without some onerous task slung around her shoulders. She glanced irritably at the Horace lying on the dressing table. And a fat lot of use that had turned out to be! She picked it up and thrust it into the drawer with her other Venetian souvenirs, a harlequin figurine, postcards and a set of Burano table mats.

CHAPTER TWENTY-ONE

Gradually, with shock subsided and police interviews over, life in the Palazzo Reiss resumed its customary calm. Thus on an afternoon not long after the event Cedric sat alone on the veranda sipping his lapsang souchong and enjoying the westering sun. Felix with unexpected zeal had taken Caruso to 'walk the block', or rather to perambulate endlessly through tortuous alleys and slumbering squares. In its plodding way the dog seemed to enjoy such outings and its minder too was becoming inured to the daily task, viewing it even with a twinge of tacit pleasure. And today, after the general turbulence, Felix found the walking ritual a calming antidote to the dreadful drama.

Cedric too, warm in the sun's declining rays and settled with book and tea, was able to savour the peace and withdraw his mind from recent upheavals. For twenty minutes or so, relaxed and detached, he basked in a comfortable limbo. He could have been any tourist in Venice – tired from earlier sightseeing and now slumped in idle siesta. He laid the book aside and closing his eyes began to doze.

Yet slyly images of the disaster came creeping back; and with eyes still shut he saw again the bridge, the figure, the sudden dive, the wildly waving arms and Hewson's gallant and abortive rescue.

He frowned and opened his eyes. It had been so grossly unfair – the wretched youth had been making some kind of floundering progress towards the side, a few more yards and he could probably have got his feet on the bottom. Still, he could hardly have known that; his mind doubtless numbed by panic. Must have taken in a lot of water by the time Hewson reached him; probably three-quarters drowned already . . . and yet he had obviously mustered some sort of energy in those final moments. Hewson said he couldn't hold him, that he had kept breaking away and going under. Were his struggles so manic that one as muscular as Hewson couldn't hang on to him? Presumably. From the sound of things there had been an awful lot of plunging and threshing about (and there had been a shout at some point though from whom he couldn't be sure). Yet Hewson was strong; much older than the boy of course, but tough and clearly a capable swimmer. Had the victim been so intractable, so resistant to his efforts?

The teacup half way to Cedric's lips stayed suspended in the air and then replaced in its saucer liquid untouched . . . Resistant to his efforts? What efforts: to pull him up or *push him down?*

Shocked by his own question Cedric stood up, leant on the railing and fixed his gaze on a distant spire trying to steady his thoughts. Surely he was being absurdly fanciful, perverse even. Just because the chap had been surprisingly ineffectual in his attempt to save the youth did not mean he had deliberately engineered his death! . . . Ah, wrong word. He certainly hadn't *engineered* it; that was obvious. The whole episode had been so unexpected. Nobody could have foreseen Edward losing his rag like that and taking off into the night to play silly beggars on top of a bridge, least of all leaping off it. The charade had been patently random – but then random events could be exploited, opportunities seized. The war had taught one that. And if that had been Hewson's opportunity then he had certainly grasped it well . . . No, he could hardly have engineered the circumstances but he *could* have contributed to their outcome.

Cedric lit a cigarette and pondered, switching his gaze from spire to the nearby jetty and Hope-Landers' boat. His eye rested on the name painted on its prow: 'La Speranza'. Yes of course. What else? But what was the skipper hopeful of? Landing a fish perhaps . . . He blew a meditative smoke ring as his mind slipped back from the realm of laboured puns to the more intriguing realm of possible murder.

All very well there being capability, he thought, but presumably such things were not done on a whim: a motive was customary. Clearly there had been animosity between the two, a mutual disdain; and the younger man had obviously gone out of his way to provoke the other. But was that cause enough for murder? It seemed a trifle extreme. Cedric sighed. Doubtless his first reaction had been right – it was he himself who was being extreme: imagination overwrought by too much drama and too little sleep. Still, he might just mention the matter to Felix when he returned . . .

And at that moment, moving slowly along the tow path, appeared the figures of his friend and the droop-eared dog. Cedric smiled remembering the Shakespearean line, 'And pat he comes like the catastrophe of the old comedy', though in this case his own cue would be far from 'villainous melancholy' but rather a genial welcome and a shared early cocktail while he apprised Felix of his startling notion. He leant over the balustrade and waved. Felix waved back and Caruso gave a reciprocal bark. Evidently the hound was starting to recognise him. Should he take a hand in its custody? Hmm. Exercise perhaps – but he drew the line at the creature's grooming.

'Did anything strike you as odd about that drowning business?' Cedric asked once they were settled with martinis and the hound snoring gently beneath the harpsichord.

'*Odd?*' exclaimed Felix. 'The whole thing was bloody

odd! Whatever do you mean? My nerves are in shreds!'

'Yes, but in particular – about Hewson's efforts to save the boy.'

Felix raised his eyebrows and shrugged. 'Well they didn't exactly work did they.'

'Precisely my point. Why not?'

Felix gave another shrug. 'Not being a professional lifeguard I wouldn't know – met his match I suppose. Short of breath, got cramp, water too wet or something . . .'

Cedric interrupted and proceeded to give a detailed résumé of his doubts.

At first Felix was unconvinced; it all sounded just a teeny bit speculative . . . But then of course Cedric was good at speculation, his forte one might say. There was that time, only a few months ago, when Cedric's speculations had proved only too right and his instinct for danger fully justified. Goodness, hadn't that had been a lucky stroke!

'Well he's not my type of course,' he replied, 'far too hearty; and does he *have* to wear that absurd cap all the time? Though I notice he did remove it before flinging himself in the canal. However, I suppose I can't really hold—'

'Hold your prejudices against him? My dear Felix, if every person you held a prejudice against were proved a murderer the scaffold-makers would be in clover!' Cedric gave a series of thin chuckles and topped up their glasses. 'But seriously dear friend, bias apart, do you think there could be something in it?'

Felix swirled his cocktail stick and mused. 'On the

whole,' he said slowly, 'from what you've been saying I should think there could be a fair amount in it. But,' he added hastily, 'there's nothing we can do or indeed should. The last thing we want is to get ourselves embroiled in such matters. I haven't recovered from that other business yet!' He closed his eyes and shuddered in recollection. 'We're here on holiday – and after all I do have my Royal Appointment to think of: when you've got one of those warrants stuck over your door it doesn't do to be linked with the indecorous, however remotely. Besides, there's the dog's welfare to consider.'

'Oh absolutely,' agreed Cedric. They studied Caruso comatose under his musical canopy, scuppered by the recent exertions and his guardian's solicitude.

The dog's welfare notwithstanding, the subject was inevitably resumed at supper.

'Do you think Rosy has got similar thoughts?' Felix asked.

'I doubt it. Miss Gilchrist is not the suspicious type, and besides I imagine she is still agitating over the errant book – which actually may be just as well; she was pretty cut up about the young man and I don't think all that police and press questioning helped. She looked distinctly woebegone. In fact at some point I suppose we ought to telephone and enquire how she is.'

Felix agreed; and then confessed that after Cedric's conjectures he was actually rather more interested in how Bill Hewson was.

'Probably lying doggo in his studio and planning his next move – a low-key departure from Venice I imagine . . . always assuming that there's truth in my theory of course.'

'Huh! Truth or not, he's more likely playing the modest hero in Harry's Bar and guzzling bellinis bought by the paparazzi. Shall we drop in later for a nightcap?'

Cedric laughed. 'For one so fearful of getting involved you do seem to be showing an avid curiosity.'

'It's the quizzical mind,' Felix asserted airily. 'It goes with the flair for flowers and all things rare.' He sleeked his spiky hair with a gesture that Ivor Novello might have envied. 'And you are right, I do *not* want to get involved – but there's no harm in a little spectating. Besides, if Hewson is going around drowning people it's as well to be on the qui vive!'

Cedric looked at him sternly. 'Do not anticipate the facts. My idea admittedly, but when all is said and done it is only a hunch as the Americans would say. Or, as I would prefer to say, a reasonable interpretation as viewed from the man on top of the Clapham omnibus – or in this case from the canal bank. There's no tangible proof, all circumstantial; and as for motive, well that might be anyone's guess!'

'Yes but you have a gut feeling.'

Cedric took a sip of wine and considered. 'On the whole I like to think that my feelings originate in my mind rather than my entrails.'

'In that case,' replied Felix briskly, 'let's get down

pronto to the Calle Vallaresso and see what's cooking; that's bound to supply some mental stimulus.'

'Well I'm not sure—'

'Come on!'

In fact to Felix's disappointment Harry's Bar was virtually empty and with certainly no sign of the American. They should have come earlier. Therefore opting instead for the gaiety of an evening with Pucci & Paolo they were about to leave, when a voice hailed them from the corner behind the door.

'Why it's the Professor and Mr Smythe isn't it!' a grey-haired lady exclaimed. She beamed and beckoned. 'Duffy will be back in a jiffy, she's just gone to the loo. But where's handsome Caruso? He's *such* a good boy! Don't you just love him?'

'Not entirely,' said Cedric taking the extended hand. 'How nice to see you again, but actually we only just looked in on our way home; we're not stay—'

'Oh but you *must* stay! Come and sit down.' She patted the place beside her and directed Felix to pull up a chair. 'It's Duffy's turn and she won't be long, so order anything you like.' She gestured to the barman and despite the proffered choice cried, 'Our guests will have brandies, Marco. Nice ones please!'

The brandies were duly brought, large and golden, and her twin returned from the loo. More handshakes and jolly greetings.

'Well now, dear friends,' began one, 'what news on—'

200

'—the Rialto?' finished the other.

There was a brief pause as Felix and Cedric adjusted to the dual approach. 'Er, well actually things have been a bit fraught,' ventured Cedric. 'You see just recently a rather awful thing happened – to that young Edward Jones we met here.'

'Indeed it did. We've heard all about it from poor Guy this morning. He's most upset, blames himself for not having stayed,' the twin on the left said.

'But we didn't know *you* were involved,' chimed the one on the right.

'Oh we weren't involved,' said Felix quickly, 'helpless bystanders merely.'

'It was Bill Hewson who was the hero of the hour, a remarkable effort,' Cedric added. 'But alas he couldn't quite pull it off.'

'Yes *such* bad luck!' they chanted in unison. And then Dilly (or Duffy) picked up Cedric's cue: 'You'd have thought Bill could have managed it if anyone. According to that friend of his who came to stay he did something terribly valiant in the war. A troop ship went down in the Atlantic with tremendous loss of life but Bill was responsible for rescuing at least three of the seamen: dived in and somehow towed them to the dinghies, and I gather conditions were frightful – icy water and monstrous waves. Still he was a lot younger in those days. Anno Domini – it catches up with us all in the end.' She turned to Cedric: 'Don't you find?' (Cedric didn't find, or chose not to, and feeling slightly nettled said nothing.)

'I say,' giggled her sister, 'talking of things naval do you remember that rather peculiar rear admiral who had the hots for you in 'forty-one? Or was it for me? One was never quite sure.' She paused. 'Actually I don't think he was too clear either.'

'You mean old Desmond? Oh yes, wasn't he awful! But a U-Boat got him in the end. So sad . . .'

'Dreadful days,' interrupted Felix hastily. 'But tell me, what about poor Edward Jones? You don't think it could have been suicide do you?'

Pulled back abruptly to the present the ladies stared at Felix and then at each other. 'Oh *no*,' was the collective cry, 'far too self-centred!'

'True he may have been unhinged, it runs in the family,' observed the greyer of the two; 'but when it came to Number One and pursuit of lolly Edward was clarity itself. Survival of "me" was the name of the game with that young man. Even Lucia complained. Tried to touch her for his bar bill only the other day but she stood firm. He didn't like it . . . I wonder how she is.' The placid eyes showed only mild concern.

'Doubtless surviving,' replied her sister dryly.

'Doubtless.'

Cedric coughed. 'Uhm – do I take it you find her a little tricky?'

'Hmm. Yes you could say that. Not our sort really: what our parents would have called showy and snooty. Isn't that so, Dilly?'

The other nodded vigorously. 'Exactly dear. Snooty

and showy! And of course although it is all very tragic and one shouldn't speak ill of the dead, but I have to say that Edward could be really very *bold*.' She leant towards Cedric dropping her voice: 'Do you know he was sacked from school for blackmailing his housemaster. Imagine! Some minor breach I gather, but Edward had the effrontery to demand money with menaces as the saying goes. There was an awful shindig though I don't think he cared one jot. Bold as brass . . . Still, poor boy, he won't be doing that any more.'

The pair gave a collective sigh and stared pensively at their wine. Cedric and Felix felt it was time to leave.

'Rescued sailors from the storm-torn Atlantic and yet couldn't fish out that youth from a sleepy canal in Venice,' Felix exclaimed. 'Sounds pretty rum to me!'

'Yes, yes it does rather,' Cedric agreed. 'But as you rightly said it has nothing to do with us . . . Perhaps tomorrow after we have phoned Rosy Gilchrist a little potter on the Lido might be congenial: a tribute to Mann's Aschenbach as it were.'

'Hmm,' said Felix doubtfully, 'and he came to a sticky end too.'

'Then we must avoid the deckchairs.'

CHAPTER TWENTY-TWO

The next day Felix had persuaded Cedric to accompany Caruso and himself to the flower market before embarking on their visit to the Lido. 'We don't need to get there before midday,' he had said, 'and the gardenias in the salon need refreshing. We can leave the dog at home when we go off but he really ought to be given a walk first.' Cedric had agreed, and the three of them set out to garner the flowers and inspect the fish on the nearby stalls. Caruso wasn't fond of fish (Felix had tried him) but for some reason seemed to like its smell. Thus he trundled along amiably, sniffing the air and grunting approval.

As they neared one of their favourite cafés Felix suggested they went in for an espresso. 'Huh,' Cedric said, 'I doubt if you'll stop at an espresso; bound to want one of those almond cream things you are always drooling over.'

'I might,' retorted his friend carelessly. 'Got to line my stomach for lunch somehow, it doesn't do to drink on empty. Besides the dog needs a rest, hasn't found its second wind yet.'

He pulled the animal towards the café. And as he stood hovering on the pavement debating which would be better, an inside or outside table, a tall figure appeared in the doorway. It was Guy Hope-Landers.

He greeted them enthusiastically. 'I say what a happy coincidence! I saw you from the window. Giving the hound its constitutional I see. Do come and join us.' He laughed loudly and before they had a chance to say yea or nay had hustled them in through the open door.

Cedric was a trifle surprised at such early morning effusions and wondered who the other parts of the 'us' would be. He saw immediately. It was Lucia Borgino. She was sitting at a corner table swathed unrelievedly in black; skin luminously pale (thick eyeliner, no lipstick) and looking immensely stylish. She also looked immensely peeved to see the newcomers. Presumably her companion's welcoming rush to the door had not been her idea.

Feeling rather uncomfortable Cedric and Felix took their seats at the table. Felix bent down to the floor and made great play of settling the dog and tying its lead to the leg of his chair – and then untying it and starting again. By absorbing himself in such essential manoeuvres he was able to leave the task of commiseration to Cedric.

The latter discharged his duty deftly and kindly but

his words were clearly of scant interest to Lucia. 'Most thoughtful,' she murmured indifferently, and proceeded to give orders to the waitress about the level of froth on her cappuccino.

A pencil and folded copy of *The Times* lay in Hope-Landers' place; and having completed his fumblings with the leash and chair leg Felix noticed this and was rather shocked. Was the man still filling in clues at this delicate time? No wonder the Borgino woman looked sour! But then he saw sticking out from under the newspaper a notebook. Its owner must have seen his glance, for picking it up he said, 'It's bad enough Lucia having to cope with the awfulness of the tragedy itself but there are so many *functional* matters to attend to as well. We've been trying to list some of the more pressing ones, or at least I have. Poor Lucia is still rather too numbed to concern herself with practicalities.'

'He means shipping the corpse and paying the creditors,' the numbed sister said with startling brutality. 'All that boring business,' She turned to the other. 'I keep telling you, Guy, grandfather and his solicitors are dealing with the whole of that palaver. He likes doing it, increases his sense of power. And the executors have already fixed the funeral – a service at Paddington Crematorium I believe. Something quick and quiet. The last thing one wants is to hear some lugubrious priest prosing on endlessly . . . In fact the only thing that I have got to do is to decide on the flowers. Grandfather says that should be my responsibility though I really can't see why.' She looked at Felix.

'You're some sort of florist aren't you? Manage a shop or something I gather. What do you suggest – or doesn't your firm service the funeral trade?'

Hope-Landers' face showed a look of mild dismay and Cedric froze. The dismissive tone had been gratuitously insolent and he knew Felix would be incensed. The Royal Appointment's gilded lettering flashed before his eyes and he shot a covert glance at his friend trying to gauge his reaction and expecting to see the familiar flush of fury. He just hoped the retort would not be too violent.

Felix (who as predicted had succumbed to the almond gateau) laid down his fork and with face unflushed appeared to cogitate. And then he said: 'I do indeed manage a shop, Mrs Borgia, and funerals are *absolutely* my forte. And as to your brother's, I would strongly recommend pansies – pink pansies. In fact the pinker the better. Couldn't be more fitting.' And smiling primly he returned to the almond cream.

There was an explosive silence during which Cedric noted Hope-Landers' mouth twitch gently, while Lucia gazed at Felix in unconcealed anger. But there was nothing she could say and he continued to sample his cake with dedicated relish.

'I don't think she likes you,' said Cedric thoughtfully as they retraced their steps through the flower market.

'She's not meant to,' replied Felix with satisfaction. 'I can't think why Guy Hope-Landers wastes his time with such an arrogant bitch.'

'He's useful to her as an escort and is too good-natured, or too lazy, to ditch her. Some men are like that: they let things ride – a tiresome state of affairs but less painful than the trauma of confrontation.'

'So I suppose that's why your marriage lasted for the five years it did. Too idle and good natured to get out of it?'

Cedric stopped abruptly. 'My dear Felix,' he protested, 'surely you are not accusing me of being good-natured are you?'

'You? Good lord no. Banish the thought!'

Bearing a large golden bream and bunches of gardenias the two men and their dog ambled back to the Palazzo Reiss.

CHAPTER TWENTY-THREE

It would be strange not to have her brother continuously loitering in the background, mused Lucia. It wasn't that she had disliked him exactly; merely that he had been such a source of annoyance. A liability too: one was never quite sure what jam he was going to get into next or who he was going to offend. She thought grimly of the blackmailing episode at his school when he had put the frighteners on that ridiculous little housemaster. There had been an awful hullaballoo and he had been expelled. It wasn't the expulsion as such that had mattered but its repercussions. It was when she had been invited to stay in a rather grand house in Wiltshire and had her eye on the hostess's son. When the lady learnt of her brother's expulsion and its cause the invitation had been hastily withdrawn. The memory still rankled.

And then there had been the time when he had approached her then current beau for money: had brazenly tapped him on the shoulder when the two of them had been getting rather snug in the tool shed, and said: 'My sister doesn't come cheap you know. How about a few fivers?' The swain had fled never to be seen again . . . Yes he really had been such a little beast!

The more Lucia dwelt on Edward's failings and his talent to annoy the more incensed she became, and the more quickly any incipient pain over his loss evaporated. The whole thing was still very shocking of course but it was also strangely liberating. In fact without the nagging fear of Edward fouling things up she could now proceed unencumbered to pursue Guy and the title. Not that there was much money there of course; but play her cards right and her grandfather might help – although that was by no means certain. *So* tight-fisted!

She frowned and then gave a little smile. Actually there was always the possibility of finding that Horace book, the one that Edward had been engaged to get hold of. After all, as she had explained to him, she knew exactly where that Murano vase was – or where it certainly had been the last time she was at Bill's studio. Secure that and she was half way to fortune. And the other half? Well Carlo might still have his uses. He had been rather cagey the last time she had enquired of the book, when Edward was pursuing it; in fact he had been tiresomely vague. She would have another go and pin him down; he was bound to know something. She could also try Lupino *when* he elected to open his shop again.

Of course it would be just her luck for that British Museum woman to have already found the thing and whisked it off to London; though presumably if that were the case those two friends of hers would surely have said something in the café the other day. She pictured the two men. She hadn't liked them from the start, when Guy had first introduced them on the Accademia Bridge – not one tiny bit. And now she liked them even less, especially the flower seller: *such* a sardonic little face. And how appallingly rude he had been. Totally unwarranted! Why Guy felt he had to be so civil to them she had no idea. Things would certainly change once she had got him to propose and she had the title: he would be steered away from such obnoxious nonentities!

And thus like her deceased brother Lucia too allowed her imagination to ramble – not so much over Ferraris, tailored suits and private planes but rather to playing hostess to venerable members of the Scottish aristocracy. As her canny grandfather might have warned, 'The best-laid plans of mice and men . . .'

CHAPTER TWENTY-FOUR

'I hope you weren't disturbed by the hammering,' said Mr
Downing as Rosy was about to go up the stairs, 'a dreadful
racket and I do think we might have been warned; it was
most distracting. It's bad enough having to write letters at
the best of times, let alone with that sort of noise going on!'

Rosy shook her head explaining she had been out all
morning (fruitlessly searching unlikely bookshops and
dodging spectral Oxford librarians) and only just come in.
'What was it, something to do with the plumbing?' she asked.

'Oh no, nothing useful like that. *Decorative* I am told.'
Whatever it was, clearly Mr Downing was not impressed.
'You'll see them on the landing: very large and very
modern. I don't care for them at all.' He pursed his lips in
disapproval.

'Ah, I see. So you are talking about pictures?'

'Some might call them that. I just call them splurges of paint. I am rather surprised Miss Witherington was so accommodating. With luck they are only here temporarily.'

Rosy was interested and wondered whether her own view would accord with Mr Downing's. 'Where do they come from – are they done by a local artist?'

'In so far as he lives in Venice, yes,' Downing said tartly. 'But certainly not local in the full sense of the word: he arrived from America five or six years ago. Some of his stuff used to be all right, quite pleasant really albeit a little derivative perhaps . . . He's evidently trying something new; a poor move I should say. Apparently they are intended as a pair: *Venice in Daybreak, 1 & 2*. Personally I would call them "Venice in Two Scrambled Eggs"! He laughed, keenly impressed with his own witticism.

Rosy continued up the stairs and paused on the landing to inspect the two paintings. As she had guessed they bore the signature of William Hewson. She stood back to get a better view. Downing had likened them to scrambled eggs. Well she wouldn't go as far as that, but the virulent yellow streaks heaped on tones of grey and blue did not strike her as particularly Venetian nor indeed evocative of daybreak. Still, doubtless the cognoscenti might dub them 'challenging'. Unchallenged she went to her room.

On the way back to the *pensione* she had bought a local paper – out of principle rather than interest. Struggling with news items would in theory help her language skills.

Though whether the exercise was truly helpful she wasn't convinced; probably a book of nursery rhymes was more her level. Perhaps it would have been sensible to buy an Italian whodunnit from the dead Pacelli or even one of those risqué paperbacks she had seen piled on his table; what wasn't understood could doubtless have been surmised! However, with an hour to go before supper she dutifully persevered with the newspaper.

Thinking of Pacelli prompted her to scan the pages for any more news of his murder. By now there may have been further revelations – though she just hoped the police were no longer seeking help from the public. With luck they had found all they needed.

The name plus an accompanying smudgy picture turned up on the third page. Photography did little to enhance the bookseller's saturnine features, and to Rosy's eye he looked less like the victim than the assassin. From what she could make out nothing new had emerged although apparently it was now fully established that the killer had been of 'huge physique' and 'frenzied mind', the journalist going so far as to assert that he (or she) was of fiendish intent and comparable to the Phantom of the Rue Morgue. Well at least I can manage to grasp all that, Rosy thought, but my God what tosh!

Slinging the paper aside she went to the wardrobe and took out something suitable for supper: a dress with matching handbag. She snapped open the bag's clasp and started to empty it of the usual detritus of pens, aspirin, hankies and lipsticks. But there was something else there – a small crumpled envelope. With a start she remembered that the bag was the one she had been carrying on the night of Edward's drowning. The envelope had slipped from the youth's trouser pocket when he had jumped up from the table and made his dramatic dash from the terrace. She recalled the thing lying on the ground among the coffee cups and smashed wine glasses, and herself stooping to retrieve it. She had stashed it in her handbag meaning to give it to him later. But subsequent events had decreed otherwise.

The envelope was sealed and slightly to her surprise on the front bore the name of William Hewson. It was written in bold ink and underlined with a thick flourish.

Had there been no addressee Rosy would have opened it. But not only was there a name but it was someone's she knew. It would be only right to give it to him, although it was presumably of little relevance now (and perhaps even slightly discomfiting). However, it had been clearly intended for Hewson and thus she must ensure that he got it. Easy: he had invited her to his studio the following afternoon and she could take it then.

CHAPTER TWENTY-FIVE

'I told Rosy Gilchrist to come round for a lunchtime aperitif,' Cedric announced. 'She's probably still upset about what happened the other night and might want some company. I take it you don't object?'

'Not unless she is beastly to Caruso I don't. The last time she was here I thought she showed a marked indifference. Clearly didn't appreciate his finer points.'

'Does anybody?' asked Cedric.

Felix pursed his lips and resumed his embroidery.

Rosy appreciated Cedric's invitation. It had been a kindly gesture; and while she had recovered from the horror of Edward's tragedy, an aperitif with the two friends would be a refreshing distraction.

At the palazzo Rosy had been about to ring the Hoffman bell but was forestalled by Guy Hope-Landers who was on his way out. 'Any joy with the Horace yet?' he asked.

She grimaced. 'No not at all. I *thought* I had it and then I didn't. Wrong one apparently. My boss isn't going to be too pleased, he had set his heart on it.'

'Never give up, that's my motto,' Hope-Landers said genially. 'Life is full of surprises.'

'Yes but they never seem to be quite the right ones,' she had laughed.

'Hmm. You have something there . . . Ah well, I must go off to my boat. Who knows, I could get one of the better surprises for once – the engine might start first time!'

Rosy climbed the long staircase and found herself puffing. This won't do, she thought. Too much pasta and delicious pastries. Perhaps she should lay off for a bit. Lay off? Nonsense, she told herself sternly, plenty of time for that when she returned to the Museum with its sombre fare! She thought of Dr Stanley and the rather functional canteen. Both seemed extraordinarily remote.

She sipped the Prosecco they had given her, and admiring its sprightly bubbles sank back gratefully against the sofa cushions. 'Gosh! I'm quite worn out,' she exclaimed. 'It's all those stairs. Don't they tire you?'

'Not really,' Felix lied casually. 'What you need is a dog; that would keep you fit.'

'But you don't keep a dog – well only here and that won't be for much longer.'

'Ah but you see,' Cedric cut in, 'dear Felix has plans: he is now thinking of getting such a creature. In fact I rather gather he is angling to buy Caruso from his cousin and take him back to London.'

Rosy took a contemplative sip of her wine. 'Really? It strikes me there could be a number of snags there. First there are the awful quarantine laws – six months if you please. Secondly, is Felix's apartment really suitable for an animal? I mean his furnishings are so exquisite it would be awful to see them destroyed by canine rampage! And then of course there is the question of its current owner. From what you were saying Cousin Violet is devoted to the dog. I can't see her parting with it easily.'

'Exactly what I have been trying to tell him,' said Cedric triumphantly; and turning to Felix he added, 'You would do much better to have a cat like mine.'

'*Not* like yours,' was the acid retort.

Tactfully changing the subject Cedric asked Rosy if she had seen anything of Bill Hewson since the tragedy.

'Yes I have. We had lunch together not long after. Actually as it happens I am going to his studio later to look at the paintings, they sound quite interesting.'

'Alone?' asked Cedric.

'What? Oh no, I don't think so. He said something about there being one or two others dropping in.' She hesitated, and then proceeded to tell them about the note fallen from Edward's pocket.

'Have you got it with you?' Cedric asked.

'Well yes. I thought I could give it to him when I went there this afternoon.' She took it from her bag and handed it to him.

He studied the envelope thoughtfully. 'Feels pretty flimsy; no more than half a page I should think. Whatever it says I doubt if it will be of much use to Hewson now. We may as well open it.'

'Oh but I really don't think—'

But Rosy's protest came too late. With a deft movement Cedric had picked up the paperknife from the desk and slit opened the envelope. There were only a few lines scrawled and no salutation or signature. He read it aloud to them:

I need to see you again. On reflection, and given the circumstances, my stated terms were rather meagre. However, throw in the vase too and you will find me accommodating. Ten o'clock tomorrow at Alfredo's.

Annoyed by what she saw as Cedric's high-handedness Rosy had not given her full attention to the words. 'Obviously some transaction they were engaged in, probably to do with one of Hewson's pictures,' she said dismissively. 'Oh well whatever it was it's too late now. But really, Cedric, I think that was a bit of a liberty opening it like that. I can tell you I am a bit cross!'

'Have some more Prosecco,' said Felix soothingly,

'you'll feel so much better.' He leant over and filled her glass to the brim.

'Yes it was,' Cedric agreed. 'Sorry.' He didn't sound the slightest bit sorry and began to study the note again while Rosy and Felix turned their attention to Caruso, the length of his ears, his military tail, and his insatiable greed for olives and titbits.

After a while Cedric looked up, and laying the note aside said: 'You were right about a transaction but I doubt if it was to do with a painting. The style is too curt for that, too abrasive. If Edward was keen to buy one of the paintings and felt he hadn't offered enough wouldn't he sound more emollient? Admittedly he says he can be accommodating but the tone hardly suggests that. Besides what are these *circumstances* he mentions? And since he was always bleating about a lack of funds I doubt that he was in a position to purchase fine art!'

'And what about the vase bit? It sounds a funny sort of thing for Edward Jones to want,' Felix added.

'Not if it was the one belonging to Farinelli Berenstein it wouldn't,' Rosy said quietly.

They looked at her quizzically. 'You mean that glass thing?' asked Felix. 'But why on earth should Hewson have that?'

'Well he may not of course. But I did overhear Edward and his sister (at least that's whom I assume she was) discussing a vase in Tonelli's and Lucia saying that she knew where it was – on somebody's mantelpiece apparently. Edward seemed very insistent she should get hold of it however inconvenient the means.' Rosy took another sip of her drink recalling their words, and suddenly to her embarrassment began to giggle. 'There seemed to be some question regarding the viability of the task . . . I mean,' she spluttered, 'Lucia seemed uncertain whether her efforts would be entirely eff, eff – effi*cacious!*'

'For God's sake,' cried Felix, 'let's give her something to eat. It must have been that third glass!'

'You should curb your generosity,' Cedric admonished, 'though it is always a tonic to witness such high spirits in the young . . . Now Miss Gilchrist, once you have sobered up let us give further thought to the meaning of this note while Felix prepares some antipasti. I think you will find we have a most choice variety.'

When Felix returned from the kitchen bearing a tray of assorted canapés certain assumptions had been made regarding both the significance of the note and the conversation overheard by Rosy in Tonelli's. The speculators looked thoughtful.

'Cedric has decided that Edward's note is hostile,' Rosy said, 'that there was some sort of deal involved in which he was the instigator or dominant partner.'

Felix passed her a plate of antipasti. 'You mean like blackmail,' he said.

'Er . . . well yes, I suppose it could be that although we hadn't quite—'

'Defined it? But doubtless that is what Cedric thinks. You know he has the most suspicious mind – don't you dear boy? In my experience most professors do.' Felix winked and Cedric looked mildly pained.

'It is as well to be alert to the latent duplicity of human nature,' he replied, 'there's a lot of it about,' and then looking at Rosy added, 'Felix is right, that is indeed what I was thinking.'

'But why should Edward have been blackmailing Bill Hewson? He doesn't seem the shifty type, rather open really.'

'Ah well now, that *is* a question. It could have been for anything: defrauding the Inland Revenue or its Italian equivalent; stealing another's paintings and passing them off as his own; bigamy in Boston; espionage; dressing up in ladies' clothes . . . anything you care to mention really.'

'Bound to be that one,' Felix tittered.

Cedric looked at him sternly. '*Do not* go down that path otherwise we shall have Miss Gilchrist doing the nose-trick with her coffee as she did with the Prosecco!'

Rosy contrived to look contrite and said, 'Well at least we are certain about the vase. From what I saw of Edward and from what you have described of Lucia it seems extremely unlikely that they were searching for a piece of glass simply for its aesthetic appeal. It must be of some financial interest, and with this Farinelli business it could well be that. Possibly Edward thought that if he could nose out the Horace he could pair it with the vase. Anyway somebody must be harbouring the thing, and given the reference in Edward's note I bet it is Bill Hewson.'

Cedric beamed. 'Well then, Rosy, since you are visiting his studio this afternoon you can test your bet can't you? Cast an eye over his mantelpiece, assuming he has one. Who knows, perhaps he props his social invitations against the thing. Make a point of admiring it and watch his reaction.'

'All right. But what about the note? How can I give it to him now that you've so conveniently slit the envelope? With his name scrawled across the thing I can hardly say I thought it was for me.'

'He doesn't need to see it. You said yourself that it was too late to be relevant.'

'Yes but—'

'Miss Gilchrist, one can overdo the adherence to scruples: it's all a case of nice judgement, and in this case showing him the note serves no useful purpose. There's simply no point.' Cedric folded the scrap of paper and slipped it into his breast pocket. 'Now would you like to powder your nose before setting out on your reconnaissance? The palazzo has the most capacious guest bathroom. Felix will show you the way.' He smiled graciously. It was clearly her cue to leave.

After she had gone, Cedric said, 'That was quite interesting. I wonder if the vase really is with Hewson. Though if he does have it I very much doubt if it's still on the mantelpiece. Still, one never knows; he doesn't strike me as having the brightest brain.'

'Hmm. I notice that you refrained from mentioning your suspicion that he may have drowned Edward.'

'Most certainly. No point in spreading unnecessary alarm; and besides it might have deterred Miss Gilchrist from going to his studio. After all, one doesn't want to spoil her afternoon!'

'It's intriguing about the note though,' Felix mused, 'if it is really part of a blackmailing threat then that certainly supports your theory that he shoved him under.'

'Yes, and if he did then we can assume that young Edward was dunning him for serious money, i.e. based on something fairly crucial.'

Felix winked. 'Not like women's clothes then.'

'Not unless he had been wearing them when committing robbery or murder.'

CHAPTER TWENTY-SIX

After their siesta the two friends took Caruso for a ramble. Pausing to lean against the balustrade of the Accademia Bridge they gazed mesmerised at the vista of sepia and ochre and fusion of water and sky that stretched before them. The late afternoon light was particularly dulcet and gave the scene an air of magical theatre.

'Pretty damn good,' Felix murmured.

'Hmm,' agreed Cedric. 'Extraordinary.'

They stood quietly enraptured. And then Felix felt around in his pocket and drew out a lira. 'Do you think it's like the Trevi Fountain in Rome: throw in a coin and you will be sure to return?'

'Worth a try,' Cedric smiled.

His friend lobbed the coin and it fell not into the water

but into a passing gondola, narrowly missing the boatman.

'Quick – look the other way,' Cedric urged. 'They won't like that!'

But it was too late. The grey-haired occupants had seen them and the next moment there were shrieks and wild gesticulations.

'Oh dear, that's torn it,' Felix giggled, 'we'll probably be had up for endangering canal traffic.'

'Yes but look – they're not complaining, they're beckoning.'

'*Beckoning?*' Felix peered down. 'Oh lor, it's those twins,' he muttered.

He was right, for the next moment the ladies had risen as one and were clearly summoning them down to the towpath, the gondolier already punting in that direction.

'I think they want us to join them,' Felix said nervously. 'What about the dog?'

'He'll have to take his chances with the rest of us. Come on. It would be rude to decline.'

They made a hasty descent to the quayside where the gondola was already waiting. Caruso leapt aboard with studied nonchalance; his minders landed in a heap.

The two ladies clapped their hands in delight. 'What luck!' exclaimed one. '*Absolutely!*' chimed the other. She turned to Felix: 'No young man has aimed a coin at me since VE Day!'

'He wasn't young,' corrected her sister. 'It was Brigadier Polegate, he doesn't count.'

'Er, wonderful to see you again,' gasped Cedric from a

semi-recumbent position. 'But do you often take gondola rides? I thought it was a largely tourist thing.'

'Ah,' responded one of them, 'but you see this is *our* gondola. Daddy left it to us and it's been in the family for years. We rent it out of course for the most *enormous* fee, but every six weeks we have our own special turn.' She turned to her sister. 'Don't we dear?'

The other nodded vigorously and gestured towards the boatman. 'Yes, and Luigi is so charming and very handsome too!' Handsome Luigi preened and executed a little bow. 'Although,' she added sotto voce, 'between you and me I think he could do with a new straw hat and ribbon, that one's beginning to look awfully mangy.'

'Well it's his birthday soon,' the other replied, 'we'll buy him a brand new one and then won't he look the little Turk!' She beamed joyfully. 'Wouldn't you agree, Felix?'

Felix studied the half-shaven rapscallion and agreed that he most surely would.

Actually it was rather pleasant gliding around in the gondola (a rather superior one with a half-canopy), and Cedric and Felix relaxed against the cushions listening with amusement to the prattling of their companions. In fact much of the twins' commentary was extremely interesting as they clearly knew the city well and were a lively source of information and anecdote. The dog, indifferent to such talk, sat sternly upright at the prow like some canine mermaid.

After a while Luigi had turned off the Grand Canal

and was weaving the craft through the network of minor waterways. At one point he broke into song, something that was met with avid applause from the sisters but which made Cedric and Felix feel embarrassed. Doubtless it was typically Venetian but English reserve made them glad when it finally finished. They passed under numerous small bridges and stared up at ancient gargoyles and flaking balconies decked with pots of flowers. Now and again they would pass a corner and glimpse a crumbling monument or tiny shrine. Cats dozed, washing fluttered and pigeons dawdled undisturbed by eager feeders.

It was a soothing itinerary, until they reached a place suddenly familiar to them: the bridge from which Edward Jones had made his fatal dive. It was higher than the other ones they had passed and the stretch of water flowing beneath fairly wide. Cedric recognised the two workshops flanking the bridge and the flight of steps leading up from the quay.

'Oh dear,' he muttered, 'I fear this is where it happened, where the Jones boy lost his life.' The scene looked benevolently placid in the afternoon sun.

The twins were clearly moved and one of them gestured to the boatman to change direction. As he punted back towards the Grand Canal, she said, 'It must have been dreadful for you all . . . Oh dear that poor silly boy, what a waste.'

'Yes,' agreed her sister, 'and of course we had seen him only a few nights earlier. You remember: the night before Guy gave that party in Harry's. Considering the state he was in when we saw him I am surprised he was able to get to it. I was quite impressed by the speed of his recovery. He was out well after midnight.'

'Ah but the young are so resilient,' replied the other.

'Not when we saw him he wasn't, being sick all over the place! Just at the end of the Calle Piccolo. We should have stopped really but we did have Matilda to consider.'

'The Calle Piccolo?' Cedric asked in surprise. 'But that's miles from the Castello area – well some way at any rate. It's close to the Rialto, near that bookshop.'

She looked a little puzzled. 'Yes that's right.'

'But I gather that Edward had told Lucia he had gone to walk off his hangover in the other direction: to the Giardini Pubblici.'

She sighed. 'Edward was a mercurial creature, and to put it politely he often said things that were not strictly accurate.'

Felix cleared his throat. 'If you don't mind my asking, who is Matilda and where were you going with her at that time of night?'

'Matilda? Our cat of course. She's fearfully old and fearfully difficult. She sleeps all day and will only deign to go out after midnight, and then we have to put her in a collar and lead otherwise she wanders off and we have to call the fire brigade or the police. We can't stand her. But you can't sling people out of the way just because they are tiresome. So we are stuck with her until she decides otherwise.'

'I see,' Cedric said slowly. 'So you were exercising

Matilda when you nearly bumped into Edward looking rather the worse for wear.'

She nodded. 'Reeling, bilious and wretched. He didn't see us of course, far too preoccupied. And, as said, we didn't approach as the sight might have upset the cat's nerves.'

'Exactly,' added Duffy (or Dilly), 'and after all, she had had a nasty scare from that other encounter!'

'What encounter?'

'Bill Hewson. Pounding along like a bat out of hell.'

'Rather a fat bat,' the other tittered. 'But yes he was lumbering along at quite a pace. Sweating too one couldn't help noticing.'

'How curious,' Cedric remarked. 'I wonder where he was going at that time of night and in such a hurry.'

There was a collective shrug and the twins exchanged sly looks. One of them cleared her throat and said, 'One doesn't wish to be indelicate but there is a notorious house of ill-repute in that quarter and now and again the police raid it: a formality of course but they have to do it and names are taken. *We* think he was trying to race home before the raid started, or had slipped out in the middle. One gathers the police are fairly obliging and generally telephone ahead but sometimes they pounce unannounced especially if there's someone new in charge.'

'Did he see you?' Cedric asked, slightly startled by their fund of local knowledge.

'Oh no, we were under an awning arguing with Matilda. She was being so difficult!'

* * *

234

By this time Luigi had tied up the gondola and with much bowing and boater-doffing bid *arrivederci* to his passengers.

One of the twins gestured towards a sprawling corner house with flaking blue shutters and high filigree iron gates. 'That's our funny old place,' she said, 'we have lived there since we were in the nursery, haven't we Duffy?'

'Oh yes Dilly, and long may it last!' And turning to Cedric and Felix, Duffy executed a broad wink and in a fair imitation of a Bronx accent, said, 'Say, why don't you come up and see us sometime?'

Giggling happily the two sisters turned and walked towards the high gates.

Their companions also turned; and when Felix glanced back at the house, squashed against one of its windowpanes he saw the lowering face of Matilda.

Later, over a pot of China tea in a corner of Florian's, they reflected upon their experiences with the two ladies.

Cedric lit a cigarette and leant back against the velvet upholstery. 'A most instructive afternoon,' he declared.

'Yes they certainly know their Venice all right,' Felix agreed. 'I suppose it comes with having lived here since children. Fancy being in the same house all those years, you would think they'd get bored.'

'Which would you prefer, fifty years in an old waterside house in Venice or five years in a new bungalow in Penge? I know which I would find the more boring . . . But as a matter of fact I wasn't simply thinking about our instruction from the boat trip, absorbing though it was, but more specifically about Jones and Hewson. You do realise that from what the two Ds said both were very close to Pacelli's shop during the night of his murder. The body wasn't found till about eight in the morning but the press report said the attack was judged to have occurred sometime between midnight and two. According to the ladies that was roughly when both Jones and Hewson were in the vicinity and yet neither said anything about it – or at least apparently not.'

Felix smiled. 'But also according to the ladies Hewson was in a somewhat compromising position and was haring home to avoid embarrassing questions. And if he knew he hadn't seen anything shady en route why should he go to the trouble of revealing what he was doing at that hour? I certainly wouldn't!'

'Perhaps. But Edward had nothing to hide – except the ignominy of being drunk and sick in the gutter, though I doubt if that would have bothered him unduly. Why did he persist in his tale to Lucia of being in the opposite direction clearing his head wandering around in the Public Gardens?'

'Covering his rear: terrified of being called in for questioning simply because he was in the area. Who knows, short of anyone else the police might have marked him as a suspect. It's not unknown . . . perfectly innocent people in the wrong place at the wrong time finding a murder charge pinned on them.'

'Possible. But it occurs to me that there may have been something else. Supposing he saw something?'

'Ah light dawns! *You* think that Edward's blackmailing note to Hewson was to do with his having seen him rushing hell-for-leather from the knocking shop and that that is why Hewson shoved him under the water!' Felix chuckled and winked at the dog. 'With all due respect that strikes me as a rather inadequate reason for such drastic action. It's also a pretty ropey reason for blackmail; I mean it's not even as if the chap has a wife and children to protect. He's on his own here in Venice. And while patronising a certain type of establishment may not be the most couth of pastimes, unless the target happens to be the headmistress of Roedean I doubt if it carries much blackmailing profit.' Felix gave a dismissive laugh and Cedric watched irritably as his friend spooned large doses of sugar into his lapsang. It was a filthy habit; quite ruined the flavour!

He sighed and tapped an impatient finger on the table. 'No,' he retorted, 'I am not such a fool as to suggest that. His visit to the knocking shop, as you so charmingly put it, is very likely no more than a product of the twins' florid imagination.' Cedric slid the sugar bowl away from Felix's cup; and then bending forward said quietly: '*I* think that what Edward Jones may have seen was not Hewson fleeing a police raid but fleeing from the bookshop where he had just bludgeoned Pacelli.'

'I never did like him,' said Felix, retrieving the sugar.

CHAPTER TWENTY-SEVEN

Leaving the palazzo Rosy decided to return to the *pensione*
before embarking for Hewson's studio. That third glass of
Prosecco had been a grave error and she could already
feel the stirrings of an impending migraine. If she could
get to the aspirin bottle and sit quietly in her room for
half an hour it might be forestalled. There was plenty of
time. Besides it would mean she could dump her earlier
shopping: she had nearly left the bag at the palazzo and
it would be silly to risk it again, especially as it contained
such a beautiful silk headscarf!

Thus back in her room she threw down aspirin,
drank two tumblers of water and lay on the bed rather
wishing she could just drift off to sleep and forgo the
studio visit. She closed her eyes and mused over the

contents of Edward's note and Cedric's interpretation.

Was blackmail really what it had been about? At the time, persuaded by wine and the tone of Cedric's conviction, it had seemed plausible; but now alone in her room and her mind soothed by the aspirin she was less certain. Admittedly, as she herself had observed, the reference to the vase was curious. But there might be some perfectly simple explanation and the comments she had overheard between the siblings in the café of no relevance. She thought about Cedric and Felix: they were inveterate gossips and she sensed that they didn't much care for the painter. Perhaps she had allowed herself to be too easily drawn into their speculative musings, had become absurdly collusive in their game of Cluedo. Cedric had termed her visit to Hewson's studio a 'reconnaissance'. How melodramatic!

Yes she would doubtless glance at the mantelpiece, but other than that she would treat the visit as no more than it surely was – a congenial afternoon among an artist's paints and sketches admiring his work. She opened her eyes, and feeling much better started to get ready.

She was tempted to wear the headscarf she had bought that morning but it was so exquisitely wrapped and beribboned that it seemed a shame to open it just yet. Much nicer to wait till she returned home and present it to herself as a post-holiday gift. She opened the dressing-table drawer intending to stow it with the other things she had bought. Slightly to her surprise the postcards left in a neat pile on top were in some disorder. The drawer fitted badly and presumably they had been dislodged when she had pulled too roughly.

Resisting the urge to give the little china harlequin yet another doting inspection, she was about to deposit her new purchase when she stopped, puzzled. Where was the damned Horace for goodness' sake? Surely she had put it there; it had been cluttering up the dressing table and she had wanted it out of the way. She scrabbled under the postcards and folded lace table mats. Nothing.

At first she assumed that her memory was playing tricks and that in her haste she had put it in some other 'safe' place – suitcase, wardrobe, underneath her maps and guidebook . . . It was in none of those places; and neither was it any of the other drawers. They stared up at her in barren mockery. Extraordinary!

What the hell had happened? She *knew* she had had it; and the more she brooded the more vivid was her memory of putting it away with the other things. She paced about the room, stared out of the window, picked up her handbag and put it down again, combed her hair, straightened the bedspread . . . Yes there were only two possible conclusions: either she was going mad and suffering delusions or someone had removed it.

On the whole she thought the first unlikely – as far as she was aware there had been no other symptoms. Presumably therefore it had been taken. When? What for? And *by whom* for God's sake! Could it have been Angelina the chambermaid? It seemed unfair to immediately think of her, and besides what on earth would the girl want with a copy of Latin poems? Had Miss Witherington herself slipped into the room and deftly rifled the drawers? Unthinkable! One of the guests? Ridiculous; they were far too staid. She pulled open the other drawers again and examined them carefully. Any sign of rummaging? It was so hard to tell, she wasn't the neatest of travellers. Still there was a pair of stockings and a jumper that seemed strangely out of place, and had she really left the clothes brush on top of the blue petticoat? The problem was she couldn't be *sure*! But one thing was certain all right: the book was nowhere to be found.

She sat on the bed and stared blankly at the wall and to her annoyance found she was feeling quite shaky. How stupid! People mislaid books every day. In the scale of things it was hardly something to get upset about; and it wasn't as if it were of value. According to Carlo it was a total fake; so she didn't need the damn thing anyway and Stanley certainly wouldn't thank her for it. Yet she *was* upset. Unnerved, because she was convinced that she hadn't mislaid the thing: it had been nicked – someone had sneaked into her bedroom, searched for it and taken it. She felt slightly sick.

But there was nothing to be done. It was out of the question to enquire of Miss Witherington or any of the guests as it might be thought she was making insinuations; and it would be unpardonable to accuse the maid. Rosy tried to comfort herself by thinking that since it had inexplicably disappeared perhaps it would just as miraculously reappear. Stranger things had happened – or so one heard. But of course that wasn't really the point: the point was that someone had entered her room uninvited and taken one of her belongings. Beastly!

She heaved a sigh. There was no point getting in a panic, disturbing though it was. Presumably whoever it was had found what they were after and wouldn't need to return to filch her underclothes! She suddenly giggled: perhaps it was the mythical man from the Bodleian. She checked her watch and realised she had better start to make tracks for Bill Hewson's studio, and wondered vaguely what she should say if the host asked her opinion of the 'scrambled egg' pictures.

As she crossed the courtyard she bumped into Miss Witherington who evidently also had the pictures in mind. 'My dear,' she said, 'what do you think of our new acquisitions on the landing? I am not sure if they are *quite* what one would have personally chosen but he seemed so keen it seemed rude to decline.'

'William Hewson's paintings? Uhm, interesting,' Rosy said. And then feeling something more was required added, 'Very bright.'

'Ye-es,' Miss Witherington replied looking doubtful, 'that's what I thought but he seemed to think they would enliven a dull area. I had suggested the vestibule downstairs but he was clearly determined they should be hung up there. I suppose artists know about such matters . . . light and perspective and all that sort of thing.'

Rosy was puzzled. 'So you bought them did you?'

'Oh no. They are on a long loan – although I am not too sure what "long" signifies: until we get tired of them I suppose – or someone complains! He does this occasionally, asks friends to display his pictures in the hope that they will get exposure and hence a sale. Saves the costs of exhibitions let alone gallery commissions. Generally he hangs them himself but this time he sent one of his framers to do it. *Not* the most meticulous of workmen, he left an awful mess with dust and bits everywhere! It was Angelina's day off but Dr Burgess was most kind and offered to hoover it up. So we are all spick and span again.' She paused and then added wryly, 'Naturally Mr Downing made a complaint about the hammering, but for one who snores so heavily it did strike me as being a mite unjust.'

Rosy smiled and was just about to open the patio door when the other said, 'I say, how are your researches going? I do trust there is no news of the book otherwise I may lose my bet. Not long to go now!'

Ruefully Rosy assured her that the likelihood of its now being found was distinctly remote and that the bet was probably in the bag. 'But you never know,' she teased, 'a *deus ex machina* might still suddenly pop up from under the floorboards with Horace in one hand and the glass goblet in the other.'

'Perish the thought!' Miss Witherington cried.

Rosy went on her way to Hewson's studio amused by Miss Witherington's anxiety over her bet. And then abruptly she stopped walking and stopped feeling amused. Good Lord, she thought, supposing the old girl *had* taken the thing! Maybe she was slightly crazed and had become utterly obsessed by her prospective visit to Longchamp. Could it be that the image of Paris and the fun of the racetrack had taken such a hold of her hopes that she was prepared to go to any lengths to ensure that she won her bet?

Rosy considered the possibility and tried to put herself in Miss Witherington's shoes. Here was a lady of presumably adequate but limited means whose moderately successful guest house, while ensuring a stable income, did not permit much in the way of costly treats. Yet from what Rosy had deduced, at one time Miss Witherington had led a life of some liveliness and style. Did she now yearn to recapture a slice of that long lost gaiety, to relive her youth wearing scandalous hats and tippling Pol Roger amidst the sporting glitterati? Was this to be the final fling before the unsparing seepage of health and decline into dotage? If so, to have a guest clearly intent on finding the book just when she wanted it so securely lost must have been worrying. The chance of the Murano vase being simultaneously found with the book was remote, but one never *knew*. One couldn't take the risk: best to scupper the Horace at least!

Rosy brooded. Might that really be the answer: the snoopings of an anxious old lady determined not to be cheated out of her racing swansong? If so, perhaps if she learnt from Daphne Blanchett that it was the wrong

245

edition the next time Rosy looked she might find it neatly replaced!

However, by now she had reached her destination and thoughts of Miss Witherington and the purloined Horace were put aside as she searched for Hewson's bell. Rather to her surprise the answering voice on the intercom was female.

CHAPTER TWENTY-EIGHT

Lucia Borgino had not banked on there being other people in Bill Hewson's studio that afternoon. Using some pretext she had intended to drop in casually when he was there alone, and if the chance arose have a swift scout round for the vase. Indeed she had confidently hoped that if she played her cards right she would be able to wheedle it out of him there and then.

Thus when she arrived and found several visitors including Dr Burgess and the rather stuffy Blanchett woman, she was distinctly peeved. A general tea party had not been her idea at all! But as always with such social gatherings she adapted accordingly and assumed her customary air of patronage and brittle charm. Sympathy over her recent bereavement was met with brave smiles and a stoical shrug.

The apartment intercom had buzzed: and busy with guests Hewson asked if she would mind answering it. The voice at the other end was female and English. She surmised it might be the British Museum person. All the more the less merry, she thought irritably.

As she had guessed, it was indeed the Gilchrist woman. Lucia appraised her. Quite attractive in a rather pallid way she supposed. Legs were good as were the features, but the straight hair and shortish stature was hardly *Vogue* material. A good six inches taller and willowy in black, Lucia flashed the newcomer a superior smile and then drifted away hoping to catch sight of the vase.

A large area, and cluttered as it was with people and painting paraphernalia, the studio did not lend itself to easy surveillance. To Lucia's frustration a couple of easels draped in dust sheets now stood in front of the mantelpiece – as did Dr Burgess and some other man. They were deep in conversation. She tried to get a glimpse of the wall behind them but her vision was entirely blocked. Maddening! She hovered by the window waiting for them to move away. Perhaps then she could edge round the easels and take a quick peek; although quite possibly it wouldn't be there anyway – it was nearly two months since she had last been at the studio and Hewson could well have moved it. She glanced across the room to where the painter was talking volubly to the Gilchrist girl. The latter looked a bit bemused and Lucia guessed he might be explaining one of his pet theories. Hewson had a lot of pet theories and in Lucia's estimation few of them held much water.

She returned her gaze to the pair by the far wall. Good, they were moving off. She weaved her way towards the easels and took a quick glance sideways . . . Yes! Amazingly the vase was still there and displaying a wilted geranium stalk and a couple of pencils. Nobody was looking. If she was quick she could sweep the whole lot into her straw holdall and it would be gone in a trice. She unclipped the fastening.

'Ah, Lucia,' cried Daphne Blanchett. 'How nice to see you; thought you might have left for your poor brother's funeral.'

'My flight is tomorrow,' replied Lucia soberly, hating the Blanchett woman with all her being.

Meanwhile Rosy was rather enjoying herself. Like Lucia, she had been surprised by the crowd; but in a way was glad. Amusing though he could be she felt Hewson's extravert personality was something to be taken in small doses; and after the recent 'tantrum' at lunch she wondered if he was quite as carefree as he seemed. Thus the presence of others (English and Italian mostly) made for a relaxing diversion. A few were obviously prospective purchasers, but like herself most were there simply out of interest or were friends who had dropped in for a casual chat. Among the latter she was glad to see Mrs Blanchett and Dr Burgess who were helpful in making introductions.

'We don't know him terribly well,' Daphne Blanchett said, 'but I did once buy one of his early paintings of Torcello at dusk which pleases me very much; although,' she added lowering her voice, 'I have to say that his later work is not entirely to my taste.'

'She means,' Burgess explained, 'those pictures outside your bedroom – or for that matter those over there.' He gestured towards a couple of indeterminate abstracts propped against the wall. 'He *says* they are all about form and texture.'

'And then what?' asked Rosy.

'Exactly. And then what?' Burgess echoed.

She wandered around eying some of the unfinished canvases and inspecting the completed ones displayed on the walls. Like Daphne Blanchett, she found the occasional one distinctly compelling, whereas the majority struck her as a trifle bland and the recent ones raucous. There seemed a curious lack of direction and she wondered if Hewson would have done well to follow the habit of established musicians and retain the guidance of a professional mentor.

She asked him about his current work and was given a fulsome account of its concept and aim. His words were not especially enlightening but she assumed the fault lay with herself rather than the confident exponent. Despite Cedric's suspicion and the cryptic nature of Edward's note, Rosy felt that there was a frankness and lack of subtlety about Bill Hewson which made him an unlikely target for blackmail. Still, as directed, she would endeavour to carry out a 'reconnaissance' for the wretched Murano thing. According to Lucia's remark in Tonelli's it was supposed to be on the mantelpiece. Well, she would take a look once that tiresome woman had got out of the way.

She stared across the room at Lucia Borgino standing by one of the draped easels. The cool aplomb with which she had greeted Rosy at the door seemed to have entirely vanished. She looked strangely ruffled, agitated in fact. The pale cheeks were flushed and she bore the look of a punter whose horse had fallen in the last lap. Huh! Rosy thought, with luck someone has snubbed her. At that moment there was a tap on her shoulder. 'Hello,' said Guy Hope-Landers, 'good to see you again.'

Having been variously waylaid by other guests and forced to listen to more condolences re her brother, it had taken Lucia some while to regain her original position by the mantelpiece. When she did so she had the shock of her life: the bloody thing wasn't there! Where the vase had been there was now only the geranium stalk and a single pencil – the other having fallen on the floor. She stared in angry astonishment. What had happened? Surely that old fool Hewson hadn't suddenly taken it into his head to put it somewhere else. That seemed hardly likely at a time like this with everyone milling around and chatting inanely. Besides he was being the genial impresario and showing off the paintings and answering earnest questions about his technique; he would scarcely have had a moment on his own. And in any case why suddenly decide to conceal the damn thing now? Could it have been Daphne and her sidekick Burgess? Possible but unlikely: far too smug and staid to pilfer their host's paltry ornament!

She glared across the room and saw the Gilchrist girl talking to Guy who had come in late still wearing that awful old reefer jacket he kept for his sailing trips. She regarded it with distaste. She would make sure he got rid of it once they were together – and the awful boat with it! But what about the girl smiling up at him so angelically? Being after the Bodger book maybe she too was aiming at the vase. A million pounds would set her up for life and she wouldn't have to work in that stuffy museum any more . . . Lucia's eye swept the room taking in the twenty or so other guests. Hell it could have been any of them!

For a few seconds she seethed with angry frustration and then gave a careless shrug: nothing to be done now. She must get home and pack for the flight and the funeral . . . and also plan how she was going to curry favour with her grandfather to see if she couldn't squeeze a little more money out of the old miser. Thus snapping her handbag shut (it had been reopened in preparation for the vase) she bid goodbye to her host; and smiling coldly at Rosy and blowing a lavish kiss at the intended fiancé, removed herself from the scene.

CHAPTER TWENTY-NINE

Altogether, Rosy felt, it had been a congenial event; and despite her earlier reluctance she was glad to have gone. Admittedly there had been nothing on the mantelpiece remotely like a vase or goblet. Doubtless it had been discarded or put in another place. But it certainly hadn't been her purpose to go snooping around in her host's kitchen or bedroom. So a fruitless reconnaissance after all, but the visit itself had been pleasant.

However, the thing at the end had unsettled her. It had been so unexpected! She had been leaving at the same time as Daphne Blanchett and Dr Burgess, and as they opened the door into the street they almost collided with a man coming in. He had stood back, muttered apologies and then continued up the staircase.

'Wasn't that the man who came to hang the pictures?' Daphne asked Burgess, 'the one who made all that dust for you to clear up?'

'Yes I think perhaps it was,' Burgess agreed. 'Not the most professional of workers – made an awful mess and then left the frames crooked.' He laughed. 'If Hewson uses him with other clients there's bound to be complaints.'

Rosy had said nothing, too surprised to comment. She had recognised the man instantly: it had been the same one who had approached the painter in the square after they had lunched together and who had given her that quizzical look. And as she had thought then – and on closer scrutiny now knew – it was also the same man who had been with Pacelli on the night she had gone to Florian's. If Daphne Blanchett was right, it was somehow disquieting to think it was also he who had been hanging the pictures on the landing outside her room.

She started to walk back to the *pensione* puzzled by her own unease. Just because she found the man rather distasteful was no reason to feel bothered by his link with William Hewson. After all it was no concern of hers whom he chose to deal with or employ. And yet foolishly she did feel bothered and kept imagining the man alone on the landing busily measuring, hammering, leaving his dusty mess; and then with job done gathering his tools and walking back down the stairs again . . . But more insistently she was nagged by another scenario, i.e. with job done the man cautiously trying the handle of her bedroom door, and finding it unlocked slipping inside.

She paused, exploring the possibility. It wasn't entirely out of the question. After all she had been out when the paintings arrived, and it was when she returned that she had discovered the Horace gone. Could he really have been the culprit? Was it so absurd? To steady her thoughts she stopped at a café and ordered a double espresso: perhaps the caffeine would focus her mind. Not bothering with a table she stood at the counter as the locals did, sipping slowly and thinking.

Yet why him? Certainly he had had the opportunity but was it *likely*? Well he obviously knew about the Horace (unlike presumably the chambermaid) as it had been he who with Pacelli had brazenly told her to go home and not bother with 'silly poems'. Motive? Obviously to match it with the Murano vase in the hope of getting Berenstein's vaunted prize money . . . But what on earth made him think she had found the book, and how in any case would he know which was her room?

She turned from the mirrored bar and leant against the counter watching the street outside with its fading sun and strolling pedestrians. A man stopped, bent his head and lit a cigarette. The tip glowed as he took his first puff, and then he walked on. The commonplace action triggered something in Rosy's memory and in a trice her mind had darted back to the night at the *pensione* when looking out from her window she had been so startled by that watching presence – the movement in the shadows, the flashing of a lighter and glint of a cigarette tip.

That was it! The watcher had been no Peeping Tom at all but someone who, like herself only an hour ago, had been set on a mission of reconnaissance . . . Yes it was obvious. She had been deliberately followed that night, and, as revealed by her own form at the lighted window, the position of her room duly noted. Rosy swallowed the last dregs of the espresso and shivered. It was horrible – the idea of him watching and waiting, and then later creeping into the empty bedroom and quietly ransacking the place. No wonder he had left the landing in such a mess: couldn't get down the stairs quick enough!

Leaving the café she continued her walk home, the twisting alleys seeming to mimic the twistings of her mind. There was of course the other question, a question crucial to the whole thing. What made the man think she had the book in the first place? Who else knew other than the donors Cedric and Felix, and Carlo who had spurned it? *And*, she recalled, Guy Hope-Landers and Bill Hewson. Yes of course! They had been having drinks at the palazzo when Cedric had presented her with the thing and had toasted the lucky find. She thought of Hewson and Cedric's distrust of him and his suspicion that Edward Jones had been blackmailing the painter. Was there really something not quite straight about the man, something a bit skewed?

Again she thought of Lucia's apparent assertion that he possessed the vase. If she was right – and it would seem so judging from Edward's allusion in his note – then Hewson might also be seeking the Bodger Horace. And if that were the case perhaps it had been he who had directed the picture hanger to steal it, had even had the pictures delivered there for the express purpose!

She pondered. Could that really be so? Far-fetched surely. And yet just as she was about to dismiss the thought, with a sudden jolt she remembered Edward's hostility in the restaurant and his snide confidential warning: 'Don't trust that one, my dear, he'd cut your throat given half a chance.' A common enough cliché and typical of the young man's taste for drama but the point had been clear enough: Hewson was dubious, dangerous even. She frowned trying to think what else the boy had said . . . ah that was it: 'I've got your number,' he had shouted. What number? What was it that Edward knew or thought he knew about Hewson? But the taunt could have been meaningless, merely the product of drunken pique. Yet it had been hurled with such force; he must have meant something! And if so what? That Hewson was capable of organising petty larceny? . . . Or something more sinister?

'If, if, if,' she muttered to herself and recalled her Cambridge history tutor's scathing comment on over-speculation: 'Conjecture without facts is the death of truth,' he had hammered home. But he had said something else as well: 'In pursuing fact do not discount the value of theory; it has opened innumerable doors.' Yes well, she had enough theory to open doors galore but whether they would reveal anything was another matter.

By this time Rosy had reached the *pensione* and despite her scepticism was both intrigued and unsettled. What she needed was reassurance, or at least to be able to decant her concern on to someone else. Who to confide in? Obviously Cedric and Felix. But were they 'in residence'? And in any case having entertained her earlier in the day would they want a repeat dose of her company that evening? Ignoring such consideration she decided to telephone the palazzo and find out.

The line was frustratingly poor; full of squeaks and crackles. But she managed to make out from Felix that she would be welcome to go round there later but that it would be only himself as Cedric was otherwise engaged – with what she couldn't hear. The line faltered and then she heard Felix say, 'anyway, I have just bought some marvellous cheese and salami, so we might try a little of that. The only thing is that I am not exactly sure when I shall be back – Paolo is keen to show me some of the Jewish quarter and its synagogues and I'm just about to go. But about half past eight *should* be all right. Tell you what though . . .' The line faded but then grew loud again and she heard Felix say, 'so the key is under the stone gryphon on the left.' The sound broke up and then collapsed altogether.

Admittedly she would have preferred Cedric to be there as well; he had a sobriety not always discernible in his friend. However, better one than none at all; and even if Felix shed no light at least he would be a diversion and someone to talk to. She couldn't recall a stone gryphon but presumably one was there standing sentinel and acting as guardian of the spare key should one be required.

CHAPTER THIRTY

The synagogues had been fascinating, Paolo's company amusing, and had he the time Felix would have liked to see more of the area. But he didn't have the time: there was the dog to feed and then of course Rosy Gilchrist was coming. He had no idea what she wanted but she had sounded agitated. He hoped it wasn't anything too disquieting as he had rather hoped for an early night and to curl up with a good book . . . well not a good book exactly but to reread yet again that lovely article in the *Tatler* about himself supervising the Queen Mother's flowers for her last cocktail party. It really had been most gratifying.

He arrived at the palazzo and let himself in. Rather to his surprise the door to Hope-Landers' quarters was wide open and from within he heard the sound of a raised voice. Rather more than raised actually – bellowing would be a better term. Startled, Felix paused and lent an ear. Yes the tone was very loud indeed, most unpleasant in fact. He thought he could just catch the murmuring of another voice but couldn't be sure as the other was making such a racket. Maybe it was the radio. Was Hope-Landers having an unquiet fit? Perhaps he ought to venture in although it would be easier to scuttle past. He recalled his mother's advice at such moments of crisis: 'Quick dear, look the other way!' It had, he reflected, been sound counsel except that on this occasion his curiosity was aroused. Perhaps just the smallest peek . . .

Other than a haze of cigarette smoke and the shambles of the lodger's sitting room the peek revealed nothing. The shouting, however, continued. Felix hovered at the threshold and then edging in a little further saw a half-open door to his left revealing a passage. He took a few tentative steps along this and was faced with another door slightly ajar, presumably that of a bedroom or study. It was from here that the shouting came. The voice was unmistakable: an American accent at full throttle.

'You thieving little bastard,' Bill Hewson yelled, 'I saw you take the fucking thing myself. You thought I wouldn't notice, thought I was too taken up with that Gilchrist broad. Well I wasn't, see. I saw everything. I can tell you old Bill Hewson doesn't miss a fucking trick!'

Fearful yet fascinated Felix was drawn to the doorway and stared in. Hope-Landers was lounging on a bed, long legs stretched out, arms folded behind his head. Hewson was towering over him, shoulders hunched and fists clenched. He did look very angry, and it occurred to Felix that had it been himself being thus addressed he would have been under the bed and not on it.

'Yes it was a bit rash,' replied Hope-Landers ruefully, 'but,' he continued mildly, 'I imagine you have been missing fucking tricks most of your life. Wouldn't you say?'

Hewson seemed to freeze and Felix drew in his breath and winced. Idiot! All very well affecting nonchalance but not in the face of such bitter fury: surely a tactical error. He was right for in the next instant Hewson had whipped something from his pocket, lunged at the other and started beating him about the head. Hope-Landers gasped, tried to sit up, was hit again violently and then heaved to the ground and kicked in the ribs.

It was then that Felix stepped forward. 'You can't do that,' he announced with scant conviction.

The attacker swung round: 'Why if it isn't the little hairdresser,' he jeered.

Hairdresser? Felix was enraged! However, he certainly wasn't going to argue the point because he had suddenly seen what Hewson held in his hand: a heavy revolver. He swallowed hard. It must have been the butt that he had been using on Hope-Landers. But it was less the butt that bothered Felix than the fact that the gun's muzzle was now being waved perilously close to his own nose. He took a step back. 'I am sure that's not called for is it?'

he said hastily. 'Er, what is it that you are looking for exactly?'

'You heard,' Hewson snarled, 'the vase that the bastard there took from my studio.' (The bastard there was still on the ground looking distinctly under the weather: blood poured from his nose and he was doubled up as if winded.)

'There it is,' said Felix, nodding towards a chest of drawers. 'Now I suggest you take it and then go away.' He fixed the man with a hard look; the sort of look reserved for the royal corgis when they became overly intrigued by his floral confections.

But not being a corgi, royal or otherwise, Hewson remained unquelled. He strode to the chest of drawers, grabbed the vase and thrust it into a canvas bag. And then turning towards the figure on the floor said softly, 'But there's something else isn't there, Guy; something else that you have and which I need. That book Emilio took from the girl's room was useless: he reckoned it was one of Lupino's bits of buggery. But I think you've got the real one – you must have otherwise why so keen to get at my vase? Berenstein's offer is withdrawn in three days' time. You wouldn't have bothered with it unless you already had the real frigging Horace. So I'd be obliged if you would tell me where it is.'

'Go to hell,' Hope-Landers grunted and appeared to pass out.

Hewson whirled on Felix. 'Okay, Smarty Pants, so where do you think it is?'

Felix shrugged. 'Somewhere on his shelves I imagine.

He's got a lot in there.' He nodded towards the sitting room.

Hewson frowned and seemed to cogitate while Felix regarded him with some nervousness. He had once had an uncle whom his mother had described as always having a wild look in his eyes (a permanent affliction apparently). Looking at Hewson now he was reminded of his mother's words. He couldn't remember what had happened to the uncle: something nasty he suspected. Hewson's eyes were definitely wild and he rather thought the man was off his chump. Whether anything nasty would happen to him Felix could not be sure but it would be nice to think so. Meanwhile, he told himself, the great thing was to play for time: something which according to literature was considered a good ploy.

'Er, can I offer you a cup of tea?' he asked politely. 'We have various types upstairs – Darjeeling, lapsang suchong, Ceylon something or other . . .' His voice trailed off as judging from Hewson's expression these did not meet with approval.

'Just shut up you pathetic Limey lizard,' the latter barked levelling the gun at him. 'I've things to do and I'm not having you prancing about messing things up!'

Felix dutifully shut up and found himself pushed on to a chair. He wanted to say that while he may have messed up a few things in his life he had certainly never pranced – but on the whole felt it wiser to keep quiet. The next moment Hewson had snapped open a penknife and slashed the curtain cords. Felix winced as he saw the velvet folds tumble to the floor. But he winced even more when he felt his arms and ankles being tightly bound and lashed to the chair legs and back. And then, horror of horrors, with a light tap Hewson had tipped the chair, and it and the occupant fell to the ground with a crash. Without a backward glance the man rushed from the room and slammed the door leaving Felix bone-shaken and terrified. He heard the lock being turned.

From his upended position Felix contemplated the ceiling and then called out to Hope-Landers. There was no answer and he felt terribly alone. It wasn't so much his physical discomfort that oppressed him but the deafening silence. By twisting his neck he could just make out the passage light shining under the door. Had the man gone back to the sitting room? What was he doing? Presumably hunting for the book. And if he found it what then? Would he quietly sneak away – or come back in and do Christ knows what? He shivered and called out to Hope-Landers fearful that he might be dead.

There was a groan and a curse. There followed another groan and more silence. Then a faint voice said, 'You look awful.'

'So would you if you had your effing feet stuck in the air,' Felix snapped. 'Kindly come and untie me!'

'All in good time old man. I'm feeling a bit groggy. If you don't mind I am just going to lie quietly here for a bit.'

Felix sighed. 'Oh take your time,' he said acidly.

The next moment there was the sound of the key in

the lock and Hewson reappeared looking triumphant and holding a book in his hand. He scanned the room and moved to the rug where he had dropped the canvas bag containing the vase. 'Mustn't forget this,' he sneered, 'it goes with its pal here.' And he tapped the book and brandished it in Hope-Landers' face. 'My fortune, your loss,' he taunted.

Hope-Landers shrugged wearily. 'Ah the vicissitudes of life.'

'Shut up you fool,' the other snarled.

'Actually,' said Felix boldly, 'I think it might be you who is being foolish. Don't you realise *everyone* knows you killed Pacelli?' (By 'everyone' he meant of course that he and Cedric had discussed it.) 'There were witnesses, Dilly and Duffy.'

'Huh! Those old hags! What do they know about anything?'

'Well I can assure you they've told the police,' Felix lied.

'Big deal,' Hewson snorted. 'You don't really think the police will listen to their bilge, do you? They have enough work always being called out to chase the sodding cat!'

He glared at the man on the floor, and picking up the remnants of rope used on Felix proceeded to bind his wrists to a leg of the bed. He grinned: 'I wasn't in the navy for nothing; darn good knots these!' Snatching the swag he hurried from the room again and locked the door.

CHAPTER THIRTY-ONE

Having nothing better to do and feeling excruciatingly uncomfortable Felix started to wriggle about in his chair, and with a heave succeeded in jolting it over on to one side. His limbs were still tightly bound, but at least his legs were now down which gave some relief and he was able to lie in a foetal position on his side. He looked over at Hope-Landers sprawled a few feet away by the bed. The blood from his nosebleed had dried but he looked a bit seedy. Felix sighed and tried to ease the rope on his wrists. Nothing happened.

'You do realise he is mad,' said Hope-Landers faintly.

'It had crossed my mind,' Felix replied. 'But if you don't mind my saying it was pretty stupid of you to have messed about with that vase thing. I take it that the Horace he snatched was the genuine article?'

'Oh yes it's the right one all right. I took it from your cousin's table some time back, the day after Carlo left it there, and replaced it with a counterfeit – the one Cedric found in her bookcase and gave to Rosy.'

'Oh so it was *you* who switched the book,' Felix exclaimed. 'Whatever for? And what were you doing with the fake anyway?'

Hope-Landers gave a tired sigh. 'I can answer your first question quite easily: I wanted the money. Having seen the Murano vase at Bob's studio earlier on I realised that if I could obtain the pair and get to Farinelli in time I stood a good chance of winning the old fool's favour. I hadn't anything to lose and it was worth a try.' He gave a rueful smile.

'Really?' Felix said sceptically. 'Seems a lot of effort to me. Are you so short of funds? I mean you seem to live quite an agreeable life here in Venice – convivial company at Harry's, supper invitations, a small pad in a palazzo and driving that boat around. Not too distasteful surely?'

'On the face of it no. But such things pall, especially when you have no prospect of doing anything else . . . Being fêted by elderly ladies and grateful tour guides is pleasant enough but there is more to life I suspect. In fact sometimes I get so bored that I have even considered swapping *The Times* crossword for the *Manchester Guardian*'s.'

'Good grief!' Felix exclaimed.

'And then of course there's Lucia. At first I thought she was rather amusing and she's certainly easy on the eye . . . I like people to look nice,' he added simply. 'But now she irritates me and has become a sort of albatross. One could do without her really.'

Felix knew exactly what he meant and nodded vigorously. However, his prurient curiosity was also roused: 'Uhm, if it's not an indelicate question' – it was of course – 'did you have a little fling with her?'

'Did I sleep with her you mean? Briefly; but it rather tailed off – or rather I did. I have a dicky heart you see, and one has to be a bit careful about such things . . . although to tell you the truth she wasn't terribly engaging: too self-centred and a curious mixture of the frigid and the ferocious.'

'Goodness, I don't suppose that would do the old ticker much good; sounds terrifying!' (Felix, who had a lurid imagination, shuddered.) 'It just goes to show,' he remarked helpfully, 'every cloud has its silver lining or whatever it is they say.'

'Pale copper I should say.'

'Er, yes perhaps . . . Anyway, presumably you wanted the money so you could chuck it all up and get away.'

Hope-Landers' face hardened. 'Exactly. To get *away*. But there's no point in getting away unless you escape to something utterly different and exciting, something extraordinary and exotic and fulfilling, and where you are not plagued with predatory sirens and irksome chores. I have spent too much of my life being obliging to vicars and old ladies and now I should like to *break out* – sail to foreign parts, hunt marauding tigers or ride on an elephant. Such things need funding.'

'Ride on an elephant? That's a bit rash isn't! I should stick with the vicars.' Felix was not entirely joking: he had an aversion to elephants ever since being unceremoniously pushed aside by one at the London Zoo; but it was not so much the slight that had rankled as the hiding he had received from his mother for breaking loose from his reins. The memory went deep.

However, dismissing the elephant he returned to the fake. 'But what were you doing with it?'

Hope-Landers frowned. 'Yes that is a bit of a saga but since you ask, here goes. You know that other bookshop near the Arsenale, the one that is run by Pacelli's cousin?'

'The one currently closed?'

He nodded. 'I had a flat in that area and used to know its owner Lupino moderately well – a bit slippery but in his way quite interesting and certainly more fun than Pacelli. Within certain discreet Venetian circles both were renowned for their forging skills, or at least the elder was. Lupino, the younger, was the novice – though apparently now quite the skilled maestro. I would often buy books from him and we used to share the odd bottle of wine and he would teach me Italian. One evening I asked him about the finer points of forging. He explained that he hadn't yet reached the finer points but he would show me an item he had recently done, a sort of practice job. He pointed out the methods he had used but also its flaws. It was most interesting (the sort of thing that as an undergraduate I'd like to have had a go at; more fun than Virgil I suspect. A forger manqué that's me!) Anyway I told him I was very

270

impressed but he laughed and said it was rubbish – as apparently his mentor had made perfectly clear. He then said that as it was such a botched job he had no use for it and since I seemed so interested I was welcome to have it.'

'And it was a mock-up of the Horace?'

'Yes. And as I hadn't read any of the verse since leaving Oxford and didn't have a personal copy I thought I might as well refresh my memory with a crude piece of fakery; after all the poems were the same.'

'But surely when you saw the original at my cousin's, the one that Carlo had forgotten, why didn't you just filch it and say nothing? Why bother to import your own?'

Hope-Landers grinned. 'Your cousin may be a bit scatty and short-sighted but even she would have realised that the thing was no longer where she had left it, particularly as she was expecting Carlo to come back. *Something* had to be there for her to pick up and hand to him. We had been doing the crossword together, and if she had noticed its absence the following day she could easily have assumed that I had taken it. Substituting the spare was at least a sort of delaying tactic, a holding operation you might say. And as it happens of course, I was in luck because Carlo completely forgot about the whole thing and the matter was literally shelved. Convenient!' He laughed.

'Hmm, but there was still a risk wasn't there? I mean it was pure chance that Carlo didn't return, and if he *had* then presumably at some point he would have realised the book wasn't his and started asking questions.'

Hope-Landers sighed. 'We all have to hope for the best

271

and take a gamble now and again. Haven't you ever done that?'

Felix most certainly had; and the recent escapades in St John's Wood remained horribly vivid. But nothing was as horrid as this! 'And I suppose too you thought that the rest of the procedure would be quick: snaffle the vase from Hewson, whip off to F. Berenstein, collect the prize and bugger off.'

The other nodded bleakly. 'Something like that. Silly really.'

'You can say that again,' Felix replied indignantly, 'look where it's landed us!'

He glanced up at the clock. It was roughly the time that Rosy Gilchrist was due. With no answer from the buzzer she would have to use the key and let herself in as he had told her to . . . But maybe she had arrived already! The entrance hall was too far off for them to hear anything. Supposing at this very minute she was being confronted by Hewson; supposing he had bashed her up as he had Hope-Landers – or worse still she was lying dead in a pool of blood. Felix closed his eyes: the bastard had done it before and in his present state he seemed capable of anything! He swallowed and tried to think of something better: Hewson fled, and Rosy seated in the salon sipping a dry martini while patiently awaiting her host's arrival. Helplessly he clung to the hope.

CHAPTER THIRTY-TWO

As Felix feared, no such homely scene was being enacted. Rosy had indeed arrived and getting no reply from the buzzer had found the key under the gryphon and let herself in.

A man stood in the hallway: big, bearded and unsmiling. It was Bill Hewson with whom she had been chatting only hours earlier. Behind him was the open door to Hope-Landers' apartment. The room was in chaos: desk upturned and books strewn everywhere. Rosy gazed uncomprehending.

'Wrong time, Rosy,' he said, 'wrong time.' He glanced at his watch. 'Too late for a social call. You should be at home tucked up in bed.'

'I beg your pardon?' she replied indignantly.

'And then,' he continued, 'you wouldn't have interrupted things.'

'Really? What things? What are you talking about?' Her eyes returned to the room behind him. 'You've been in there,' she said accusingly. 'My God you've ransacked his rooms!' She was suddenly fearful and felt her stomach lurch. *He would cut your throat given half a chance* she could hear the boy saying.

'Hmm, yes. I was searching for something. That's something you would understand I guess.'

She nodded. 'You are after the Horace I imagine.'

'Nope, not any more I'm not. I've found it.' He gestured to the bag on the table, and taking out a book held it up. 'See? The real McCoy this time, not that crude little fake Emilio took from your room.' He gave a mocking grin.

Anger replaced fear. 'You're a fool,' she said scornfully, 'you can't even be sure if this is the right Horace. It may be one of Pacelli's masterpieces; they say he was brilliant.'

'I don't think so,' he said evenly, 'I've looked. It's the genuine article all right and I am going to have it.' He made to replace the book in the bag and in so doing his sleeve brushed against candlestick on the console. It fell heavily and the book slipped from his grasp.

With hindsight Rosy wondered what on earth had possessed her; some kind of mad defiance presumably. But in an instant she had darted forward, grabbed the thing and made a wild rush to the main door. She yanked at the iron handle which creaked noisily but yielded nothing. She wrenched again but in vain. Oh God the thing had stuck! She turned, ducked under Hewson's upraised arm and ran in the opposite direction. Fool! Only the stairs were ahead: she was in a dead end . . . Still, if she could reach the salon she might be able to lock or barricade its doors. Besides, Felix *must* be back soon. She reached the staircase and began the long ascent. Behind her she could hear Hewson's pounding footsteps. 'I'll get you,' he shouted.

She pushed on desperately. She was lighter, more agile than her pursuer. Surely she could beat him to it! Up and up she floundered, heart racing, breath rasping. The stairs seemed endless but she willed herself to keep going, clutching the Horace in one hand and hauling herself on the banister with the other. She raised her eyes: only another flight. But behind her the thudding feet were relentless. At last she gained the landing, and scudding across the floor flung herself into the sanctuary of the salon.

Some sanctuary! She fumbled with the ornate bolt. It seemed far too flimsy to be useful – as indeed it proved. By now Hewson too was on the landing and she heard the heavy feet as he approached the door.

'Rosy,' he called, 'open the door. You might as well. Do you think I am going to stand here twiddling my thumbs?' Through the thin panelling she could hear his breath heaving.

She said nothing and backed away to the middle of the room, and waited.

He didn't take long. There was a kick first. And then after a few seconds, not built to withstand a shoulder battery, the doors burst open and he was in the room with her.

She had expected sound and fury but in fact though breathing heavily he seemed strangely calm. He regarded her for a few moments and then said easily, 'I'm sure we can come to some sort of arrangement. I don't suppose your job at the British Museum pays much; you could probably do with a few extra dollars in your purse. How about it?'

Rosy looked at him steadily. 'I have no desire to make an arrangement with you and I have a perfectly adequate salary which covers most of my needs. Unlike you I don't have a paranoiac craving to be as rich as Croesus. I suppose it's the paintings: they're not particularly special and presumably don't make the money you feel is your due. Edward Jones was perfectly right: your work *is* pretty run of the mill and you're too old now to hit the headlines.' She was mad to say it she knew; but it was anger that drove her and she couldn't help it. (Perhaps, she fantasised, if she could get to the veranda she could chuck the book over the edge and then he would damn well have to run all the way down the stairs again!)

Calm vanished and his face contorted. 'You little bitch!' he cried. 'Give me the book. Give me the fucking book!' He lunged towards her and tried to grab it. She dodged and leapt back.

'Don't you dare come near,' she breathed. He took a step towards her and thrusting his hand in his pocket produced a penknife and snapped open the blade. He placed it carefully on the table beside him.

He would cut your throat given half a chance . . . again the words hammered in her mind and fear closed on her like a vice. And yet despite the fear and still goaded by some rebel instinct she heard herself saying, 'This won't work you know. Even now you are not *quite* sure if it's the right one. You made a mess of the other all right – a ridiculous charade, sending over those ghastly paintings we were all supposed to admire and then getting your minion to search my bedroom. You are a bit of a blunderer aren't you?'

Instantly she regretted her words. The retort had not been calculated, simply the product of wayward scorn. But she knew it was stupid. She saw the glint of hatred in his eye and his fists clench in fury. And yet when he spoke the words were level. 'Oh there are no blunders this time,' he said quietly, 'that's the book all right. It's got the initials BF on the back cover: *Bodger* effing *fecit*,' he sneered. 'That pathetic little wop Carlo explained it to me once. I shouldn't have known otherwise; but I do now and I'm going to put it with that cheap bit of glass the old fool in Padua wants.' He gestured to the bag he had been holding . . . And then lowering his voice he mumbled something she couldn't catch while his eyes took on a glassy stare.

'What did you say?'

He hesitated, and then clear-eyed again scanned her face: 'I *said*, Miss Gilchrist, that if anyone blundered it was the pig Pacelli.'

Rosy gazed back sick to the core . . . *I've got your*

number Edward Jones had said. So that's what the blackmail had been about! She should have guessed. She moistened her lips and said huskily, 'What made you do it? I agree he certainly lacked charm but why bash him up like that?'

'Because, young lady, he had crossed me – rather as you are doing now.' Hewson idly picked up the knife.

Rosy swallowed. *Oh my God, Felix,* she implored, *where on earth are you? For Christ sake come quickly!* Outwardly she said, 'But wasn't that a bit rash? I mean, did you intend to kill him or was it just a mistake?' She tried to sound genuinely interested, concerned even. (As if she cared!)

To her relief he began to answer her question and she saw his hold on the knife relax slightly. He nodded. 'Yes, it was a mistake all right. One hell of a mistake but he deserved it the two-timing rat!'

For an hysterical instant Rosy thought she was going to giggle. 'Two-timing rat'. Had she ever heard that term used outside American westerns and English gangster films? She thought not, and certainly not spat out with such venom. Interesting that people really spoke like that. A picture of James Cagney slipped into her mind and she could hear herself repeating the phrase with cronies round the supper table . . . With cronies? Supper table? Dear God, she would be lucky if she saw any of those again! In a trice she was sobered and once more plunged in icy fear.

'Yes,' he continued, 'we had a deal. As you've heard, he was a first-class forger and while I had the Murano vase I knew I'd never find the Horace and certainly not in the time left. So I offered him a good price to produce a comparable book. I reckoned Berenstein was too blind and gaga to look too closely. It was a chance worth taking. But when I went to collect the thing he held out on me; said there were others interested who were willing to offer a better price. I tried to bargain but he was adamant. Well, I had already paid a percentage and I wasn't going to be messed about like that. So I told him straight that we had a deal and that if he knew what was good for him he would damn well stick to it.'

Hewson paused and Rosy could see sweat glistening on his neck. He seemed horribly big and horribly near. His eyes swept the room as if he was recalling the scene in the shop. Then returning his gaze to her went on: 'He had the nerve to laugh and said that he knew exactly what was good for him: a large increase on what had been agreed. We started to argue. The fool seemed to think it was funny and kept smirking, so I swiped him across the face and he tried to knee me in the groin. We struggled a bit and that's when I picked up the paperweight and smashed it down on his head. His legs buckled and I smashed again . . . and again.' Hewson shrugged his shoulders and added simply, 'And then I left.'

'And Edward?' Rosy whispered. 'What about him?'

Hewson frowned, seeming to reflect; and when he spoke it was in the tone of a reproving schoolmaster. 'That young man was too big for his boots, always had been . . . How shall I put it? He had no sense of boundaries,

279

no propriety. But when he started to blackmail me over Pacelli he went too far. I knew I would have to deal with him but wasn't clear how. But in the end, as I see you have guessed, the young cub laid his own trap. It couldn't have been easier.'

He moved closer and something inside her started to crumple. *Please Felix come!* 'You see Rosy my dear,' he said softly, 'charming though you are, I don't like being crossed; people have to pay the penalty . . . especially when,' and suddenly his voice changed, became rasping and thunderous, 'when they *mock* my *art* you brazen little bitch!' The knife flashed in the air and Rosy shrieked. But then he let it go and the next moment, like an ogre in a dream, he was bearing down upon her, his huge white hands outstretched ready to grasp, to wrench, to throttle . . . She gave a moan and it was as if the room exploded.

Bill Hewson fell at her feet. He lay writhing and another shot was fired.

'That's done for him,' said Guy Hope-Landers.

CHAPTER THIRTY-THREE

He walked over from the doorway and gave Hewson's body a tentative prod with his foot.

'Sorry about that Rosy,' he said, 'must have given you a shock. Are you all right?'

She nodded speechless as he took her arm and guided her to a chair. The next moment Felix appeared followed by Caruso. The dog looked disgruntled as well it might. He had been woken from his dreams and his bones in the downstairs lavatory. Felix too looked ruffled, his hair sticking up and his suit dishevelled. Rosy closed her eyes. 'Why were you so long?' she breathed.

'Long? It's amazing I'm here at all!' he protested. 'I have been trussed up like a chicken in Guy's apartment in a most demeaning position. We've only just got out.

It's been most disturbing!' His voice held a querulous note.

Rosy sighed wearily. 'Yes, I've been fairly disturbed myself.' She looked down at Hewson's hulk and shuddered. 'Can somebody cover him up please, it's not very nice.' She felt no sympathy, only disgust and residual fear.

Hope-Landers took the rug from the sofa and threw it over him. He looked at Felix. 'Where did you say Cedric was?'

'What? Oh with those twins; at their house I assume. They wanted to show him their father's etchings or was it his golf clubs? Anyway something like that . . . I say, do you think we might have a drink. I feel I may pass out otherwise.' He put a hand to his forehead.

Typical, Rosy thought crossly, he was only tied up whereas I came within an inch of being butchered! However, out loud she said, 'But what about the body – oughtn't we to do something about that, e.g. telephone the police?'

'There is no telephone,' Felix said, 'it went off this afternoon.'

'No phone, no hurry: Felix is right,' agreed Hope-Landers, 'we could all do with a brandy.' He went to the cocktail cabinet and found a bottle. 'Here drink this, Rosy, it'll put colour in your cheeks.'

Her hand still shaking she took the glass and sipped gratefully. Dutch courage after the event. She glanced down at the shape under the floral rug and for a nightmarish moment wondered if she might see it move. She flinched and took another sip.

Her rescuer must have read her mind for he said, 'Oh don't worry, he is dead all right. I'm not a bad shot – top of the school cadet corps once upon a time.'

'Ah the manifold uses of a good education,' Felix quipped, yanking the dog away from the corpse.

'Only for certain things. It doesn't always get you what you want; in fact it's often no bloody use at all.' He sounded bitter, and Rosy was about to ask what it was he wanted but thought better of it. This was hardly the time for philosophical discussion.

Instead she said, 'I can't tell you how grateful I am, you literally saved my life. He really was going to choke me to death!' She gulped and leant back in the chair feeling rather weak. 'But I am not clear – if you were both tied up how ever did you get here?'

'It was Guy,' Felix explained. 'Despite Hewson's boasting about his rotten knots they weren't as good as he thought – the clumsiness of dotage I expect. Anyway Guy was able to pull free. And then, and then . . .' (He broke off, starting to laugh.) '. . . you will never guess what we saw under the bed: Hewson's gun. The cretin had forgotten to take it with him. Must have put it down when he was tying those brilliant reefs!'

Some cretin, Rosy thought bitterly, visualising the open blade. And then out loud she asked, 'But hadn't he locked you in?'

'Oh we just shot the lock off,' Felix said carelessly. He

cleared his throat: 'Well Guy did that actually.'

Rosy looked up at the latter. 'You really have been amazing. I'll never forget this.' Something was digging into her hip, and reaching behind she pulled out the Bodger Horace. 'Oh look,' she exclaimed, 'I had forgotten – the blessed book. Safe at last!' And despite the grim presence of what once had been Hewson she suddenly felt so much better, strangely light-headed in fact.

'Ah yes, the book,' Hope-Landers murmured. He smiled and held out his hand. 'I'll take it if you don't mind.'

'What? Oh it's quite all right there's plenty of room in my handbag.' She reached for her bag and started to slip the book into it.

He remained with his hand held out. 'No, Rosy, I would like to have it please.'

She looked up at him nonplussed. 'I am sorry I don't understand. The book's mine, it's what I've been searching for; you know that.' (Really, what on earth had got into the man?)

He smiled again but this time his face held no warmth. 'It's all a question of finders keepers,' he said quietly. 'It has been in my possession for some time and I don't propose to yield it now.'

'Look here,' Felix protested, 'you may have acquired it, *filched* it from Cousin Violet's table, but the actual owner is Carlo. He was the one who originally found and bought it, not you. Now for Christ's sake give it to Rosy; you must admit she deserves it!'

'Actually,' Hope-Landers replied, 'I don't think the concept of deserts enters into this. As I told you in the bedroom, it is something I rather need – to go with the vase over there.' He nodded towards Hewson's discarded holdall. 'Just once in a blue moon things work to one's advantage: a quirk of fate when one miraculously happens to be in the right place at the right time. I am in that position now and I can assure you that – if Rosy will excuse the term – I have no intention of having things cocked up.'

He spun round and stepped towards her. She shrank back in the chair. 'Oh don't worry,' he said, 'I'm not going to attack you like that thug there, but you will give it to me all the same.' His tall form loomed over her, and looking up she meekly handed him the book. There was no point in resisting; and after her ordeal with Hewson she was too tired anyway.

She glanced at Felix knowing there was nothing he would do. What could he? He was no pugilist; and in any case what could five foot six do against six foot three, especially when the latter had a gun? She saw the dismay in his face – the sense of helplessness, and felt a prick of sympathy. She turned back to Hope-Landers. 'So what are you going to do?' she asked dully. 'No point in trying to contact Berenstein to report your luck; as you said, the phone is out of order.'

'*Telephone?* Good lord no. I'm going to Padua now, immediately – up the Brenta Canal in my boat; there is access from the lagoon and his mansion overlooks the water. It won't take long and there's plenty of petrol in the tank.' He gave a sardonic laugh. 'It'll make him happy: Santa Claus bearing gifts at midnight!'

In a swift movement he had grabbed the bag containing the vase, stuffed the book into it and made for the door. He looked very white and Rosy was startled to see how haggard his face had become. Felix, in what was presumably a flash of derring-do, took a tentative step towards him and was brushed aside.

'Out of the way,' Hope-Landers snapped. 'You may have noticed that this gun is loaded. I could blow off your kneecap or shoot the dog.'

'Shoot the dog?' cried Felix in fury – and retreated instantly.

Already he was out of the room and they could hear his feet clattering across the tiles and descending the stairs. They stared at each other in silence. And then Rosy leapt up and rushed to the banisters, and craning over watched as Guy Hope-Landers spiralled his long way down the echoing staircase. A wave of resignation swept over her and she suddenly felt terribly tired. *Carpe diem* Horace had urged: gather the day . . . Some bloody day, she thought; a corpse in the drawing room, herself nearly strangled and now a man so obsessed that he was clearly losing his mind.

However, gloom was shattered by commotion; a commotion which assaulted her ears in a two-pronged attack. Behind her the air was rent by throaty roars as

Caruso, hitherto quiet, embarked on excited comment. Below her was the sound of raised voices, protests, the slamming of a heavy door, more protests . . . She rather suspected that Hope-Landers' flight had clashed with the inconvenient ingress of Cedric and company.

To the noise of Caruso's bellows and Felix's ineffectual threats, Rosy darted to the window and peered down at the canal side. The stars were bright and she could see the fugitive's angular figure careering along the quayside towards the boat. He took a flying leap and frantically began to tug the engine's starting handle. She could see him bent over with shoulders heaving . . . Then abruptly all movement ceased. The figure seemed to stand stock still, frozen in the moonlight . . . And then jerkily, bit by bit, like some clockwork doll winding down, Hope-Landers sunk to his knees and then disappeared altogether beneath the boat's gunwale. 'Oh my God,' Rosy breathed.

By this time the returning party – Dilly and Duffy led by Cedric – had reached the landing in a state of panting indignation.

'I simply can't think why he was in such a hurry,' croaked one of the twins, 'and when I said "Hello Guy" he didn't take a blind bit of notice. Seemed not to hear at all!'

'Well at least he didn't tread on your foot, dear,' gasped the other. 'I am really quite bruised!' She turned to Cedric. 'I hope that front door is all right. He slammed it so hard I thought one of the panels would fall out – that wonky one that Violet keeps meaning to have fixed.'

Cedric too was peeved. He had spent an amusing time being shown the twins' family home – their father's etchings, sporting trophies, dusty collections of glass and silver and all the accumulated treasure of a bygone age: vestiges of Edwardian Venice and English eccentricity. Thus on a whim he had invited them back to the palazzo for a cocktail nightcap. They had accepted eagerly, and as a 'special treat' for their visitor had said they would take him in the gondola. At first he had demurred, reluctant to be subjected to further samples of Luigi's warblings. 'Oh no,' they had cried in unison, 'we will punt you ourselves; we *can* you know!'

And so at first horrified and then strangely delighted he had lolled back among the gondola's cushions as the two ladies took it in turns to glide their barque through the moonlit tributaries to the jetty of the Palazzo Reiss. There had been something pleasurably ghostly about the journey: the gentle swaying of the boat, the ethereal silence and the shadowy waters all lent a dreamlike unreality. It was something that Cedric would remember for a long while after . . .

But such unreality was as nothing compared to what lay in wait. The collision with Hope-Landers as he came rushing out of the entrance just as the three of them were going in was acutely embarrassing. The ladies had been rudely shoved aside, one of them had dropped her handbag and he himself was almost knocked to the ground. The door had been given an almighty slam and the gas lamp fell from its bracket. It had been an unceremonious greeting for his guests and Cedric was none too pleased . . . Far worse was to greet him upstairs.

CHAPTER THIRTY-FOUR

Once the sisters had recovered their breath and availed themselves of the 'facilities' (punting stirs the bladder) Cedric's intention was to usher them into the salon and ply them with the special concoction he knew they liked, 'Venice on the Razzle'. However in this he was forestalled by Felix. 'For God's sake don't take them in there,' he hissed, 'it's not nice.'

'What do you mean? Don't say the dog has disgraced itself!'

'No, no, the dog's been as good as gold—' He broke off to quell the booming creature. 'You see it is . . . well it's Hewson. He has had what you might call a turn.'

'A turn? What sort of turn?'

'*Not* a nice one.'

'Do you mean he's tight?' Cedric muttered. 'But what is he doing here anyway? I thought you were going to—'

Felix ran his fingers through his hair and said, 'Well he's not actually *here* any longer – I mean not in the technical sense.'

Cedric gazed at him startled. 'Not here in the technical sense? What sort of sense then? I don't understand – where is he?'

Felix cleared his throat. 'Under the rug.'

Light dawned on Cedric. '*Ah*,' he exclaimed in an anxious whisper, 'you mean he has lost his wits: off his head under the rug – thinks he's a bear or something. I am not entirely surprised. I always thought there was something a bit—'

'*Dead* under the rug. Shot.'

There came the sound of a cistern being flushed and the two friends stared at each other in consternation.

'Deflect them into the dining room,' Cedric said through gritted teeth.

But it was too late. Relieved and spruced the siblings emerged from the cloakroom, clearly eager for their Venice on the Razzle. Circumventing the hovering Felix they stepped briskly into the salon, exclaimed appreciatively at its beautiful blooms and cast appraising eyes towards the cocktail cabinet.

They seemed not to have noticed the shrouded heap on the floor, being evidently too engrossed in the prospect of the cocktail and issuing Cedric with earnest instructions on how to mix it. Exact measurements were apparently crucial.

'That's it,' directed one, 'just a dab of lime and a mere third of gin and don't overdo the bitters or it'll taste putrid.'

'But you can be more generous with the rum – though none of that Bacardi stuff of course. Only the dark will do,' cried the other. They seated themselves on a sofa and prattled merrily about the rival claims of French and Italian vermouth and the relative skills of their preferred bartenders. Listening to this, and despite the general ghastliness of things, Cedric was worried lest his own skills did not come up to scratch.

As they chatted Felix planted himself squarely in front of the rug-draped mound, feet apart and trying to stretch wider than his lean frame would allow. He wondered where Rosy had got to. Last seen she had been haring down the backstairs. Had she returned to her lodgings? It seemed unlikely. He recalled her squeaking something about Hope-Landers. Surely she wasn't mad enough to be pursing him for that bloody book still. Really, as if either he or it mattered now!

At that moment, just as Cedric was presenting the twins with their drinks, there was a clattering of feet and Rosy appeared at the door dishevelled and breathless. 'It's Guy,' she gasped, 'he's dead – in the boat. I tried to resuscitate him but it wouldn't work. I tried for ages!' She flopped down on the sofa next to Duffy or Dilly, grabbed the glass from the twin's hand and downed it in two gulps. Her neighbour looked mildly affronted.

There was a silence. And then the other twin, the one still in charge of her glass, said quietly, 'Oh dear, it must have been all that rushing about. He had a bad heart you know. It was very foolish of him to be in such a hurry. And I daresay he had forgotten to take his pills. How sad. I had always rather liked him.' She examined her glass pensively, and then raising it announced: 'To absent friends.'

There was an awkward silence; and then those fortunate enough to be holding a glass raised them solemnly and murmured assent. There was another pause, after which the one without said: 'I so agree. He was delightful; and when I have the means I shall toast him myself.' She glanced at Rosy's drained glass and then looked pointedly at Cedric who returned to the cabinet.

Sensing a certain *froideur* in her sibling's demeanour, the other said tactfully, 'I say, Dilly, do you think Violet has any of those wonderful Bath Olivers she used to keep? They are quite my favourite biscuit and impossible to find in Venice. Shall we go and raid her kitchen and see if we can find any?' She looked at Felix. 'You don't mind do you, Felix?'

He nodded dumbly, grateful for the respite. The sisters rose and bustled off in the direction of the kitchen.

'Quick,' commanded Cedric, 'shove Hewson behind the harpsichord. There's no light in that corner, they won't see a thing.'

Felix and Rosy dutifully stooped and began to lug the

thing to where he directed. Rosy felt numb and exhausted – out of her mind actually after that thoughtless raid on the twin's cocktail. God, had it been strong! She closed her eyes. *Dear lord, let me wake up soon!*

The pair returned from their culinary searches evidently successful. They carried a plate draped in a napkin, but judging from the crumbs on their dresses and the sound of munching they had already tested the fare. Exchanging glances they passed the plate around to the other three and returned to the sofa.

Cedric proffered the freshly mixed drink to Dilly (or Duffy) and she gave him a benevolent beam. 'Delicious,' she pronounced, 'not bad at all!' She scanned the room frowning and looking puzzled. 'But what have you done with it?' she asked.

'Done with what?' Felix asked tensely.

She hesitated. 'Well . . . with the body of course. Hewson's. It was here a moment ago. I saw his shoe, one of those American loafers.'

There was a stunned silence while each considered their response. Rosy was the first to speak. 'What sharp eyes,' she said vaguely.

Cedric merely cleared his throat; while Felix yelped, 'It was nothing to do with us – Hope-Landers, you know!'

'Well I am sure it makes a very interesting story,' said one of them, 'you had better tell us.'

'All ears!' said the other and took a bite of her Bath Oliver.

* * *

When they had finished the sisters appeared to reflect. And then smoothing her dress, one said, 'It seems to me that you have spent a very strainful evening. *Most* strainful . . . Wouldn't you say so, Duffy?'

Duffy nodded vigorously. 'What papa would have called a blinking bloomer!' She turned to Cedric. 'You were well out of it.'

'I am not now,' he replied tightly.

'So,' they both suddenly chimed, '*something* must be done!' This was uttered with such brisk purpose that Caruso barked and wagged his tail. He looked enquiringly at the ladies.

'I suppose we had better alert the medical authorities about Guy,' Rosy said, 'there must be a standard procedure for sudden heart attacks,' adding bleakly, 'and then – and then we shall have to report it all to the police . . .' She groaned visualising the palaver and endless complications.

Cedric closed his eyes. 'Tricky,' he muttered. Like Rosy he felt horribly weakened by the prospect in store. Why on earth hadn't they simply gone to Frinton!

'Take heart,' said one of the twins stoutly, 'no point anticipating trouble. There are certain pre-emptive measures that can be taken.' She nodded firmly.

'Although actually,' her sister murmured, 'it is Felix who may have the hardest task.'

'What!' he cried. '*Me?* What on earth do you mean?' He had the air of a petrified rabbit.

'Because it is you who will have to explain to dear

Violet when she returns what Bill Hewson is doing rolled up in her best rug stashed behind the harpsichord.'

'But . . . but he won't *be* there,' Felix protested, bewildered. 'He will have been moved somewhere else by that time – to a morgue, a cemetery or something!' He looked askance.

'I rather doubt it,' she replied consulting her watch, 'your cousin should be here any minute. A bit late really – she was due to arrive an hour ago. Carlo is supposed to be picking her up at the Santa Lucia railway terminus. The flight was delayed as usual I assume.'

Felix's mouth dropped open and his horrified gaze moved slowly towards the shape wedged in its darkened alcove. He closed his mouth; and approaching the body tucked the protruding foot beneath the rug.

CHAPTER THIRTY-FIVE

It transpired that delightful though Chicago had been, by late October the city had started to turn chilly. That, plus her sudden overwhelming yen to be reunited with Caruso, had prompted Cousin Violet to curtail the visit. (Talking to the hound by telephone was not comparable to feeling its hot doggy breath on knee and cheek.) Naturally she *had* tried to alert Felix but, as so often, the palazzo telephone system had proved uncooperative (the loose door panel being not the only thing requiring attention). The plane had indeed been late but she knew she could rely on her faithful friend Carlo to be at the station awaiting her arrival . . . And thus here she was, full of delicious memories and mementos – including that spiffing trombone!

'What trombone?' Felix had asked dolefully. 'I don't see one.'

'Oh,' she said carelessly, 'a little present from Jack Teagarden. It's still downstairs of course. Carlo is dealing with it and he's bringing up some of the other stuff too.' She turned to Rosy: 'My dear, I don't know who you are but you look nice and strong. Would you mind awfully just running down and giving him a hand? It should only take two goes.'

Startled, Rosy did exactly as bid. At least by the time she had struggled with the luggage the returning traveller would have been acquainted with the corpse in her drawing room . . . She would also know about the fate of her lodger, his body rocking gently under a tarpaulin in *La Speranza*. God what a mess! It was not a homecoming Rosy would have chosen for herself and she didn't relish witnessing the reaction. Perhaps she could spin out her time with Carlo and the baggage . . . From far below there came a crash and what sounded like a curse.

As might have been predicted, Violet Hoffman was none too pleased to learn of what had occurred in her absence and even Cedric's suave sympathy failed to mollify.

'It is too bad,' she protested, 'you have moved the harpsichord. It is so temperamental and now it will have to be retuned – it was only just done before I went away!' (Cedric rather doubted this, his own trial with it suggesting otherwise.) 'And why on earth did William Hewson have to choose *my* house to go on his rampage? We didn't

300

have much in common and I consider it an imposition. Couldn't you have stopped him, Felix?' she asked angrily.

'Not really, I was otherwise engaged,' he replied bleakly.

'Or you might say all tied up!' chortled one of the twins.

Violet shot her a withering look. 'This is no time for drollery, Duffy. It is a serious matter: I can't have dead bodies strewn about my premises like this. It simply won't do!'

'Actually Violet dear,' ventured Dilly, 'there is only one surely. Guy's is in his boat.'

'That boat and the landing stage to which it is attached are within the curtilage of my domain,' was the huffy response. 'I am responsible.' She glared around at them; but as her eye fell on the dog her expression softened. 'Come to Mummy, then,' she crooned. 'Has poor Caruso been frightened by a big bad man . . .' There followed the usual mutual pawings and fawnings.

Felix took his cue. 'Oh no,' he lied, 'the dog has been as brave as a lion. *So* valiant! He's a wonderful fellow and we've been such good friends, haven't we old boy?'

The old boy waddled over and gave his friend an obliging lick.

Impressed by the performance Cedric exclaimed, 'You see! They have a real bond. Felix has been a splendid guardian . . . And do you know, Miss Hoffman, he has taken Caruso to the flower market *every* day for fresh blooms. The dog loves it!'

'Really?' said the owner regarding her cousin with a

301

kindlier eye. 'Well that's reassuring at least.' She glanced around at the plethora of exquisite flower arrangements. 'Hmm. Yes I can see why you earned the Royal Appointment warrant. Most decorative.' She nodded approvingly. But then her glance fell on the shape again and she scowled. 'He really can't stay here you know: far too unsettling.'

'Well,' broke in Dilly and Duffy, 'that was just what we were saying before you arrived. You see we have a plan which—'

They stopped as Rosy and Carlo appeared in the doorway. Both looked tired, and Carlo was carrying a trombone under one arm. He placed it gravely next to Violet's chair and then, having been alerted by Rosy, peered uneasily towards the far corner.

'It won't bite you,' Violet said briskly, and gestured to them to sit down. 'The twins have a plan,' she announced.

The sisters rose and took centre stage; and in alternating sentences outlined their proposal. This fell into two parts: to detach Guy's boat from its moorings and let it drift aimlessly whither it chose – preferably into the Grand Canal and thence the lagoon (i.e. well away from the Palazzo Reiss and Violet's 'curtilage'); and secondly to weigh down Hewson's body with bricks, place it in their gondola and punt it into some backwater where it could be surreptitiously sunk.

There was silence as the plan was considered.

'Who is doing the punting?' Carlo enquired.

'Bags I!' cried Duffy.

'No dear,' her sister said gently, 'I think this particular task requires a degree of care. It would be better if I handled things. Besides I *am* the eldest.'

Duffy sighed. 'Oh well, if you say so . . .'

Cedric started to toy with his cigarettes. 'Oh do smoke if you would like,' said his hostess graciously. 'And you could give Carlo one too, he looks a little peaky.' The latter fell upon the proffered cigarette and started to puff with avid intensity. Rosy had the impression he was a man not currently at ease with the world.

'But actually,' she said, 'as far as Guy is concerned, even if the boat were to stay where it is the body will be found anyway. Suffering a heart attack may be awful but it's not sinister. Does one really have to set him adrift? What difference would it make if he were discovered here or somewhere else?'

Violet frowned. 'Because as I have pointed out it is *my* jetty – or at least I rent it. It is virtually outside my front door. Think of the publicity! And may I remind you that Hewson wasn't the only murderer in all of this: it was Guy who gunned him down. The police are by nature inquisitive and have a passion for detail. Thus the poor man may have been my lodger but the less one knows or appears to know about him the better. Keep things dark and Guy and his boat at a seemly distance, that's my answer . . . which is why I thoroughly endorse the twins' proposal. Dispose of the pair of them!'

'Provided one can locate some bricks,' murmured Carlo.

'A mere detail.'

'Not really,' he persisted. 'If the body is to sink and to remain submerged for some time I should have thought heavy weights are essential. Wouldn't you say so?'

Violet conceded the point and addressing Rosy said, 'Do *you* have any bricks by any chance?' Rosy said that she hadn't and felt rather inadequate. 'Well somebody must have some,' exclaimed Violet impatiently.

Faces were blank. And then a twin spoke (Duffy, outranked by Dilly in the punting stakes): 'We don't need bricks, we have an anchor. It's in Guy's boat.' The suggestion was met with general approval; and she beamed, clearly feeling her status restored.

'Good. So that's agreed,' Violet declared. 'Time is pushing on: we must get to work.'

'Uhm . . . would it be out of the question to have a drink first?' Cedric enquired. 'There's a heavy schedule ahead and I don't think it wise to commence on an empty stomach, especially given the nature of the task.' He gave a delicate cough.

It was another suggestion well received and drinks were duly poured. But Carlo politely declined saying it was essential that someone vet *La Speranza*, divest the body of its tarpaulin and generally check that there were no telltale signs of anyone (i.e. Rosy) having been present at, or just after, the owner's unfortunate demise. 'Let us not offer hostages to capricious Fortune,' he warned them solemnly. Rosy was grateful for such foresight, yet despite the situation couldn't help being amused by his continuing espousal of such literary English. That sergeant major must have been quite something!

Years later, as an old lady in her eighties and the other participants all dead, Rosy was to look back on that night with a mixture of horror and incredulity. Had she really been there doing *that*? It was ridiculous; and yet the events remained so vividly imprinted in her mind that she knew it to be true. What an outrageous secret – but vaguely risible all the same! She wondered whether the other old ladies in the Home had ever been engaged in such disgraceful shenanigans . . .

Meanwhile, as a young woman, Rosy joined the others in their fortifying brandies while Carlo slipped from the room.

By the time he returned, the pall-bearers, tanked up and wheezing, had managed to lug their awful burden to the bottom of the stairs.

'Have you got the anchor?' gasped Felix.

'Of course,' Carlo replied, 'it's in my pocket.'

Felix tossed his head. Typical Italian sarcasm!

It was agreed that the best procedure was to get Hewson to the jetty, heave the anchor from Hope-Landers' boat into the gondola, and then once the body was safely ensconced under the canopy attach the anchor with its chain.

'An excellent idea,' said Cedric doubtfully. 'But perhaps in addition to the anchor it might be sensible to stuff some cans of beans into his pockets. Extra ballast you know.'

'Ah,' Violet said, 'do you want to go upstairs and fetch them? There's a few in the larder.'

Cedric looked up at the winding staircase whence they had just come. 'Not really,' he replied.

'If it's not a silly question,' Rosy asked, 'how are we going to get Hewson to the gondola? It's one thing hauling him down the stairs but carrying him along the towpath might attract attention.'

'He must walk,' chimed the twins firmly.

'*What!*' she yelped.

'Oh yes,' one of them said, 'that's what they did with Crown Prince Rudolf – the Mayerling scandal you know. He was supported on either side and manoeuvred to his carriage as if he were drunk. Worked quite well I believe.'

'Good thinking,' Violet said. 'Now who is going to support him?' She looked at her cousin.

'I say was that Caruso I heard?' Felix exclaimed. 'He probably thinks we have gone and left him. I think I had better just go and see—'

Cedric became strangely diverted by a picture on the wall. He began to examine it closely. Carlo looked down at his feet.

Oh my God, thought Rosy, Violet said I looked strong! She shut her eyes.

'Oh we'll do it,' Dilly volunteered (or Duffy). 'Fortunately we are blessed with height – and in any case we got so used to shunting Pa about when he was tight that it shouldn't be too difficult.'

'Not at all,' the other agreed. 'Don't you remember? He used to become quite corpse-like.' She gave a fond chuckle.

It would be wrong of course to say that the trio set off at a brisk pace; but the two ladies handled their companion with impressive strength and dexterity. Clearly manoeuvres with Papa had proved an instructive exercise. Slowly and silently he was lurched to the jetty. Felix and Cedric skulked behind them in the shadow of the wall and then helped to heave the burden into the gondola. They thrust him beneath the canopy where he lolled on the cushions like a beached whale, or, as Felix thought, like a sack of giant turnips.

The rearguard were Violet, Rosy and Carlo: the latter pair to grapple with transferring the anchor; and Violet to provide further swigs of sustaining brandy from a flask she had had the foresight to bring. It was an exhausting business and such aid indispensable to its success. That it *was* successful was something that Rosy could never quite fathom: the drink of course, but also surely a blend of luck and desperation.

According to Felix, before they had levered the corpse into the gondola Cedric had murmured something about putting a penny in its mouth. Felix had said he hadn't a clue what he was talking about and that in any case this was Italy and they didn't have any pennies. Cedric had smiled and said perhaps a lira would do and had placed a coin in the dead man's pocket.

Initially Rosy had been as perplexed as Felix but later she learnt the significance. Meanwhile she watched as the redoubtable Dilly, accompanied by her sister and the two men, smoothly punted the gondola into the moonlit canal and thence into the shadows of some darker stream . . .

Left on the quay Rosy and Violet breathed a sigh of relief. But there was still the matter of Guy Hope-Landers and *La Speranza*. Carlo reached into his pocket and drew out a small packet. He opened the top and threw it down next to the body. A few of the contents spilt out. 'Heart tablets,' he explained. 'It will help the police when they pick him up: reduce the number of questions.' And then dropping to his knees he untied the rope mooring the dinghy, and grasping the pole lying on the duckboard pushed it gently away from the bank. The current took it immediately, and after moving in a faltering circle it started to drift down the channel towards the southern end of the Grand Canal.

Rosy thought of the great Tennyson poem. 'Do you think he will be crossing the bar?' she whispered.

'Oh I think he has done that already,' Carlo replied.

They walked back slowly along the towpath to the palazzo – or rather Rosy and Carlo were slow; Violet, eager to get back to Caruso and attend to her unpacking, moved ahead with an energy which Rosy found draining. It was four o'clock in the morning and she had narrowly escaped a knife, been nearly strangled and helped dispose of two dead bodies.

'You can stay the night if you like,' Violet had offered. 'I shall be rather busy myself but I am sure Felix can fix you up all right when he gets back.' She scanned Rosy's face. 'If you don't mind my saying, you look rather awful. I suggest you tell him to make you some black coffee, it may help. A bit of lipstick wouldn't come amiss either. Well now, I must get back to my poor boy!' And giving them both a vague wave she hastened on towards the staircase.

Rosy and Carlo watched her in silence. And then, as one, slumped on to the ancient settle outside what had been Hope-Landers' quarters. Carlo took out a cigarette case, offered Rosy an Abdulla, took one himself and flicked open his lighter. In the half-light his features looked drawn – as, according to Violet, were Rosy's own. For a little while they smoked in silence each immersed in private thoughts . . . although actually Rosy was not thinking at all. Her mind was stripped of everything, a state she found remarkably soothing. She rather wished she could stay like that all night or what was left of it. How pleasant to sit in the dark on that hard bench, just puffing slowly and not having to move or speak. Bliss.

But just as it seemed she was on the edge of sleep, a thought did strike her – rather a vital one. 'My God,' she said slowly, 'Guy had those two things he was taking to Farinelli Berenstein, the vase and the *book*. They'll still be in the boat with him, in that canvas bag!' She sighed ruefully. 'Oh well I suppose that's the end of my Bodger search. Dr Stanley won't be very happy . . . Still, do you realise that if the boat doesn't capsize before it's spotted and the police recognise the two items and latch on to their significance I assume somebody could be a millionaire.'

'No they couldn't,' said Carlo. 'They will find only one item and that's the trashy vase. I've got the other here.' He tapped the inner pocket of his raincoat.

CHAPTER THIRTY-SIX

Rosy took the cigarette from her mouth and with her heel absently ground the butt on the stone floor. She cleared her throat, and turning to him said, 'I see. So when did you get hold of that?'

'When you were all throwing down the drink. You may recall that it was then that I went down to inspect the boat: to remove the tarpaulin and to ensure all was shipshape. As you say, the holdall was of course with him and naturally I removed the book.'

'Yet ignored the vase.'

Carlo gave a light laugh. 'You think I ought to brandish the pair at the idiot in Padua and claim the prize? The man's in his dotage – always was really, and flaky with it as you English would say. He has his pet lawyers naturally, but I very much doubt if the arrangement has much legal validity. He would wriggle out of his commitment somehow, if only by saying he didn't recognise the objects. Besides it would mean I lost the Bodger Horace.'

'So you wouldn't trade the Horace for that amount of money? Is it really so special to you?' Rosy asked in some wonder.

'If I were a poor man I would indeed consider yielding it for that sum. Probably jump at the chance. But mercifully I am not poor. Not rich, you understand, but sufficiently comfortable not to have to worry too much about life's necessities – or indeed about its little pleasures. I have the wherewithal for my books, my domestic comforts, my music, my friends; and I live happily in this beneficent city. Why should I so desperately require a million pounds? As we used to say in the Sussex POW camp, it's not worth the flipping haddock!'

Rosy considered his words and then said wryly, 'Well you will have made somebody happy: Miss Witherington, my landlady. She has a bet on that the two things won't be produced by the prescribed date and is terrified they might turn up.' She grinned to herself, and added, 'Although I suppose it's not beyond the realms of possibility that the vase is recovered from the boat when they find it and that I simultaneously suggest someone burgle your apartment.'

'Ah I thought of that,' he replied gravely. 'I gave it a tap with a mallet. There was one lying in the stern; most handy. Belt and blooming braces as—'

'Your sergeant major would say?'

'Exactly. And now Miss Gilchrist, if you will forgive me I must go home. Your friends the professor and Mr Smythe will be back at any minute, and delightful though they are I do not feel I am in a fit state to renew their acquaintance just yet. Sleep summons. But one thing I ask: please do not forget my invitation for tea and toast before you embark for England. It would be a great honour. I will contact you shortly, i.e. once I have regained my equilibrium.' Carlo rose from the bench, walked to the palazzo door and slipped out into the mist of a Venetian dawn.

Ah well, out goes the Bodger I suppose, Rosy mused ruefully . . . And two minutes later, dank and whey-faced, in came Felix and Cedric, mission accomplished.

When she returned to the *pensione* after midday it was to be greeted by Miss Witherington full of sly giggles. 'I suppose you've been on the tiles have you? I hope he was nice!'

'Er . . . well I, I uhm . . .' Rosy was flustered, having given little thought to an explanation and being ill-prepared.

'Oh don't worry, my dear; I was awful at your age. Awful!' Miss Witherington clapped her hands in nostalgic mirth. 'But I tell you what,' she said conspiratorially, 'I told Mr Downing that you were struck down with a migraine.'

'Really? Why?'

'Oh when he saw you were not at dinner last night or here later this morning he was *most* concerned.' She lowered her voice further: 'Between you and me I think he has a bit of

313

a pash on you!' There were more knowing giggles.

Rosy closed her eyes. That was all she needed! 'I am perfectly well,' she said, 'but I *am* quite tired. I think I will go and rest in my room.'

'Very sensible. One always needs to be soothed afterwards.' Afterwards? Rosy was startled, but escaped thankfully to her room where she got into bed and slept for five hours. It was obviously a very persistent migraine.

When she emerged she found a note waiting for her in the vestibule. It was from Carlo inviting her to meet him at Quadri's the following day. Evidently he had found his equilibrium more quickly than she had found hers.

She met him at one o'clock. Thankfully there was no tea; but they did indeed eat toast – spread liberally with a luscious duck pâté and accompanied by oysters from the lagoon and a bottle of pink Billecart-Salmon. Considering the ordeal of less than twenty-four hours previously Carlo looked exceedingly well and spruce . . . doubtless the result of getting his hands on the Bodger again, Rosy thought rather sourly.

By tacit agreement they made no mention of the night's activities but talked easily of more agreeable things, wandering over a range of topics from literature (specifically English comics which he had so loved as a prisoner of war) to Venetian baroque music and the newly released Fellini film *La Strada*.

But as they neared the end of the wine Rosy broached the subject of his library collection. 'Have you finished the cataloguing yet?' she enquired. 'You must be pleased to be able to include the Bodger in your inventory,' and added teasingly, 'I trust you haven't left it on somebody's table this time. That would be too bad!'

He assured her it was perfectly safe and that he had taken much pleasure in examining and handling the thing. 'As we know, the translations themselves are unremarkable, a trifle stilted I would say but the notes are perceptive and it has been interesting to see the actual signature and dwell on the inscription. A pompous man, but it was a work of love all the same: a privilege to have owned it for a while.' He smiled and called for coffee.

As they were leaving he said how much he had enjoyed Rosy's company and that were she ever in Venice again, free and at leisure, he would be delighted to be her guide. 'But this time,' he added wryly, 'you can be assured I would deflect you away from any dubious bookshops.'

He gave a little bow and presented her with a crumpled paper bag . . . containing, of course, the Bodger.

'So you see, Dr Stanley,' Rosy explained down an unusually clear line, 'all being well I shall be in on Monday with the Horace.'

'Excellent,' he said. 'How much did it cost?'

'Cost? Er – oh nothing really. Or at least, nothing of any consequence.'

'Hah! That's a mercy. I shan't have to do battle with the accounts department. You've no idea how difficult they are. Now tell me Rosy, you *are* absolutely sure it is the right one? It would be most unfortunate if you had blundered . . . Oh and by the way, did that bastard from the Bodleian ever show up?'

She assured him she had not blundered and that the bastard had never appeared.

There was a dark chuckle. 'Probably still wandering around the back streets looking for the damn thing. Bad luck for some!'

Rosy agreed that it was indeed bad luck for some. And she thought of William Hewson, Guy Hope-Landers and Edward Jones.

'Well,' he said graciously, 'on the whole I think you've done rather well. I knew you wouldn't let me down. Tell you what, when I'm in hospital with my hip you can have my lunch vouchers, a pity to waste them.'

She thanked him for his generosity and was about to put the receiver down, when he added, 'You see – I told you it wouldn't be too difficult.'

'Yes,' she said, 'you did tell me.'

Bolstered by champagne and First Class cushions on the *Simplon-Orient*, Cedric and Felix reflected upon their Venetian venture. They agreed that it had been singularly diverting but not something that they would care to repeat, or certainly not for a considerable time.

'Rather fatiguing, wouldn't you say?' Cedric remarked.

'Taxing I would say,' Felix replied, 'and then some!'

There was silence as each dwelt upon the various aspects of the experience. 'I was a tremendous hit with

Caruso you know,' mused Felix. 'I am clearly the sort of person he has a natural affinity with.'

'Oh clearly,' Cedric agreed. 'Tell me: did you prefer him to the corgis?'

Felix closed his eyes and shuddered. 'Much.'

A further silence ensued as they gazed out of the window admiring the darkening Swiss scenery with its neatness, order, and reassuring safety.

'Do you know,' Cedric mused, 'I dealt with that matter most adroitly. A little heavy but it slipped into the water without a hitch, hardly a bubble.'

There was the merest hesitation and then Felix said, 'Well . . . the gondola did nearly capsize, but other than that I think you showed remarkable deftness. The ladies were very impressed too. I heard one of them say that even their father couldn't have done better. High praise I think coming from that pair. Oh by the way, they said something about coming to London in the spring.'

'What!' Cedric cried dropping his newspaper. 'We must decamp to Hunstanton!'

'I think Deauville might be preferable,' suggested Felix, 'very salubrious and safe. A chic guest house on the promenade would be ideal. Sand, surf and ozone – most refreshing. One can have rather too much of palazzos and canals.'

Cedric nodded. 'Just a little,' he said.